TWO TIMES MURDER

Also by Adam Oyebanji

The Quiet Teacher series

A QUIET TEACHER *

Novels

BRAKING DAY

* *available from Severn House*

TWO TIMES MURDER

Adam Oyebanji

SEVERN
HOUSE

First world edition published in Great Britain and the USA in 2024
by Severn House, an imprint of Canongate Books Ltd,
14 High Street, Edinburgh EH1 1TE.

Trade paperback edition first published in Great Britain and the USA in 2025
by Severn House, an imprint of Canongate Books Ltd.

severnhouse.com

British Library Cataloguing-in-Publication Data
A CIP catalogue record for this title is available from the British Library.

ISBN-13: 978-1-4483-1245-0 (cased)
ISBN-13: 978-1-4483-1701-1 (trade paper)
ISBN-13: 978-1-4483-1244-3 (e-book)

MIX
Paper | Supporting responsible forestry
FSC® C013056
www.fsc.org

Typeset by Palimpsest Book Production Ltd., Falkirk, Stirlingshire, Scotland.
Printed and bound in Great Britain by TJ Books, Padstow, Cornwall..

The manufacturer's authorised representative in the EU for product safety is Authorised Rep Compliance Ltd, 71 Lower Baggot Street, Dublin D02 P593 Ireland (arccompliance.com)

Praise for The Quiet Teacher series

"A clever, intricately-plotted murder mystery wrapped in a tense spy thriller"
Chris Merritt, author of *Committed*

"Meticulously plotted, nimbly paced, and devilishly fair play"
Lauren Muñoz, author of *Suddenly a Murder*

"Hooks you right from the opening, and ratchets up the tension all the way to the unexpected finish— I couldn't put it down"
Marsali Taylor, author of the Shetland Sailing mysteries

"Outstanding . . . A must for both Agatha Christie and John le Carré devotees"
Booklist Starred Review

"A tense and topical thriller"
The Times

"Satisfying . . . Readers will eagerly await Oyebanji's next mystery"
Publishers Weekly

"Well-plotted . . . Oyebanji demonstrates a confident and developed voice and style"
Library Journal

"Oyebanji's hero is complicated and sure to win readers' sympathies"
Kirkus Reviews

"Greg Abimbola is a likeable, intriguing protagonist with some interesting tricks up his sleeve. I don't know if he'll ever appear again, but, if he does, I'll be waiting"
lesasbookcritiques.com

About the author

Adam Oyebanji was born in Coatbridge, North Lanarkshire. He recently took the big step of moving east to Edinburgh by way of Birmingham, London, Lagos, Chicago, Pittsburgh and New York: a necessary detour, because the traffic otherwise is really, really bad. A graduate of Birmingham University and Harvard Law School, Adam works in the field of counter-terrorist financing, helping banks choke off the money supply to rogue states, narcotics empires, and human trafficking networks.

He is the author of acclaimed SFF novel *Braking Day*, as well as the acclaimed mystery/spy novel *A Quiet Teacher*, featuring Black British expat Greg Abimbola, a seemingly mild-mannered Russian-language teacher with terrifying secrets. *Two Times Murder* is the second novel in the Quiet Teacher series.

www.adamoyebanji.com

For Alex and Barbara, without whom nothing is worthwhile.
And for Elaine Connolly (1969–2023)

MONDAY, THE SIXTH
6:52 A.M.

Try as he might, Greg Abimbola was unable to shake the feeling he was being followed. Morosov had found him, after all, and if Morosov had found him, so could others. He kept his one good eye on the rearview mirror as he turned into Joseph Avenue. Even now, the glimpse the mirror afforded of his other eye, the one hidden behind the eyepatch, still caught him by surprise. Not the face he remembered. Not the face he wanted to remember. WESA Pittsburgh, the public radio station, burbled unheeded out of the car's speakers.

There was a small wash of relief as the gray van behind him failed to make the turn and continued on its way.

If he were planning his own abduction, he thought to himself, a van would be the way to go. Nothing fancy, just wait for the right moment, knock the target unconscious and bundle him into the back. Then it would be off to some deserted shithole where the fun could really begin.

Or, if God were feeling particularly vindictive, he'd wake up in Moscow.

This latter thought evinced a wry smile. It was still there when he arrived at Calderhill Academy and pulled into one of the few remaining parking spaces. With a certain amount of effort, he squeezed his dark-green Mini Cooper between a high-end minivan and an equally high-end SUV. Brisk spring air filled his lungs as he trotted across the road. A pale sun cast his shadow on to the asphalt, the shape of it warping as it flowed across a pothole.

It had been weeks, he reminded himself. Weeks since Mikhail Morosov, former Russian intelligence officer, had climbed the stairs to his apartment in search of Grigoriy Petrov, the man who'd betrayed Mother Russia to the British. The man whom the British, with US assistance, had spirited away to Pittsburgh under witness protection. The man Russia's military intelligence outfit, the GRU, wanted very, very dead.

If only they knew where he was.

Morosov had known. But Morosov, keen to make a profit, had kept the knowledge to himself.

Or so Greg hoped.

Stifling his uncertainty, he skipped up the broad steps to Calderhill's vaulted entrance, waving at the security camera as he did so. The door buzzed open a split second before he reached it.

'Morning, Stacey.'

'Morning, Mr Abimbola.' Stacey glanced out at the sunlight streaming through the lobby windows. 'Looks like it's gonna be a nice one. About time too.'

'Couldn't agree more.'

He passed the security desk with a smile, crossed the opulent marble atrium, and climbed the stairs to the second floor two at a time. He took a deep, cleansing breath at the top.

Morosov was out of the picture, his knowledge of Greg's whereabouts beyond the reach of Russian intelligence.

Or so he hoped.

Deputy Werner at witness protection had been unexpectedly tight-lipped about Morosov's status. As had Dianna Aldis, whose precise role at British Intelligence Greg had never figured out. That, though, had been less unexpected. Spies, after all, are not known for being chatty. He'd confronted both of them with the news story in the *Pittsburgh Post-Gazette*: the washed-up body at the foot of the Rachel Carson Bridge; the description that sounded suspiciously like his one-time pursuer.

Who'd been in their custody less than twenty-four hours earlier.

'Morosov's present status isn't your concern,' Werner had said, his voice less friendly than usual. 'What you need to do is get the hell out of Dodge. It's not safe for you here, and you know it.'

Aldis had played the same tune, albeit with an English accent disturbingly similar to Greg's own. 'I wouldn't worry about Mr Morosov if I were you,' she'd said soothingly. 'But – and excuse me for saying this – you'd have a lot less to worry about if you'd simply *move*. America has many fine cities, I'm sure. Pittsburgh will get on perfectly well without you.'

'I like it here,' Greg had told her. Which was true as far as it went. That he was sick of running, that God would either have him tortured and killed or let him live in peace, was too much trouble to explain.

Either way, he would end up in hell.

Leaving the stairs behind him, Greg turned right, in the direction of his classroom. There was always a slight feeling of relief when he did this. Turning left meant entering the glass-walled maze of the admin suite, at the center of which lay the principal's office. Greg, whose teaching skills had benefited from neither training nor long experience, spent more time there than he would like. It was no coincidence that his classroom was as close to the admin suite as it was. The principal liked to keep an eye on him.

The *previous* principal. As for the new one . . .

'Hey, Greg, wait up.'

Out of the corner of his eye, Greg could see a tall, loose-limbed figure coming through the frosted glass door that marked the exit from the admin suite. For a brief moment, Greg thought he was being summoned for yet another telling off. But as the person coming through the door was Demetrius Freedman, Greg put the idea to rest. The chemistry teacher closed the door behind him and strode toward Greg with a broad smile, unusual in itself where Demetrius and the administration were concerned. Demetrius's clashes with the principal's office tended to be more political than Greg's, but Greg doubted Demetrius enjoyed those interactions any more than he did. A smiling Demetrius merited investigation. Greg eased his pace, allowing the taller man to catch up to him.

'Good morning, Doctor Freedman. And what can I do for you on this very fine day?'

'You can congratulate me is what,' Demetrius said, still beaming as he followed Greg through his classroom door.

'Happy to. Why, exactly?'

'I just handed in my notice to Principal Eisner. You are looking at the new Head of Science at the Edgeworth School.'

'No!' Greg had intended to break into a surprised, happy smile but felt a frown forming instead. He perched on the edge of his desk, allowing curiosity to get the better of him. 'I thought you were *persona non grata* over there. You know, with Brian Delcade and the—'

'The little shit's no longer on the board of trustees.' Demetrius favored Greg with a glance that was intended to be meaningful. 'Criminal indictments can have that effect.'

'I'm sure they can.' Greg refused to be drawn. Brian Delcade, the now former trustee of the Edgeworth School and a Calderhill parent, had stymied Demetrius's previous application to Edgeworth in a row over grades. The murder of Delcade's wife in the Calderhill basement and its recent, headline-grabbing denouement – for which Greg had striven to take zero credit – had come with obvious consequences. Obvious, that is, once he bothered to think about it.

'So the Delcade veto has been removed?'

'Exactly right, my man. Exactly right. With that *gentleman* out of the way, the politics over there look a lot different.'

Greg nodded.

'Yeah, so the last guy has gone to be deputy principal at some big-deal school back in Chicago. I have an in – kind of an in – with the chair of the Edgeworth board of trustees. Guy by the name of Alan Mester. We go back a ways. He couldn't stop Delcade doing what he did last time around but this time, with that asshole well and truly toast, Alan and Principal Ferguson asked me if I'd be interested in giving it a go. They came to me, man.' Demetrius's smile returned in full force. 'They came to *me*. Can you believe that?'

'I can, actually. You are more than qualified for the job.'

'Damn right I am.'

'Yes. But—'

'But what?'

Greg hesitated, conscious of the need to pick his words with care. Demetrius was Black. Greg was also Black. According to the rules, they belonged in the same bucket. Except the rules, which neither he nor Demetrius had any part in crafting, were ridiculous. Demetrius was African American. He, on the other hand, was a bi-racial Russian of African descent pretending to be English. The lines of communication could get easily and fatally scrambled.

'Principal Ferguson and this Alan Mester guy must want you very badly,' he said slowly, picking his way. 'But what about the school? Brian Delcade was only one man. If he didn't have significant support, he'd never have got away with what he did. And then there's PEACE—'

'PEACE is just a handful of hysterical, backward-looking parents who can't get their heads around the fact that the world is changing. They're nothing to worry about. You start changing your behavior to please a bunch of white supremacists, you might as well go back to picking cotton. The way to deal with those assholes is to take the job, not run away from it.'

Greg suppressed a sigh.

'You're not worried about being isolated there? About not getting enough support?'

'You mean like I am here? Gimme a break.' He nodded savagely in the direction of the admin suite. 'You think these clowns are any better?'

Perhaps this was the time, Greg thought, to keep his own counsel.

Demetrius, taking a cue from something in Greg's expression, took it down a notch.

'Look. First, the Edgeworth School has offered me a step up, which is more than can be said for this place. Second, Alan Mester and Principal Ferguson are pretty progressive guys in a not-so-progressive school, but they're getting somewhere. For real. They have an anti-racism program now. Again, unlike here. And they're going to open a DEI office.'

'A . . .?'

'DEI. Diversity, Equity and Inclusion.' Demetrius clearly couldn't decide whether to be exasperated or amused. 'Jesus, Greg, what planet are you from?'

'Worcestershire, England.'

'Like in the sauce?' Demetrius's expression tipped into full-on amusement.

'The very same.'

'That, my man, would explain a lot.' The chemistry teacher became slightly more serious. 'You had your interview with the principal yet?'

Something Greg didn't care to examine too closely wriggled to life in the pit of his stomach.

'No. But I'm due to see him later today. I can't say I'm looking forward to justifying my existence.'

Demetrius favored him with a wry smile.

'Yeah, well. One less thing for this here departing hero to worry about. Science costs money. We need labs, equipment, expensive shit. We're the Thanksgiving turkey with the longest neck. Standing in front of a whiteboard teaching verbs and adjectives is a lot easier on the cashflow.'

'You really think he'd swing the ax at your department?'

'It's the easiest way to save money. You can't have a murder on school premises without parents getting spooked and taking their dollars elsewhere.'

'I get that. But he'll cut humanities first, surely. This is America, Demetrius. The whole country is built on science. It's why it's the most powerful nation on earth.'

'Sure, but it's run by people with arts degrees, including our new principal. Those folks? They don't think like that.' He drew a slow, graphic finger across his throat. 'Chemistry, physics, bio? You mark my words: they're on the chopping block.'

'Well, I certainly hope you're wrong.'

'Don't hope too hard, bro.'

'Why ever not?'

'Because, if I'm wrong, you'll be the one getting the pink slip.'

1:07 P.M.

With a rising sense of horror, Greg realized there was a stain on the lapel of his jacket. An errant splash of mayo. A small one, to be sure, but a stain, nonetheless. There was no way he was going into a meeting with Principal Eisner looking like that. Truth be told, there was no way Greg would have a one-on-one with *anyone* looking like that. The jacket was new, and Harris tweed, and expensive. Greg had been pleased with the purchase. He looked good in clothes. He liked clothes. As long as they were stylish. The rumpled, mismatched fabrics that constituted faculty fashion offended him, but he'd no choice other than to fit in, parading through the corridors of Calderhill in a series of ghastly outfits that he'd shrug off as soon as he got home.

The Harris tweed jacket was different. It appeared rumpled but wasn't. Even though it didn't look at all out of place in a high school classroom, he could feel the quality of the material pressing against his shoulders as he taught.

And now it was covered in mayonnaise. He popped into the nearest restroom.

Fresh as it was, the stain wasn't too bad, easily removed with a damp paper towel dabbed carefully over the affected area. This, of course, resulted in a wet patch. He took the jacket off and exposed the lapel to the hot roar of an air dryer.

Perhaps, if he'd been less absorbed by the stain, less deafened by the machine, he'd have heard the faint sound earlier. Realized he was not alone. Hairs prickled on the back of his neck. He stepped away from the dryer, allowing the wheezy blast to fade away. He changed his stance, adjusting his balance in the silence.

There it was again.

The tiniest shuffling of feet.

Behind a locked cubicle door.

Greg sighed.

He was in a high school restroom, not the grimy facilities of a biker bar in Minsk. He forced himself to relax. If the past was going to find him, it wasn't going to be here. He allowed himself the luxury of embarrassment. Slipped his jacket back on.

A sob, desperately stifled.

'Hello? You all right in there?'

He heard a quick intake of breath.

'Anything I can do to help? You want to talk about it?'

Nothing. Not even the sound of breathing.

For a moment, Greg gave serious thought to kicking the door in, effecting some kind of rescue. But rescue from what? He was on the second floor of an upscale, very expensive private school, knee deep in privilege, so it was almost certainly nothing. Adolescent angst. Dumped, probably. Or parents insisting he drive a used car. Best to let the kid cry it out and get on with his life. Besides, if he waited to see how this played out, he'd be late for his appointment with Principal Eisner.

He stepped out of the restroom and continued on his way. As ever, he entered the admin suite with a faint sense of foreboding.

'Come in, Greg. Take a seat.'

Greg did so, trying very hard not to get distracted.

It wasn't simply that Principal Eisner's office looked different from that of his predecessor, although it did. Despite the furniture and décor being completely unchanged, it was like sitting in a brand-new room. There was a sense of tidiness and order in place of the previous chaos. Books fit neatly on the shelves, alphabetized and, so far as Greg could make out, arranged by subject. Various certificates hung on the walls in matching frames, the more important ones arranged so that they were easy to read from where Greg was now sitting: summa cum laude from Pitt; PhD from Yale; a public service award from the San Antonio chapter of the Sierra Club. The desk, the surface of which Greg could not recall seeing during the previous regime was, to be fair, slightly untidy. But it was the sort of mess that could be cleared away with a couple of minutes' effort at the end of the workday.

Décor aside, a great deal of Greg's distraction stemmed from the fact that Principal Eisner was a startlingly good-looking man. He was tall and athletically built, in a neatly pressed suit that fitted well enough to be tailored. Cheerful, hazel eyes twinkled out at him from behind a pair of rimless glasses. Greg forced himself to meet the man's gaze. The alternative risked focusing too much on the way the principal's chest pressed against the smooth fabric of his shirt. The feeling that Greg had tried to ignore when talking to Demetrius earlier in the day reasserted itself. His heart was beating a little faster, his mouth was dryer than he would like, there were butterflies in the pit of his stomach.

A condition worsened by the one framed object more prominently displayed than either the degrees or the eco-prize.

A photograph of Principal Eisner and his very male partner, heads pressed gently together, a beach and attendant ocean stretching out endlessly behind them.

A chill spread down the back of his neck and across his shoulders. Somewhere behind him, somewhere out of sight, the Devil was taking a seat.

Don't just look, the Devil whispered. *He likes you. You can do more than that.*

Except it was a sin, and he wasn't made that way. Not normally. He wasn't a—

Eisner was looking at him, clearly expecting an answer to . . . something.

'I'm sorry?' Greg said, relieved his voice sounded nowhere near as flustered as he felt.

'I was just asking how your day's been.'

'Fine. Good, actually.'

'Great. Great.' Eisner settled back in his chair. He had the air of a man who had said the same thing many times already. 'As you know, Greg, I've been meeting members of the faculty one on one to get a sense of how things are with all of you, where you think the school is in light of the recent difficulties, and what your view is of the best way forward. Though we do have to bear in mind, obviously, that things will have to change. We can't go on as we are.'

'I understand.' He had a sudden, vivid image of the school basement. The custodian's room. The bloodstained floor. Vernon Szymanski sloshing pink-stained water down the drain, its rusted grating deep-set in the concrete.

There'd been a murder, and a subsequent scandal, and he'd been caught up in all of it.

Bad memories, to be sure. But he was grateful to be thinking of something other than the man on the other side of the desk.

'We've lost some kids this year and admissions inquiries are down,' Eisner continued, 'so it's real important we stabilize the situation. That we project an image of normality.'

'Does an image of normality include mass firings of the staff?'

Eisner smiled at that.

'They told me you could be surprisingly blunt. I guess that English accent of yours kind of lets you get away with stuff, huh?'

Greg inclined his head in agreement. Eisner chuckled.

'OK. I'll learn to deal with it, I guess. And to answer your question: I hope not. The finances are in decent enough shape, though I don't think we can weather a prolonged slump. But as long as we all pull together, I'm hopeful we can avoid the worst. This is a great school: best in the region. We just need to remind people of that.' Eisner's expression turned shrewd. 'But if I *were* thinking of reductions, you wouldn't be on the list. Know why?'

Greg had a pretty shrewd idea.

'I bring in too much money.'

'Exactly. Now, why is that?'

'Cultural funding. From the State Department.'

'So everyone keeps telling me. I've never heard of such a thing.'

'And yet, here I am.'

'Here you are. Care to tell me what's really going on?'

Witness protection asked me if I had any 'life skills'. I lied, channeled my mother and said I knew how to teach.

'Absolutely. The State Department is concerned that a lack of language skills hampers US diplomacy. My funding is part of a program to increase the number of people culturally exposed to countries in which the US has a strategic interest, Russia being one of them.' He made sure to keep his expression guileless. 'There's a lot more Mandarin being taught these days, too.'

'And that's it? Nothing more?' Eisner didn't look even slightly convinced.

'Nothing more.' Greg allowed himself a small smile. 'What is it that Freud is meant to have said? Sometimes a cigar is just—'

'—a cigar,' Eisner finished, laughing. 'Have it your way. I guess I shouldn't look a gift horse in the mouth.' The hazel eyes crinkled. 'Not that I'm comparing you to an actual horse, you understand. Besides, I hear good things about your classes, so there's that.'

The talk turned to the school's current situation and the way forward. Matters of great interest to Eisner, obviously, but not at all suited to Greg's skillset. He could barely teach, never mind run a school that had been in the headlines for all the wrong reasons. He tried to be constructive, but all that came out of his mouth were bromides and platitudes. Eisner listened politely, but it was clear to Greg that he wasn't saying anything the man was finding useful. The interview wound down toward its natural conclusion.

'I look forward to seeing you at the game tonight,' Eisner said, as they rose from their respective chairs.

'The game?' Greg was almost certain the Penguins weren't playing that evening, absolutely certain they weren't playing at home, and beyond certain that he didn't have a ticket.

'Basketball?' Eisner prompted. 'Against the Edgeworth School? It's the playoff decider, Greg. A lot's riding on it. You gotta be there. Show some school spirit.'

'I—'

'Great. I'll see you then. It'll send a message of solidarity to the parents. Ours and theirs.'

Eisner clapped him on the shoulder on the way out. Long, powerful fingers rested briefly atop Greg's Harris tweed jacket.

The feel of it stayed with him far longer than normal.

3:50 P.M.

'Is that thing on?' Greg tried not to let his irritation show, but he couldn't help himself. He was staring down the barrel of a video camera.

'No, sir. Sorry, sir.' Caitlin Bell, looking alarmed, took a step back and pointed the offending instrument at the floor instead. Long strands of purple hair, suddenly disheveled, fell across her face.

'Sorry to bark at you,' Greg said, unnerved by the effect he'd had on her. He was continually surprised at how easy it was to frighten students, and he particularly regretted doing so to Caitlin. While he made a conscious point of not playing favorites, Caitlin would have been a front runner for the position. 'Old man. Technology in face. Frightening.'

Much to his relief, Caitlin decided to see the funny side.

'I'm sorry it wasn't on, sir,' she said, pushing the stray locks back into place. 'It would have been a great reaction shot.'

Greg fell in step beside her, swept along in a river of students.

'You off to the game?' he asked.

'Yes, sir.' A loaded pause. 'Are you?'

'Of course. Why are you looking at me like that?'

'Because you're not the basketball type.'

'I like all sports.'

'No, you don't. You like ice hockey. And maybe soccer.' Dark eyes twinkled at him from beneath lightly glittered eyelashes. 'Did the principal make you come?'

'Busted,' Greg said, laughing. 'So: what do I need to know? It's a big game, yes?'

'Yes,' Caitlin agreed. 'It's a big game. Last of the regular season, and the winner goes to the playoffs.'

'And we have home field advantage?'

'Yes, sir. Which we're definitely going to need because the Essies are good this year.'

'The Essies?'

'Edgeworth School. Keep up, sir.'

'Sorry.'

'They beat us at their place with a freak three-pointer just before the buzzer, seventy to sixty-seven. But a couple of their starters fouled out early; otherwise, it might not have been as close. I doubt that'll happen again tonight.'

'Does that mean we're the underdog?'

The question gave Caitlin pause.

'No,' she said at last. 'We're playing in our own house, and we have Caleb, who was injured last time out.'

'Caleb Freedman?'

'Yes, sir.'

Demetrius's eldest son. Greg had forgotten he was on the team.

'He's that good, then?'

'Sure is.'

'And what's your role in all this?' He nodded at the video camera, still pointed safely away from him. 'Most people use phones when they want to film something. This looks a bit more serious.'

'It is, yeah. Will Zuckerman and I are making a sports documentary for Media Studies.' Caitlin's free hand swung out in an expansive arc. '"From Training Camp to Championship – A Season with the Calderhill Cougars."'

'"Championship", eh?'

'Gotta aim high, sir. We can always change the title if it doesn't work out.'

The river of students had carried them into the gym. Greg eyed the rows of tiered aluminum benches without enthusiasm. He watched Caitlin meet up with a boy – Will Zuckerman, presumably – armed with some kind of furry microphone. They headed off to a raised platform already occupied by a professional-looking and very grown-up camera crew. The game was big enough for the local media, apparently. Greg looked at the cameras with an increasing sense of disquiet, trying to figure out where he was most likely to be out of shot. Immediately below would—

'Greg! My man!' Demetrius Freedman wrapped a limb that was more tentacle than arm around his shoulders. 'I did *not* expect to see you here.' An expression of mock sympathy took ahold of the chemistry teacher's face. 'Principal got to you, yeah? Well, don't worry. You're not alone.' Demetrius directed Greg's attention to the benches directly across from where the cameras were setting up.

Three rows of teachers were huddled together, some more happily than others. Principal Eisner was right in the middle of them, his face alight with enthusiasm.

All of them sitting in the worst possible place for someone intent on keeping out of the limelight. Greg's gaze flicked unhappily between the TV cameras and the benches.

'Faculty's all here,' Demetrius said. 'I guess we'd better go join 'em.'

'But—'

'But what? I know basketball isn't your jam, but you might as well make the best of it. Hell, you might even like it. And you'll get to see Caleb play.' Demetrius clapped his hands together. The sound hit Greg's ears like a gunshot. '*Man*, I am so looking forward to this.'

And, just like that, Greg found himself being steered toward the rest of the faculty, directly across from the unblinking gaze of a news camera. He took a seat beside Demetrius. But not before reaching into the pocket of his tweed jacket and pulling out a Calderhill baseball cap. The rear strap was adjusted in such a way that it was too big for him, allowing the brim to slide down his forehead and cover half his face. Demetrius opened his mouth to say something, eyes twinkling with amusement. In the end, though, he decided to let it go.

Greg spent most of the game with his chin tucked into his chest. The result, of course, was that while his face was invisible to the cameras, the game was pretty much invisible to him. Teenage feet in expensive rubbery shoes pounded this way and that, soles squeaking on the floor, the ball a thumping bass as it bounced up and down the court. Sometimes the ball went into the basket, sometimes it didn't. Whistles blew and play stopped from time to time seemingly at random, even though Demetrius assured him there was nothing random about it. Either some rule had been broken or the referee needed a brand-new pair of eyes. And often, after the whistle had blown and Demetrius had opined on the rightness or otherwise of the call, someone would step up to a particular line marked out on the gleaming parquet floor and get a couple of free shots at the basket. Sometimes the ball went in, sometimes it didn't.

Unless the shooter was Caleb Freedman, in which case the shot went in far more often than not. Greg didn't need to look at Demetrius to feel him beaming with pride. Nor would it have escaped

Demetrius's notice that his son was the only Black player on the court. A fact that, in other circumstances, he would have complained about vociferously. Calderhill were edging ahead. A two-point gap became three, became seven, settled back to five. Stayed there. Sometimes the ball went in, sometimes it didn't.

The clock was winding down toward the end of the third period. Caleb Freedman was standing at the free-throw line, ready to make the first of two attempts. In Greg's mind, the gap had already increased to seven. Caleb spun the ball in his hands, eyeing the basket. The spinning stopped, the ball settled, Caleb took aim, bent his knees just a fraction and—

'Chain him up!'

A male voice. Adult. From the middle of the Edgeworth School's traveling support.

Demetrius stiffened. The ball smacked impotently against the rim and fell limp to the floor.

The ball was put back in Caleb's hands. He took aim. Bent his knees—

'Chain him up!'

The ball swished through the net. The scoreboard ticked over. Caleb glared at the Edgeworth School parents and trotted back to the opposite end of the court.

The only thing stopping Demetrius from leaping to his feet was Greg's grip on the chemistry teacher's arm.

'Let go of me!'

'So you can get up and make a scene?'

'Yes, goddamn it. That's my son! I'm going to find that smug, racist fucker and break his goddam neck!'

Greg refused to let go.

'That smug, racist fucker is a parent at the school you've just accepted a position at.' He waved his free hand in the direction of the cameras. 'A position that will be rescinded the moment you punch him out in full view of a local news crew. And which will be followed, sure as eggs is eggs, by an assault charge and your present employer suspending you without pay.' Greg's grip tightened a fraction. '*Think*, Demetrius. Please.'

The ball was thudding down the court again. Rubber soles squeaked against the floor.

Demetrius slumped back in his seat, sighed air hissing through his lips like a deflating balloon.

'This is fucked up, man. Fucked *up*.'

The clock wound down to zero.

As the teams changed ends, Principal Eisner got to his feet. Greg watched, intrigued, as he had a quick word with the referee and then made straight for the Edgeworth School's coach.

This time, Demetrius was too quick for him. Eluding Greg's grasp, the chemistry teacher's long legs stepped from bench to bench and down on to the floor, where he intended, no doubt, to be a factor in whatever Principal Eisner was up to. Fearing the worst, Greg followed, baseball cap down, head angled away from the cameras, which, for the moment, were blessedly oblivious to the drama unfolding before them. Caitlin Bell and her partner were touching heads, exchanging *sotto voce* technicalities. The grown-up crew were focusing on center court, waiting for play to restart.

'They can take a walk around the block and cool their heels,' Eisner was saying, as Greg arrived within earshot. 'They can't stay here.'

Edgeworth's coach, a short, barrel-chested man with a florid face and thinning hair, shook his head in apparent disbelief.

'I'm sure you misheard,' he said.

'I'm sure he didn't,' Demetrius growled, looming over Eisner's shoulder. The coach's expression displayed a flash of nervousness.

'You can't eject people for harmless banter. It's gamesmanship, that's all. Trying to put your best guy off his shot.'

'Then it's gamesmanship of the worst sort,' Eisner said, before Demetrius could speak again. 'And a very unfortunate choice of words. You can't demand that the only Black kid in the game should be chained up.'

The coach was looking at him blankly.

'Slavery? *Chains*?' For the first time, Eisner's voice carried an edge. 'I'm not here to debate with you, sir. This is my school, and the dads have to go. Moms and kids can stay.'

'And if they refuse?'

'Then this game is over.'

A smile wrinkled the coach's face.

'Fine by me. You'll forfeit.'

'Sorry to interrupt. But I have an awful feeling the fire alarm's about to go off.' The words fled from Greg's mouth before he could stop them. Three heads turned toward him, expressions comically identical in their surprise. Greg was left with no choice but to style it out. 'Everyone will have to leave, of course. But I dare say we can finish the game once everyone realizes there's no actual fire.' He allowed himself an expression of insincere concern. 'I don't imagine we'll be readmitting everyone to the building, though. It might not be safe, after all. School IDs and players only, I imagine. No forfeit, naturally. And no support at all for the, ah, *Essies*. A shame, really.'

'You wouldn't dare,' the coach said.

Eisner's lips quirked in a vain attempt to keep a smile from his face.

'Don't bet on it, pal,' Demetrius said, his expression fierce. He towered menacingly over the coach, hands clenched into large fists.

A faint stir rippled through the crowd as it dawned on them that something was going on. Cameras, amateur and professional, swung in their direction. Greg presented them with his back.

'Fine,' the coach said. He was looking warily at the cameras. Perhaps, Greg mused, he was thinking about how the tape would play elsewhere. Edgeworth, after all, was about to set up an office of 'Diversity, Equity and Inclusion'. Being the subject of its first inquiry would not be a good look. The coach turned toward the traveling support, uncaring that Greg, Demetrius and Eisner got to hear his final word on the matter.

'Assholes.'

Greg headed home significantly later than he'd intended – well after dark, in fact. Edgeworth had collapsed in the fourth period, returning to the suburbs nursing a seventy-one to fifty-eight loss. Celebrations in the school turned into pizzas with the team and the team's parents at a local restaurant. Demetrius had insisted that Greg come along and, despite Greg's entreaties, had regaled anyone who would listen with tales of the end-of-third-period confrontation.

'A fire alarm,' he'd said, laughing. 'Can you believe that? A goddamn fire alarm!' Demetrius's fist had pounded the table, causing the nearest pizza slices to wobble. 'That was too funny, man. Too funny.'

Greg had tried not to cringe. But now, having parked a little farther up the hill from his apartment than he would have liked, he got to thinking that it was a fun episode in a life that didn't have too many of them. A small injustice had been avenged, the new principal turned out to have a spine, and Calderhill was in the playoffs. Better yet, Demetrius had been kept out of trouble.

And it had all been accomplished without his face being caught on camera. He would not be coming to the attention of anyone who could do him harm.

With regard to this latter thought, however, Gregory Abimbola could not have been more wrong.

As he rounded the curve that brought his apartment building into view, a car door opened maybe fifty yards ahead of him. Standing under the streetlight was a tall female figure in a long coat and a pantsuit that had seen better days. The coat, unbuttoned at the front, rippled rebelliously in the spring breeze. The woman's hands were jammed into its pockets. She didn't wave in greeting or say anything by way of hello. She just stood there, waiting.

Detective Sergeant Rachel Lev of the Pittsburgh Police.

7:32 P.M.

'So it's lieutenant now?'

'Acting lieutenant.'

Surreal, Greg thought, didn't cover the half of it. He seated himself in a newly acquired leather chair, wearing an expression he hoped was coming across as confident and friendly. Sergeant or, rather, Acting Lieutenant Rachel Lev was inside his apartment, perched across from him on the living-room sofa. She was still wearing her coat, as if expecting to be thrown out at any second. An expectation that Greg would have been happy to meet but for the bounds of common courtesy and the fact that Rachel Lev was here for a reason. And if Rachel Lev had a reason, it was probably best to find out about it now rather than get blindsided later. Hands that had waved away his offers of tea or vodka clasped each other instead, their grip tight enough to whiten her knuckles.

'I like your apartment, Mr Abimbola.' Her eyes, as dark and thoughtful as he remembered, refused to meet his gaze. They stared at the walls instead. 'Nice, er, prints.'

That's when it dawned on him.

Rachel Lev was even more nervous than he was.

'I do what I can,' he said quietly. 'And the rent is very reasonable.' A tentative stab at humor. 'Nothing here is stolen, if that's what you're wondering.'

'What? No. That never even crossed my mind.' Lev looked desperately serious until she caught the twinkle in his eye. She broke into a relieved grin, followed by something far more earnest. 'Fact is,' she said, 'I need your help.'

'*My* help?' Greg scratched at the underside of his eye patch to cover his confusion. A trap, surely. What the heck was she playing at? 'I'm just a teacher, Lieutenant. I don't see how I can be of any help to you at all.'

Which provoked a dry, slightly cynical laugh.

'Oh, you're far more than just a teacher, Mr Abimbola. I think we both know that.'

Greg's heart thudded in his chest.

'You're also a quite good amateur detective. We might never have solved the Delcade case without you.'

His sigh of relief was too quiet for the police officer to hear.

'You're giving me more credit than I deserve.'

'Yeah, right. Anyway, that's why I'm here.'

'As far as I know, Lieutenant—'

'Rachel. Please.' She had a lovely smile when she put her mind to it.

'As far as I know . . . *Rachel*, no one has been murdered on school premises lately, so, regardless of my alleged extra-curricular abilities, I don't see what I have to offer that you could possibly want.' He was chagrined, however, to hear the note of intrigue in his voice. The longing for something more challenging, more dangerous than a room full of privileged, mildly resistant teenagers.

'I'm going to tell you a story, Mr Abimbola.'

'Greg,' he said, finding himself smiling in return. 'It seems only fair.'

'Greg it is.' Her expression turned wry. 'The details of this story are new, but the plot, I'm afraid, is kind of dull. Dull and annoying and the sort of thing we've all seen before.' Rachel leaned forward. 'So, once upon a time, there was this girl – because girl was all she was allowed to be – who wanted to be a police officer. And she succeeded, up to a point. She made it through the academy with only a few grabs of her ass, out of uniform and into plain clothes with the usual levels of harassment, and from there to investigations and homicide. She even made sergeant, if you can believe that.

'But then she got kinda stuck. Good at her job but not quite one of the boys. She needed to try harder to fit in, they said. And she tried and made a fool of herself trying, and stayed stuck where she was anyways. Good at the detail, they'd say, but not able to see the big picture. Not like the boys. More like a secretary with a badge.'

Greg made a move to object, but Rachel waved him down.

'And then some Hispanic kid is pulled in for murdering a woman in a school basement. This doesn't feel right, the girl said, but the boys ignored her. Then some weird-ass teacher weighs in on the kid's behalf. The boys ignore him but the girl . . . the girl listens.

And when the weird-ass teacher fingers the real murderer, the girl is there to bring them in and get all the credit.'

'A happy ending, then.'

Rachel gave him a wan smile.

'Almost. The girl is taken more seriously, seriously enough for a promotion: the big LT. In Collision Investigations, maybe. Or the Nuisance Bar Task Force. But Homicide? Robbery even? Nah. She can't see the big picture. HR will find her a suitable slot in a few months, and in the meantime she can do what she does best, assisting a real LT on another homicide. An unidentified man washed up in the Allegheny, by the Rachel Carson bridge.'

Morosov. Or someone uncannily like him.

'I read about that,' Greg said slowly. He couldn't quite put his finger on the swirling sensation in the pit of his stomach. More than curiosity, for sure. Fear, maybe? Excitement? A connection to home? His real home, that is. Not this steep-sloped city in the foothills of the Appalachians. 'I'd no idea you were working on it.'

'*Assisting* on it. Until the LT in question – a man you are familiar with, by the way – suffers a minor heart attack and has to take medical leave.'

Greg didn't insult Rachel's intelligence by pretending to be sympathetic to the man's plight. Brendan Cassidy was a dick.

'Anyway, *now* the girl gets her chance. The LT had come to a dead end. No one else wants the gig, so why not let the girl have a go? She wants to prove she has what it takes to be a homicide detective? Great. Let's see what she can do.'

'Sounds like a poisoned chalice.'

'You think? But, poisoned or not, this is the only chalice she's going to get. She seizes it with both hands. And quickly realizes she's just as stuck as the LT. Because maybe they're right, after all. Maybe I don't have what it takes. All detail, no big picture. Perfect for collision investigations.'

Rachel's eyes glittered with unnatural brightness.

'Anyway,' she said, after a deep breath, 'the girl's not giving it up without a fight. She needs help. A mind that works differently from hers. If she asks inside the department, they'll use it against her. So she has no choice, does she? Not really. She has to go outside. To the weird-ass teacher who got his Hispanic friend off the hook and solved a murder that Pittsburgh PD couldn't.'

Greg knew he was staring.

And dumbstruck.

'Say *something*, goddammit.'

'You mean it, then. You actually want my help?'

'I think I've made that pretty damn clear, don't you?'

Greg slumped back in his seat. The seat may have been newly acquired, but it was almost two hundred years old. He was still getting used to it. The worn antique leather of its arms was soft beneath his hands. How many of its previous owners, he wondered, had sat here like he was sitting now, contemplating some off-the-wall proposal? How many had accepted? How many not? How had it gone for them?

Maybe Morosov was dead and dumped in the Allegheny, maybe not. WITSEC had told him nothing, MI5 even less. If Morosov *was* dead, who had killed him and why? Did the killers, like Morosov, now know who Greg Abimbola was? And if so, were they a threat or had they done him a favor and hidden him from further pursuit?

Enquiring minds want to know.

Rachel Lev could help him get answers he'd never get otherwise.

But Rachel Lev was a police officer. And Rachel Lev was no fool. What if it *was* Morosov dead in the water? Like it or not, he and Morosov were connected. What if, somehow, Rachel Lev made the connection? He'd be exposed, his cover story blown. He'd have no choice but to leave town. And much as he railed against the quiet life of a Russian language teacher, truth was he was beginning to like it. For the first time in his life, he was putting down roots, making connections with people. So what if it was boring? It was also warm and comforting.

And safe.

Rachel Lev, the woman who was no fool, could end it in a heartbeat.

The antique leather pressed against his palms, history in every stitch, every irregularity. Proposals accepted. Proposals turned down. Railroad investments maybe, marriages, some old-time run for the Senate.

'How can I be of service?' he said.

A Rubicon crossed. For both of them. Rachel leaned back in the sofa with a sigh.

'Let me tell you some of what we know, and then, if you could maybe think on it and we can talk some more?'

'Sounds like a plan.'

'Great!' Her expression became immediately businesslike. 'Our vic is a Caucasian male, mid-forties. Six foot tall, two hundred pounds and physically fit for his age. He'd been shot twice by a nine-millimeter: once in the shoulder, which didn't kill him, and once in the head, which most definitely did.' Her dark eyes raked him over, the look appraising. 'You're not squeamish, I hope?'

'I deal with teenagers. So, no.'

Rachel smiled at that.

'The reason I ask is because the head shot took out most of his face, so we don't know what he looked like. Which, as you can imagine, is a problem.'

'Quite.'

'We do have some dental, though, which is interesting. A lot of the work is Eastern European.'

'Is that why you think he might be Russian?' In response to Rachel's quizzical look, Greg hastened to explain. 'It was in the news reports. They said he was either Russian *or* British. Which seems . . . odd.'

He chose not to dwell on the irony.

'Not as odd as you'd think. One of the weirder things I've picked up on this case is that London is crawling with Russian oligarchs. It's like a little Moscow over there. "Londongrad".' The moniker provoked a wry smile. 'This guy isn't an oligarch, though. People like that don't go missing without *somebody* noticing. But he might be oligarch adjacent, if you know what I mean. We've floated some inquiries with local law enforcement but nothing doing so far.'

'Eastern European fillings don't make him Russian, necessarily. There's more to Eastern Europe than just Russia, you know.'

'True. But he has a surgical pin in his right shoulder – the one that wasn't shot, by the way. The pin has a Russian serial number. We tried to get information about it from the Russian authorities, but, again, nothing doing so far.'

Had Morosov ever had surgery? Greg couldn't remember. But even if he had, Russia being Russia, there was no way on earth Rachel Lev would ever hear back.

'OK. I get the pin thing. The guy's had surgery in Russia, so he's probably Russian. What makes you think he's British?'

'His clothes. Every last thing he had on was British. Savile Row shirt and tie, suit pants from Moss Brothers, underwear from, er, someplace called Marks and Spencer.'

Greg could feel a smile quirking at his lips.

'No suit jacket?'

Rachel gave him a thoughtful look.

'Not that we found, no.'

That did not sound like Morosov at all. The man always wore a jacket. Unless he thought it was going to get creased or he was . . . working on someone. Greg's hand strayed to his eye patch.

'All right,' he said. 'That makes sense. Your deceased is a man with a very close connection to Russia, who has lived in Britain long enough to buy his underwear at Marks and Sparks – Spencer,' he added hastily in response to the frown forming on Rachel's brow. 'He's been shot twice and killed. But, given he was found in the Allegheny, I'm assuming the crime scene was somewhere else.'

'We don't have a crime scene.' Rachel grimaced. 'Best guess is he was dumped. Either there or farther upstream.'

'And no one saw him thrown into the water?'

'No. If we had a witness, *any* witness, I probably wouldn't be sitting in your apartment risking my career, reputation and dignity.'

'I'm just a teacher,' Greg said gently. 'You have to allow me the odd stupid question.'

'Yeah. Sorry.'

Greg's eyebrows climbed up his forehead. He was surprised at the detective's apology, the speed of it. She must be genuinely desperate to be here at all, he reminded himself. The last thing she could afford to do was alienate him. In a department where the men were holding her back, here she was, looking to another man for help.

Which, all things considered, did not put Rachel Lev in a good place.

He found himself channeling his mother. Someone who'd spent her entire life in the petty, back-biting and overwhelmingly male environment of Russian academia. Who'd thrived there. Reveled in it.

'Don't be sorry when I'm the one being thick,' he said. 'In fact, don't be sorry on the job, *ever*. That's one of the ways they keep you down.' He thought of Rachel Lev's ass of a superior. The man who wouldn't listen. 'Would Lieutenant Cassidy say sorry? Even when he was completely and totally wrong?'

Acting Lieutenant Rachel Lev gave a rueful shake of the head.

'There's plenty of people in the world who'd be happy to put you down,' he continued. 'And absolutely no reason why you should give them a hand, OK?'

'I guess not.'

'Anyway, moving on. Any gunshot residue on the deceased?'

She threw him that thoughtful look again.

'Why are you asking?'

'I'm trying to figure out what sort of situation he'd got himself into. Maybe he was in a gunfight. One that he lost.'

'Hmm. Worth thinking about. Definitely.' A long sigh. 'To be honest, we didn't test for it. I'll speak to the medical examiner.' Seeing the expression on Greg's face, she felt compelled to add, 'Our vic was in the water for several hours, which has a nasty way of screwing around with the forensics, so Lieutenant Cassidy didn't see the point of spending the department's budget on a useless test. The gunfight angle may make it worth the effort, though, even if it's a long shot.' Her expression brightened a little. 'But I can tell you this: he wasn't shot point blank. There'd have been burn marks and stippling that the river would have been unable to erase. But whether he was armed at the time? We don't know.'

A gunfight, Greg thought, would almost certainly rule out Morosov. Not that the man was averse to shooting people – far from it. But when Greg had last seen him, when Greg had laid him flat out with a dumbbell to the temple, he had most definitely not been armed. Not with a gun, anyway. And he'd left Greg's presence in the custody of the US Marshals.

'Any sign of a robbery?' he asked.

'Hard to say. There's no wallet but, like you pointed out, there's no jacket, either. So we can't tell if the wallet was stolen or if it's wherever he left his jacket. But there was also no watch, and shading on the left wrist indicates he was a habitual wearer, which weighs in favor of some kind of mugging.' Another sigh. 'But then again, if he removed his jacket voluntarily for some reason, maybe he took the watch off, too. Or maybe the whole kit and caboodle was stolen and this is just a robbery gone bad.'

Morosov, Greg recalled, was a great lover of watches. Big, chunky, expensive ones, always with metal bands, and with his initials engraved on the back. He claimed the bands would cut through rope if you gave them enough time, so, really, a big expensive watch counted as survival gear.

Greg had chuckled politely. Polukhin had called him a corrupt, bullshitting *kulak*.

Try as he might, Greg couldn't remember whether Morosov had been wearing a watch or not.

He became aware that Rachel was looking at him expectantly.

'Yes, well, that's a lot to think about,' he said. He pursed his lips, wondering how far he could push his luck. Rachel Lev, despite the present bizarre situation, was a highly competent, highly professional police officer. There was only so far she would go with a member of public.

On the other hand, though, she was drivingly, perhaps recklessly, ambitious. Otherwise, the present bizarre situation would never have arisen in the first place.

He came to a decision. Turned the smile on his face all the way up to charming.

'Is there any chance,' he asked sweetly, 'of seeing the file?'

TUESDAY, THE SEVENTH
5:21 A.M.

When it came to his morning runs, Greg had a love–hate relationship with Pittsburgh's hills. He loved the extra boost they gave to his fitness; he hated the dump truck of pain that came along for the ride. His younger self wouldn't have loathed them quite so much, he thought between gasps, before discounting the idea as delusional. It was important to remember what he'd actually been like back then. His younger, less disciplined self would have hated them even more than he did. It's just that he would have gotten to the top a hell of a lot faster.

The wry smile that was the usual by-product of thoughts like this refused to form. It was too hard. He was climbing the steep grade of Centre Avenue out of Oakland, headed toward downtown and moving far too fast. Weak, widely spaced streetlights did little to dispel the Stygian, pre-dawn darkness. He pounded along beneath an overhang of not quite leafless trees. The gritty sidewalk, unused to pedestrian traffic, scrunched beneath his feet as he fought to maintain a steady rhythm.

Too fast. Too old.

His heart pounded in protest.

He needed to slow down, to give his body a chance.

A car swooped by on his left, headlights splashing the world with sudden color, its driver blissfully uncaring of the gradient, of the extra work the motor was putting out simply because he'd pressed a little harder on the throttle. The vehicle reached the top in mere seconds, disappearing from view beneath a green traffic light. Greg was alone again. Feet pounding. Rhythm somehow maintained.

Too fast. Too old.

He really ought to slow down.

Greg was alone on the road because few runners used this stretch of Centre. Whenever he mentioned his route to one of the faculty, there would invariably be a discreet silence, or some opaque comment along the lines of 'You should be careful.'

What they meant, of course, was that he was running through the Hill District, which pretty much guaranteed that he would be mugged and murdered by Black people.

At five in the morning.

As if. Black people had better things to be doing with their lives than mugging middle-aged joggers.

The traffic light at the summit was growing slightly closer. Pain lanced through his legs and lungs.

He tried to slow down and failed miserably.

Because the thing that was propelling him at this ridiculous pace, the thing he didn't quite have control over, was the sheer excitement of working on the maybe-Morosov murder case.

Rachel, after a moment's hesitation, had agreed to bring over the file or, more accurately, to share some of the contents with him. In the disjointed fashion of hypoxic runners, he wondered whether he should have another go at Werner and Aldis, tell them what he now knew about the case, see if he could shake something loose.

Yeah, right. Neither Werner nor Aldis had a career-related incentive to be indiscreet. They'd give him nothing. Worse yet, a quiet call to the Pittsburgh chief of police would cut off his new-found access and wreck Rachel Lev's career all in one go. Not one of his better ideas.

A car appeared at the top of the hill, its headlights on high beam, dazzling him. It hurtled down and past, engine aroar, intent on reaching wherever it was going as quickly as possible. Greg, having decided that this behavior meant the driver was some kind of reckless narcissist, had tried to get a look at whomever was sitting behind the wheel. But it was too dark, his vision was too blinded, and the target was traveling too quickly for any kind of identification.

The traffic light at the summit was definitely closer now. Pounding heart or not, he was going to make it.

Perhaps, if he hadn't been dazzled by headlights, or too deafened by engine noise, or too out of breath to think straight, he would have been more aware of a vehicle approaching from behind. Of the same vehicle slowing to a crawl alongside him. Perhaps he would have remembered that the bulky, unmarked silhouette was on his left side, the side without a working eye. And, perhaps, he would have made the effort to turn his head to get a better look. Had he done so, it might perhaps have occurred to him that a vehicle that had come up from behind him with its headlights off was a cause for concern.

Perhaps.

Only when he heard the too-loud rumble of a sliding door did it occur to Greg Abimbola that something was wrong. Large, powerful arms wrapped around his shoulders and bundled him to the ground. The man's hot breath blasted against his ears, filled his nose with the stench of stale alcohol. Something stabbed into his neck, the pain sharp and short as his body went into shock.

The faculty had been right, after all, he thought as he struggled to free himself. He was going to get mugged. And worse.

He moved to break the hold they had on him, the motion instinctive, the result of endless training and real-world practice. But nothing happened. His limbs were too sluggish. Rubbery to the point of uselessness.

'We've got you now, you bastard.'

Incongruous, egocentric satisfaction bubbled up alongside the rapidly rising terror.

The faculty was wrong, and he was right.

After a fashion.

The snarling words had not come wrapped in a Black accent. Of course they hadn't.

Because every single syllable had been Russian.

It was the last thing he registered before the world disappeared.

Time Unknown

For several moments, Greg Abimbola was unsure as to whether his good eye was open or closed. His head thumped in the pitch blackness, there was a burning pain in the deep muscles of his neck, his mouth was painfully dry. He grabbed what little spit he could muster, tried to moisten his lips with a leaden tongue.

And tasted cloth. Thick. Velvety. Hard to breathe through.

They'd put him in a hood. He could feel the cord biting against his throat where they'd tied it just a little tighter than necessary. He struggled to control his breathing. To stay calm.

This, after all, was only the beginning.

He was sitting in a hard wooden chair, wrists tied to the arms – with duct tape by the feel of it. His ankles were attached to the chair legs in the same way, he guessed. He couldn't be entirely sure because he couldn't feel so well through his socks.

Which was interesting. He'd have expected to be barefoot. Yet his socks and running shoes were still on. Definitely *not* protocol. Bare feet not only lessened the chance of escape, they made you feel vulnerable, robbed you of a sense of dignity, made it clear you were less than.

A standard precursor to a long and painful interrogation.

So maybe this wasn't an interrogation at all. Maybe they were planning on making it quick.

Greg's heart, driven by conflicting impulses, thudded harder in his chest. Terrified by his impending death, relieved there'd be no torture.

But if they were simply going to kill him, why hadn't they done so already?

Think, idiot. If I had me *in this situation, why would I keep myself alive?*

He let out a slow breath. Put like that, the answer became straightforward. They wanted him to know he was being executed – and why. They wanted to look him in the eye. See him recognize that it was over. Send him to the other side with one last message ringing in his ears.

Don't fuck with us. Ever.

And once he got there, once he reached the other side, the tortures he would endure then, the eternal kind, would make him wish he were still on earth, dealing with the very worst the GRU had to offer.

He bit back a sob, ashamed of himself for being so weak.

And then angry.

Fuck these guys. He wasn't going to give them the satisfaction. Not yet, anyway. Whatever they thought of him, of his treachery, the color of his skin, he was still Russian. If they wanted him to scream and beg, they'd better do the work.

The duct tape around his ankles was affecting his circulation. He wiggled his toes in an attempt to keep the blood flowing.

Then stopped, puzzled, before starting again.

There was something weird about his running shoes. No. Not the shoes. The ground beneath them. It was hard to be certain, given the thickness of the soles, but it felt like he was on open ground, that his feet were resting on uneven, rock-strewn earth.

Yet there was no sound, no breeze. The air was damp and oppressively still. There was no rustle of leaves in the trees, or the distant roar of traffic, or the uncaring chitter-chatter of birds. Nothing he would associate with being outside.

He had to be mistaken.

His left foot was too closely tied to the chair for any sort of movement. But his right . . . it was tight, too, but he sensed a little bit of give in it. Perhaps, if he made the effort . . .

He managed to slide the sole of his shoe across the ground. Was rewarded with the gritty, scraping sound of pebble against pebble.

A fist slammed into his stomach.

'You're awake. About fucking time.'

Russian again.

Greg was still gasping for air as the cord around his neck was untied and the hood removed. Light lanced through an over-dilated pupil, provoking tears. It was hard to see, to make sense of his surroundings.

But he made the effort.

He was sitting in an unfinished basement, the floor little more than an expanse of uneven gray gravel, ready to be dug out and floored. Construction tools leaned haphazardly against whitewashed brick walls, the whitewash blistered brown in places by damp. The tools within his field of vision comprised shovels, a couple of pick-axes and a sledgehammer, none of them a stranger to hard use, all blotched with gritty, cement-colored dust.

Tucked just under the low ceiling was something that looked like a narrow, horizontal window. He couldn't be entirely sure because the space was wadded with the orange fibrous fluff of roofing insulation. It cut off any connection to the outside world, to any source of light that might give him a sense of time or place.

How long have I been out? he wondered. The bruising ache in his neck was from a roughly applied needle, he guessed. Some fast-acting drug, which would also explain the pounding in his head. But had he been given one dose or several? Hours or days?

Somewhere behind him, a low-wattage ceiling bulb was bathing the room in insipid off-white illumination. As his eye adjusted to its surroundings, he realized that there was barely enough light to read by.

But more than enough to see what was right in front of him, what he'd known, instinctively, would be there. The one thing he'd purposely, desperately, tried not to look at.

The workbench. The tools.

Not for construction, these. These were for finer, wetter work. The bulb elicited a dull gleam from their smooth, lifeless surfaces.

A car battery, its jumper cables draped carelessly over notched, deeply scarred wood and an incongruous manila folder. Hammers. Pliers. Knives, serrated and not. The vicious curve of a bone saw.

A dental drill.

And beyond them all, atop a bulky tripod waiting for the action to begin, a video camera, its single large eye a distorting, disinterested black. For the folks back home.

So. It was to be torture, after all.

Greg's heart thudded even harder in his chest.

And almost burst under the force of the fist that smashed into his stomach.

'Mr Gregory Abimbola. A pleasure to meet you.'

English, this time.

The fist slammed in again. Greg couldn't breathe. Not even a little bit. His spasmed diaphragm refused to move. Waves of red rushed across his vision.

Just as he thought he would pass out, his diaphragm unstuck itself. Air rushed into his lungs in great wheezing gasps. Greg rode it out, fear replaced by an insensate fury that he was being attacked in this way.

Anger was his friend, now. Better than terror. Than snot-nosed begging. It wouldn't be his friend for long, he knew that. But he clung to it while he could, directing a hot glare at his assailant.

The man who'd hit him was tall and broad, blond hair buzzed savagely short to hide the fact he was starting to go bald. Disdainful blue eyes stared down at him from a face that might have been handsome had it not been disfigured by the broken nose of a boxer. He was dressed in a gray suit that was trying too hard to look expensive, the sheen of the cloth so bright as to be almost metallic in appearance, a match for the cheap-looking watch on his left wrist. Unlike Morosov, or himself for that matter, he hadn't bothered to take off his jacket before going to work.

Or anything else.

With his breathing barely under control, it was difficult for Greg to contort his face into the right kind of sneer, but he just about managed it.

'I'd been hoping to be interrogated by someone more professional. Not some *zhopoliz* from the provinces who's too stupid to ditch his shoulder holster.'

The not-quite-handsome face darkened in anger.

'Your Russian is very good for a *negr*. Let's see where that smart mouth of yours gets you.'

The fist slammed into him once more. Air abandoned his lungs in an agonized groan.

'I think that's quite enough, don't you?' a voice drawled from behind him. 'Besides, Mr Abimbola is entirely right. Why the fuck are you getting up close and personal carrying a gun?'

His assailant, face a mask of confusion, looked down at his shoulder holster. The blocky, red-brown grip of a Makarov PB, the GRU's weapon of choice, was clearly visible under his jacket.

'What if Mr Abimbola gets free?' The voice behind him turned rueful. 'Not impossible in his case, I assure you. He'll have that gun of yours before you have time to think to yourself – assuming you *know* how to think, comrade major – "Oh fuck, I'm a dead man."'

The speaker strolled into view. He was a small, slightly built man, on the older side of middle-aged, his hands thrust deep into the trouser pockets of a rumpled, off-the-shelf charcoal suit. The shirt beneath the suit was immaculately pressed, though; the tie precisely knotted; the black dress shoes polished to a gleam and unbesmirched by the gray grit of the basement floor. The shoes moved with a slow, languid precision until their owner was standing right in front of him.

Vladimir Vladimirovich Polukhin looked down at Greg with an expression that bordered on amusement. The humor, however, failed to reach his eyes. The gaze that raked Gregory Abimbola from head to restrained foot was distinctly cool.

'Leave us, Major.'

'But—'

'I'm not in the habit of repeating myself.'

'Yes, Comrade General.'

Heavy footsteps scrunched across the lumpy ground. Somewhere behind him, a door opened and closed with a petulant squeak. Polukhin watched the major depart, his expression contemptuous.

'The guy's a fucking idiot,' the general murmured. 'He should be pushing paper in Vladivostok. Or worse. But his mother . . . Ah! What a woman. A delight, Grigoriy Adamovich. A delight. How could she have birthed such a creature, I wonder?'

Polukhin's hands withdrew from his suit pockets and produced a pack of cigarettes.

'Want one?'

'No. Thank you.'

Polukhin fished a cigarette out of the pack, surveyed its dark length and lit it. The acrid tang of Russian tobacco filled the room. Greg's nose twitched on the edge of a sneeze.

The general wandered over to the workbench and picked up one of the knives, examining it with care. The wicked, serrated blade gleamed dully in the artificial light.

He turned toward Greg, knife in one hand, cigarette in the other, his gaze reptilian in its lack of pity. Greg tried not to tense up. Failed.

'We need to talk,' Polukhin said. And then, to Greg's utter astonishment, jammed the cigarette in his mouth, knelt beside one of the chair arms and started sawing away at the duct tape binding his wrist.

'Aren't you afraid I'll kill you?' The words burst out of him unbidden, the shock of it loosening his tongue far quicker than any beating.

Polukhin's rapid sawing didn't pause.

'Not really. Killing isn't your style, Grigoriy. You and I both know that.' He nodded sharply toward the back of the room. 'Besides, Major Dobrygin, having followed my orders to the literal letter, will no doubt have his ear pressed firmly against the door, trying to figure out what the hell is going on. Should he hear something untoward, he will no doubt use that recklessly worn sidearm of his to kill you where you stand. He's an excellent shot, by the way. He might kill me too, if you try to use me as a shield, but that won't stop him pulling the trigger. Not much of a thinker, that one.'

The sawing stopped, the job only half done. But the grip of the duct tape had loosened enough for Greg to wince at the painful return of circulation.

Polukhin looked thoughtful.

'As our friend Dobrygin *is* listening, it might be prudent to make his task more difficult.' The sawing began again. 'Your French remains good, yes?'

'*Oui*.'

'Excellent.' Unlike Greg, who had never quite managed to purge his French of a faint Russian accent, Polukhin's was flawless. '*La belle langue* is not one of Oleg's strengths. Not that he has many.'

The sawing began again. One of Greg's hands came free. He flexed it violently, hoping to banish the small agony of pins and needles. Polukhin moved to the other side of the chair.

'It was quite a shock to discover you were alive, let me tell you. Even more of a shock to discover you were hiding *here*, given that Pittsburgh is not unknown to us. And, of course, having reacquired you, an example should have been made.' Polukhin glanced meaningfully at the workbench and its assorted, brutal tools. 'In normal circumstances, anyway.'

The duct tape on his other wrist gave way with a gooey creak.

'In normal circumstances?'

'Precisely.' Polukhin dropped the knife on to Greg's lap, inviting him to free his legs. 'Circumstances have changed.'

'How?' Greg asked, bent over. He was trying not to slice open an artery in his hurry to be free.

'Not so much how as who. The who being one Mikhail Sergeevich Morosov.'

Few people would have noticed the brief pause in Greg's sawing. Greg knew, however, that Vladimir Polukhin was one of them. Angry at himself for providing the man with any kind of insight, he freed the first of his ankles with a savage tug.

'Morosov, as I'm sure you know, tried to kill me.' He moved on to the last of the restraints.

'So you killed him instead, is that it?'

Greg made no attempt to mask a snort of derision.

'If you believed that, I'd still be tied to this chair.'

'I believe,' Polukhin said slowly, 'that mention of Mikhail Sergeevich makes you uncomfortable. And I observe also that you have no trouble accepting he's been killed. Why would that be, I wonder? Unless, of course, you know he's dead. Which would raise an interesting question or two.'

Polukhin, Greg noticed, was standing off a little ways, one hand casually inserted into the pocket of his jacket. It was entirely possible that Dobrygin's boss, like his subordinate, was armed. If Greg charged him with the knife – it was no good for throwing – it was fifty-fifty as to which one of them would end up dead.

And there was Dobrygin, of course. Waiting on the other side of the door.

The final piece of duct tape peeled away from his ankle.

'I don't *know* he's dead,' Greg said carefully. 'I do know the police have pulled a body they think is Russian – or connected to Russia – out of the Allegheny. Maybe it's Morosov, maybe it's not.' He shrugged artfully disinterested shoulders. 'But it's not my problem.

'Knife?' He stood up, offering the weapon to Polukhin hilt first.

The general's polite smile contained the merest hint of relief.

'On the table. Please.' Greg moved to comply, slightly unsteady on feet lanced by pins and needles. 'As for problems, I'm afraid you're very much mistaken, Grigoriy Adamovich. Mikhail Sergeevich Morosov *is* your problem.'

'I don't see how.'

'Oh, it's very simple. Let's assume for the moment that the body your Pittsburgh police have in the morgue is, in fact, Morosov. If you can't tell us who killed him, and soon, the next, ah, *conversation* you and I have will be your very last on earth.'

Time Unknown

Polukhin approached the workbench, lifted the jumper cables attached to the battery and pulled out the manila folder lying beneath them. Clearing a space between a lump hammer and a pair of pliers, he opened it up to reveal a small pile of photographs, the first of which depicted Morosov. He was wearing an unbuttoned raincoat and appeared to be stepping out of a UPS store.

'Morosov told us he'd found you but refused to tell us where,' Polukhin explained. 'We arranged it so that he needed to collect some equipment in order to carry out his mission, the result being that we acquired him here, in Washington, DC.' Polukhin tapped the photograph with an elegantly manicured finger, then turned it over to reveal a second. 'We tailed him to Reagan National, where he boarded a plane to Pittsburgh. Pittsburgh was a lucky break for us because we already had an asset in place. If you can call Major Dobrygin an asset.' Polukhin smiled wryly. 'He's good with a camera, though.' Another photograph. 'We reacquired him at Pittsburgh International and tailed him, ah, *here*.'

Greg's drug-dry mouth became drier still as Polukhin turned over the photo. And then another. Morosov entering his apartment building. Greg himself following not long after, dressed, like now, in running gear. The pounding in his head intensified.

'We weren't there, of course, but clearly things did not go as Mikhail Sergeevich had planned.' The next picture in the series showed Morosov in the company of two US marshals, each as big as he was, being bundled into an SUV. 'And that, I'm afraid is the last that we saw of him.'

'Really?'

'Really.' Seeing the look on Greg's face, Polukhin added, 'Major Dobrygin followed them, of course, but lost contact in the city traffic. Since then? Nothing. He hasn't returned to London and there's fuck all sign of him back home. Friends? Family? Business associates? Absolutely nothing.' Polukhin, having finished his cigarette, immediately lit another. Smoke rushed from his lips in a long sigh. 'It's possible the Americans have him at a . . . what do they call it here? Yes. A black site. But our analysts are adamant that US marshals wouldn't dirty their hands in an operation like that. Prim and proper bastards, apparently. And then, a day later, we have an unidentified man, thought to be Russian, dead under a Pittsburgh bridge. Coincidence? Maybe. But in this business . . .' He gave an eloquent shrug of the shoulders. 'That's where you come in.'

'But why do you need me? How hard is it to break into a medical examiner's office and obtain a DNA swab, for God's sake? What's really going on here, Vladimir?' He fixed Polukhin with a hard stare.

The GRU man looked pained.

'Look, Grigoriy, you need to understand that things have changed since you, ah, decided to leave us. Resources are . . . constrained. Our operation here is delicate, and I only have Dobrygin to carry it out. Breaking into a facility like that is a two- or three-man operation. And even if the oaf managed to do it on his own, the risk that the break-in was detected somehow and reported to American intelligence is too great. They can't know we're here.' He waved his cigarette so close to Greg's face that Greg could feel the heat from it. 'I don't want you anywhere near the medical examiner's office, understand? Don't even *think* about the medical examiner's office!'

A cold, icy sensation was forming in the pit of Greg's stomach.

'I have two questions,' he announced, although the first was just a means of delaying the inevitable. 'One: since when have you allowed GRU agents to operate alone? Always in pairs. That's the rule: one to keep an eye on the other. And yet you allow your Major Dobrygin, a man you've just described as an "oaf", to run free? In *America* of all places? Why?'

'Oleg, despite his shortcomings, has certain skills that are useful here. And like I said, he's here on his own because resources are limited. We need to be more flexible these days, Grigoriy Adamovich. More efficient.' Polukhin's expression became sour. 'More like the West.'

He took a slow drag on his cigarette. The tip of it glowed an angry red.

'And your second question?'

Greg took a deep breath, steeling himself.

'Why are you telling me all this? Why am I seeing . . . all this? A major general—'

'Colonel general.'

Greg felt his eyebrows lifting in surprise.

'A *colonel* general of the GRU has revealed his presence to a known traitor.' Try as he might, Greg couldn't stop the shame and bitterness from leaking into his voice. 'And this same colonel general has not only admitted that there's an active operation taking place on American soil, he's also identified the agent responsible. Major Oleg Petrovich Dobrygin.

'What's to stop me walking straight out of here and picking up the phone to MI5? Or the US Marshals?'

Greg was surprised by the genuine warmth in Polukhin's smile.

'Ah, Grigoriy. That's what I most miss about you. Always thinking, always moving the pieces around in your head before you play them. It makes life easier sometimes – for me, not you.'

His hand went to the folder. Revealed one last photograph.

'She looks good, yes?'

Greg turned his head to one side, trying to hide his stricken expression from Polukhin's probing gaze.

The woman in question was short and slightly built. She wore an elegant raincoat that had been buttoned up against a no doubt bitter Moscow wind. A few strands of dyed-black hair poked out from beneath a warm-looking beret, while a gloved hand clasped at the strap of a ridiculously large shoulder bag. She was walking along Lomonosovsky Prospekt, by the university. Greg knew this because the building in the background was one he was intimately familiar with: the Faculty of Foreign Languages and Area Studies.

'Your mother, may God bless her and keep her from harm, is a quieter, sadder woman these days. Her only son is "missing, presumed dead", after all.' Seeing Greg's sharp look, Polukhin added, 'Well, what was the point of telling a good Russian woman that her son was a fucking traitor? Isn't "presumed dead" bad enough?'

'Thank you,' Greg said, his voice choked.

'Yes, well.' Polukhin sounded almost embarrassed. He took a couple of drags on his cigarette before continuing. 'Enough of that. The point is that as a bereaved mother, albeit of a traitor, Yulia Petrovna is a person deserving of sympathy, of support, even. But as the mother of a living, breathing former agent, she becomes a – how shall we say this? – a point of *pressure*.' The general's gaze went deep. 'Do I really need to say more, Grigoriy? Do I have to spell out what will happen to her if we should have any reason to bring her into a room like this one? With Major Dobrygin?' Polukhin's voice hardened. 'Tell your Western masters about any of this and your mother will live to regret it. Try to hide from us again? Same result. Do we understand each other?'

Greg, to his horror, found he was standing at attention. He forced himself to slouch.

'Find out if the drowned body is Morosov's,' he said, the tone insolent, even though he was faking it. 'If it is, find out who killed him, or face the consequences. Don't squeal and don't run. Does that pretty much cover it?'

Polukhin's smile was feral.

'Not quite. If Morosov *was* murdered here, I want the bastard or bastards who did it dealt with. *Painfully*, Grigoriy. Slowly. And then I want the remains left somewhere public. A message to any other fucker who thinks they can kill my people and get away with it.'

He patted Greg on the shoulder.

'And you, Grigoriy, you're going to be the one to do it.'

8:39 A.M.

'Feel better,' the voice on the other end of the phone said before hanging up. Calderhill had no substitute teachers for Russian, so his kids were in for a pleasant surprise.

Greg slid his cellphone underneath the band on his arm and stared blindly into a wide blue sky.

He was having trouble accepting what had just happened. Only three hours ago, he'd been gasping his way up Centre Avenue. Now, an eternity later, it seemed, he was standing outside a GRU safe house in Lawrenceville. They'd rented it through Airbnb, apparently.

Having been given his orders by Polukhin, what then followed had passed by in a blur. The general had called an angrily astonished Dobrygin back into the room and instructed him to provide Greg with every assistance in the 'unlikely' event that Greg would ask for it. Mr Abimbola, Polukhin told him, was to ascertain whether the corpse pulled from the Allegheny was Morosov's. Morosov was a traitor to the Motherland, and if it was him, Greg was to recover certain information the man had stashed somewhere before the Americans beat him to the punch. Greg's few personal possessions had been restored to him, protocols for making contact, both live and dead drops, had been established and, weirdest of all, Polukhin, uncaring about security, had escorted him up the stairs and out of the building.

The general had glanced at his watch.

'Oleg will look after you,' he'd said, no doubt conscious that his words could have more than one meaning. 'I have a plane to catch. Before your Western friends realize I'm not in Moscow.' Polukhin turned back inside without so much as a backward glance, leaving him on the sidewalk like trash on collection day.

Which is where he now found himself, on the painfully steep slopes of 44th Street, good eye watering in the sunlight. A couple of hundred yards downhill, rush-hour traffic was rumbling along Butler Street.

Greg turned in the opposite direction and started trudging toward home, head still pounding from whatever drug they had stuck in his neck, legs too drained of energy to run.

Suddenly, everything was Morosov, he thought wearily. Rachel Lev wanted her dead body identified and the killer or killers brought to justice. Which, in her case, meant arrest, arraignment and trial. And justice – assuming the dead body was, indeed, Morosov – was what Polukhin wanted too. Except Polukhin's justice involved long, drawn-out torture, followed by another murder, with the body dumped in a suitably public place, the equivalent of DON'T FUCK WITH THE GRU scrawled across its forehead.

And both of them expected Greg Abimbola to make justice happen.

He reached the top of the climb, stopping to catch his breath at the corner of 44th and Penn Avenue. He groaned and bent over, clutching at his stomach. He could now add nausea to his list of post-abduction symptoms. On the far side of Penn, a woman looked at him curiously but moved on without speaking.

There was no way he was getting home in this state. He pulled out his phone again and called for a rideshare, which took its sweet time coming. So long, in fact, that Greg started to feel marginally better. Well enough to dive back into the rideshare app and change his destination.

'Greg?' the driver asked, as he slid into the back seat of a spotlessly clean Toyota sedan.

'I am indeed.' Greg fumbled with the rear seatbelt, clicking the thing into place more clumsily than he would have liked.

'And you're headed . . . er . . . Downtown? The Point?'

'That's right.'

The vehicle slid smoothly away from the curb.

'Been running?' the driver asked.

'Oh, yes.'

'Got too much for you, did it?' A sympathetic chuckle. 'Me? Every time I try to exercise, it gets too hard, and I give up.'

Greg managed a faint smile.

'I hear you. I'm giving up, too. I turned my ankle coming up Forty-Fourth Street, so I need you to get me home.'

'No worries. You live by the Point, then?'

'Uh-huh.'

Why, Greg wondered briefly, did he still feel the need to lie about *everything*?

Old dog. New tricks.

'Man, that's some run you've been on.' The driver glanced at him through his rearview mirror. 'Mind you, you look helluva fit.'

'Thank you.'

The conversation lapsed then. Greg leaned back in his seat, grateful that the pounding in his head seemed to have stopped. Even though it still hurt, the worst was definitely over. The pain of healing rather than ongoing injury. His stomach, however, jumped rebelliously as the Toyota lurched through a pothole. He stifled a grimace.

The driver was listening to a local news station that Greg didn't recognize. Local enough to report that Calderhill was going to the state championships at Edgeworth's expense, incurious enough to omit any reference to the sudden departure of male traveling support.

The channel, though, was not finished with the Edgeworth School. The part of Greg that was turning into a committed, bona fide teacher sat up and paid attention.

'Not only has Edgeworth School's boys basketball lost its shot at the state championships, more drama is due to take place later today, when the school's board of trustees meet to discuss the growing backlash against Edgeworth's new anti-racism policy. A group known as PEACE, standing for Parents and Edgeworth Alumni Concerned about Education, has focused attention on what it says is the school's increasing support for a politicized, "woke" agenda. An agenda that PEACE alleges is failing to provide students with the knowledge and skills needed to be successful in the modern world. Of particular concern, according to the group, is the teaching of so-called critical race theory.

'One senior at the school, Cameron Archer, poured cold water on PEACE's concerns. He claimed PEACE was "interested in making sure that only certain types of kids are made to feel welcome". Edgeworth, he said, "should be welcoming to all, regardless of their background".

'While most students seem supportive of the school's new approach, some were more critical. One, Brad Leclerc, claimed that as a conservative student, he felt judged by some teachers and classmates for his views. So judged, in fact, that he had—'

'This good for you?' the driver asked, slowing down. Startled, Greg focused once more on his surroundings. They'd arrived at the far western edge of downtown. To his left, the last of Pittsburgh's buildings, the tall, silvery tower blocks of the Gateway Center, rose up to greet the morning sun. To his right lay the green expanse of Point State Park, infested, as always, with joggers and people riding absurdly expensive bicycles.

'Perfect. Thanks so much.'

Greg hopped out of the rideshare. He waited until the car had moved out of sight before heading away from the park, past the Gateway Center and deeper into the city. But for ice hockey and the theater, Greg had little cause to come downtown, so his knowledge of its geography was sadly lacking. But he had a vague sense that he was headed in the direction of a small but useful row of shops.

He got there – eventually – popping into a small general store with an inward sense of triumph. He quickly found what he was looking for: a copy of the *New York Times*, a half dozen prepaid cellphones and a bag to carry them in. He paid with the credit card he always went running with in case of emergencies. Using a credit card was not ideal in the circumstances, but given it was the GRU he was worried about rather than US law enforcement, he wasn't too concerned. The GRU would not be tracking small-time credit card transactions in the middle of America, so his purchase of a bunch of burner phones would not raise any flags.

He wandered back the way he'd come, heading mostly west until he'd left the buildings behind. He crossed a last, wide road and entered Point State Park. The Point, as it was more usually called, got its name from the fact that this was where downtown Pittsburgh ran out of land. Squeezed by the Allegheny River to the north and the Monongahela to the south, Point State Park was a sharply constricted triangle of open ground, the apex of which – the Point – marked where the two rivers met to form the Ohio. Some people referred to this part of town as Three Rivers, an appellation that made no sense to Greg given that it was two rivers merging into one. To Greg's way of thinking, the decision of the early settlers to give the Ohio River and its sources three different names did not three rivers make. Reasonable people might disagree, he supposed, but that didn't stop him being right.

He headed toward the Point and its huge fountain, quiescent now in anticipation of a summer yet to come. Sitting on the edge of it, he positioned himself facing east, which allowed him to see the whole of the park spread out before him. He didn't seriously think Polukhin had bothered to have him followed, but old habits die hard.

He cracked open one of the burner phones. Dialed a number.

'Crevice Rye Suits, bespoke tailoring. How can I help you?' The accent was clipped and very, very English.

'It's Mr Abimbola. I'd like to speak to Mr Rye about a fitting, please. I need something run up for a function.'

'Mr Rye is busy right now, sir. Is this function of yours on the immediate horizon?'

'It's not deathly urgent, but very soon.'

'I see.' A pause. 'As I said, sir, Mr Rye is busy at the moment, but he can call you in an hour if that's OK. Can he use this number?'

'Yes, he can. I look forward to speaking with him.'

The line went dead. Greg pulled out the *New York Times* from his bag and started reading.

Exactly sixty minutes later, the burner phone chirped to life. There was a slight delay in completing the connection, evidence of heavy-duty encryption.

'So, Greg, what can I do for you?' Dianna Aldis asked.

Greg bit back his disappointment. He'd been hoping to get someone more junior. More malleable.

'How lovely to hear your voice, Dianna. Are you my full-time minder now?'

'Not officially. But as you know, I take a keen interest in your welfare.'

'I'm flattered.' He allowed himself a small pause. 'What I'm less flattered about is the fact that you've been lying to me.'

'Really?' Aldis refused to be drawn. Her round, Home Counties accent was infused, if anything, with amusement. Greg had no option but to shake the tree as hard as he could. To see if anything fell out.

'I have it on good authority that, contrary to what I've been led to believe, Mikhail Morosov is in the offices of the Allegheny County medical examiner. Lying on a slab.'

'And what makes you say that?' If Dianna had been amused, that was gone now.

'Never you mind how I know. I know. The man was in your custody. And now he's dead. How did *that* happen and what does it mean for my safety?'

'I would remind you that you live in the United States, Greg. We aren't allowed to take custody of people. Not our jurisdiction, remember? That's a question for the US Marshals, not the Security Service. And, just to be clear, I have absolutely no idea what you're talking about.' She paused briefly, to gather her thoughts or draw breath or both. When she spoke again, her voice was softer, almost maternal. 'As for your safety, you are and always will be in extreme peril so long as you choose to stay where you are. Please, please, *please* let us pull you out.'

'No, thank you. I like it here. And they haven't even turned the fountain on yet.'

He hung up without bothering to explain.

Taking a direct run at Aldis hadn't been a complete bust, he decided. *Something* had happened with Morosov. Instead of telling him that Morosov was safe, or that it was none of his business, her first, knee-jerk reaction had been supremely institutional: it wasn't us, guv. Whatever happened to Morosov, it wasn't our fault because it wasn't our op: blame the Marshals. Only afterwards had she thought to say she had no idea what he was talking about. A lot of weight to put on very few words, perhaps, but Greg was willing to trust his instincts. Dollars to donuts, something bad had happened after Morosov had been escorted from his apartment. Morosov was either dead or he'd somehow escaped. But if the latter, what possible reason did he have to hide from Polukhin?

Unless, of course, his failing to put an end to Gregory Abimbola had put him on the general's shit list. Maybe the steaming pile of BS Polukhin had shoved down Dobrygin's throat, about Morosov being a traitor, had a tiny element of truth to it. If Polukhin was *hunting* Morosov, the identity of the man on the slab was not so much about justice; it was about whether the GRU was wasting its time.

Without conscious thought, Greg twisted the burner phone over and over in one hand, scanning the flat, green reaches of the Point as he did so. Still no sign of surveillance. He took a long, slow breath.

And smashed the burner phone against the rounded stone of the fountain.

He walked slowly west until there was nowhere left to go.

Three Rivers. As if.

He stared out at the brown waters of the Ohio, made suddenly broad as it began the long, slow journey to the Mississippi. With a graceful flick of the wrist, he sent the broken burner phone arcing through the air. It hit the surface with a faint plop, sinking without protest.

As he turned away, a middle-aged cyclist, dressed like an extra from some sci-fi movie, rolled past him with an accusing stare, no doubt appalled at his wanton act of pollution.

'It was a bad breakup,' Greg explained.

He walked on, never bothering to look back.

WEDNESDAY, THE EIGHTH
7:49 A.M.

'What's going on?' Greg asked, stepping through the door to the faculty lounge. It closed behind him the same way it had opened, with a loud creak. 'Somebody die?'

'Kind of, yes.'

There was no mistaking the note of intrigue in Amy Tsai's voice. Calderhill's Chinese teacher, and the head of Greg's department, was seated in a well-worn armchair, surrounded by several of their colleagues. She lowered the faculty's hard copy of the *Pittsburgh Post-Gazette* just enough to meet his gaze.

'Iain Ferguson's resigned.'

'*What?*'

By way of explanation, Amy returned her attention to the newspaper.

'"A late-night meeting of the Edgeworth School's board of trustees ended in high drama yesterday evening, with the resignation of school principal, Iain Ferguson,"' she read. '"The meeting was convened after a group of parents calling themselves PEACE (Parents and Edgeworth Alumni Concerned about Education) sent a letter of complaint to the school community. In it, PEACE criticized what it called political and ideological indoctrination masquerading as education, not least the teaching of so-called critical race theory. The last straw, according to the letter, was the proposed creation of an office of Diversity, Equity and Inclusion (DEI). DEI, the letter said, was simply a fanciful mechanism for implementing 'the race-baiting socialism of the radical left agenda'. Complaining about falling enrollment at the school, the letter blamed Principal Ferguson and the school administration for 'failing to provide an academic environment that prioritizes academic excellence and parental choice over left wing propaganda and ideological indoctrination'.

'"A visibly angry Alan Mester, chair of the executive committee of the school's board of trustees, announced Principal Ferguson's resignation before leaving it to a fellow committee member, Clyde

Leclerc, to explain the decision. Mr Leclerc, reading from a prepared statement, said that—'"

Amy's recitation of events was interrupted by the creaking open of the lounge door. Demetrius Freedman, wearing the expression of a man determined to down one last cup of coffee before class, came to a surprised stop, taking in the scene before him.

'What's going on?' he asked. 'Somebody die?'

8.31 P.M.

This time, at least, Rachel Lev felt comfortable enough to take off her coat when she entered Greg's apartment. Although she would undoubtedly have preferred coffee, she sipped black, sugarless tea from a delicate porcelain cup. A cup Greg had just filled from a matching teapot. If he was going to start entertaining people at home like a normal person, he thought, he might have to start stocking a selection of beverages that extended beyond either that or vodka.

Rachel set the teacup down with exaggerated care, clearly worried she might break something.

He made a mental note to add some less frou-frou kitchenware to his shopping list.

As before, the detective was sitting on the sofa. Light from his hastily muted TV washed across her face, making her look paler than she actually was. Unlike before, she carried a large shoulder bag, similar to his mother's, which now rested on a cushion beside her. She pulled a small manila folder out of the bag and proceeded to open it. A number of photocopied documents rested inside. She made no offer to share them with Greg.

'Not a lot to add to what I told you on Monday,' she said, leafing through the pages. 'Dental, clothing, surgical pin – all like I said. Caucasian, six foot even and a shade under two hundred pounds. Nine-mil shots to the head and left shoulder, blood type O-positive, which doesn't tell us much. DNA, which could tell us a lot if we had a match, but we don't, so not in any of our criminal databases.'

'At least it tells us he's not a legal US resident,' Greg said.

Rachel looked at him quizzically.

'If you're a resident alien with a green card, or a naturalized citizen, you have to give DNA and fingerprint samples as part of the process. Presumably because all immigrants are criminals who haven't been caught yet.' He shrugged. 'It just adds to your theory that he's Russian or British, with few connections here.'

Greg wondered whether he'd ever known Morosov's blood type and decided he hadn't.

The height and weight were bang on, though.

Rachel nodded, a gesture she accompanied with a small grimace. 'Slipped my mind,' she said. 'But you're right. We'd have run it against the immigration database as well.' She turned back to the photocopies. 'I had them run a gun residue test like you suggested. Nothing.' Now it was Rachel's turn to shrug. 'But like I said before, our John Doe had been immersed in water, which screws up everything.' She closed the folder. 'And that's pretty much it, Mr – Greg.' She favored him with an ironic smile. 'Any bright ideas?'

'One, actually.' He tried to block out the penumbra of associations attached to it. GRU overseas operations. The thudding impact that had driven him to the ground. The sharp stab of drugs entering his neck. Polukhin.

'And?'

'Pardon? Oh. Yes.' He forced himself to focus. 'Russian, British, both: it doesn't matter. What does matter is that he's not from around here. This gentleman is almost certainly based in Europe. Which means he arrived here by plane.'

'Go on.'

'He would have rented a car.'

Rachel's eyes widened at the thought.

'As our man was in no condition to return it,' he continued, 'there's a pretty good chance you have a rental company somewhere with a missing automobile.' In his mind's eye, he was thinking of a Hyundai sedan with Alabama plates, the vehicle Morosov had been driving when Greg first realized he was under surveillance. Morosov, knowing he'd been spotted, had made off before Greg had got close enough to ID him, and he'd given the car little thought since. The one thing he was certain of, though, was that it was nowhere near his apartment. He'd have seen it, otherwise. Morosov must have parked it at a safe distance and approached the building on foot. 'Find the paperwork for the missing vehicle,' he said, 'and there's a good chance you'll have an ID for your, er, "John Doe".'

Rachel Lev's smile was completely genuine. It lit up her whole face. It was like looking at an entirely different person.

'Now *that*, Mr Abimbola, is an idea.'

She left shortly after, her feet scampering down the stairs in a hurry to be out and about and doing things. For his part, Greg couldn't understand her need to rush. The people she'd have to talk to would be at home, or somewhere else that wasn't work. She wouldn't be able to get ahold of them until tomorrow, at the earliest. Running down the stairs was a waste of both enthusiasm and energy.

Clearly, he lacked what it took to be properly American.

Smiling to himself, he closed his front door and returned to the living room, bent on clearing away the tea things. The still-muted TV was striking reflections off the polished surface of his coffee table. Local news.

On his way to the kitchen, hands weighed down with porcelain, he came to a halt, staring at the television.

The screen was showing a wide shot of the Edgeworth School, its low-rise, mock-Georgian architecture instantly recognizable. It looked more like an Ivy League college than a high school, Greg thought; all the better to lure in the high-income parents needed to keep a place like that running. The picture was old footage, with a summer-blue sky and out-of-season foliage. The chyron across the bottom of the screen made the context clear.

SURPRISE RESIGNATION OF HIGH SCHOOL PRINCIPAL

The scene shifted to night. Last night, without doubt. The camera, wobbly and a little grainy due to distance and poor lighting, was zooming in through one of the tall, paned windows. Two middle-aged white men and a glamorous Middle-Eastern-looking woman could be made out on the far side of the glass. Members of the Edgeworth School's board of trustees.

To say the body language looked intense would have been the grossest of understatements.

To Greg Abimbola, ex-GRU officer and unofficial consultant to the Pittsburgh PD, it looked more like a prelude to murder.

THURSDAY, THE NINTH
9:55 A.M.

Greg didn't get lacrosse. The rules about when you could run and not run continued to elude him. And carrying a ball around in something that looked like the mutant offspring of a tennis racket and a fishing net struck him as all kinds of pointless. The equipment looked expensive, though. Perhaps Demetrius was right, he thought. Maybe it's just a way for rich white kids to get sports scholarships. Like fencing.

On the other hand, it looked very difficult to do well. And impenetrable rules or not, there was a lot of running.

God knew, he needed the distraction. Between Polukhin, and Rachel Lev, and Dianna Aldis, his mind was awhirl, a flurry of random, unconnected thoughts. For the last day or two, he'd been teaching on autopilot, and he wasn't a good enough teacher to get away with that. Kids that usually followed his every word sat mutely at their desks, faces clouded in puzzlement. He could feel the attention of his various classes slipping away from him, drawn instead to the warm spring weather beckoning through the window. And as for the written work . . .

He needed to pull himself together.

Which is how he came to be at the back of Calderhill's main building, standing on the edge of the school sports field and watching a bunch of middle graders learn to play lacrosse. A light breeze took the edge off a morning that was promising to turn hot. Squeals and laughter accompanied the pounding of small feet on turf. Greg took a deep breath, savoring it all.

He could think of no better place to get his thoughts in order.

He'd jogged along the Allegheny earlier that morning, on a route that had taken him under the Rachel Carson bridge. It would have been possible to dump a body there, he'd decided, but risky. There were apartment buildings overlooking the riverbank, giving rise to any number of potential witnesses. And given that the murder had occurred elsewhere, it was quite a distance to lug a dead body from the trunk of a parked car to the riverbank. Particularly that of a big, powerful man like Morosov. Unless the murderer was an idiot – and the absence of usable clues suggested otherwise – the body had been tossed into the water somewhere upriver. Somewhere where it would be easy to park. Where you wouldn't have to carry the body more than a few feet. Where, if you timed it right, there'd be no witnesses.

Like the side of some other bridge. In the early hours of the morning.

Greg felt his lips quirk into the beginnings of a smile.

The City of Bridges. One of Pittsburgh's many appellations and entirely apt. There'd be no shortage of dumping sites. Sixteenth Street, Fortieth, Sixty-Second, the Highland Park bridge.

The smile, if that's what it had ever become, slipped away.

Knowing what had happened didn't explain how Morosov – if it was Morosov – had managed to get tipped off the side of a bridge in the first place. What had happened after Dobrygin lost contact?

One of the middle graders was having a meltdown on the field.

'Why aren't I winning?' they yelled at their teammates. 'I should be winning by now!'

There's no 'I' in 'Team,' Greg thought, grinning. And then, thinking of Dobrygin and his boss: *There's no 'We', either.*

Whatever had happened between Greg's apartment and the Allegheny, he knew two things.

One: Polukhin was unlikely to have told him the whole truth. It wasn't the GRU way. The GRU way was to tell people only what they had to know and then lie about the rest. Particularly if 'the rest' made either the teller or the GRU look bad.

Two: the same logic applied to Dobrygin.

One plus two equaled consequences.

Calmer than he'd been since his kidnapping, Greg turned his back on Calderhill's fledgling lacrosse stars and returned to the main building. Not needing to access the gym or the locker rooms, Greg started up the nearest of the school's back stairs, this one little used as it was on completely the wrong side for freshly showered students heading back to class. His shoes made a scraping sound on the painted-over concrete.

There was a child sitting at the top of the first flight, staring intently at a tablet and scrolling furiously. So deep was his concentration, in fact, he seemed completely unaware that he was blocking Greg's progress. Or that Greg was there at all.

'Hello, Malik. Free period?'

The child looked up, startled.

'Uh . . . yes, sir.'

Malik Freedman was, Greg knew, the younger of Demetrius's two sons. He didn't take Russian, so Greg didn't know that much about him. Bright, he'd been told, particularly on the STEM side, and decent at sports, although, given his stockier build, unlikely to be a standout ball player like his older brother.

No one had pegged the boy for a loner.

Malik moved to make room on the stairwell, tablet tight against his knees. He didn't even bother to look up, so absorbed was he in whatever it was he was doing. Greg stepped past, glancing down at Malik's screen as he did so. Kids were allowed access to their personal devices when not in class, although scrolling through social media during free periods wasn't actively encouraged. Greg, though, had no intention of lecturing the boy about the brain-rotting downsides of modern tech. As far as he was concerned, free meant free. If Malik wanted to spend that time looking through his feeds, it was a matter for him. Except . . .

'What are you doing?' he asked, unable to stop himself. The tablet's screen contained neither cat videos, nor dancing teens, nor bubbles of text. So far as Greg could see, limited as he was by having only one eye, Malik's tablet contained line after line of arcane letters and symbols. Complete gibberish, in fact.

Unless, of course, one was a computer nerd.

Greg had to repeat himself in order to get the boy's attention.

'It's a robotics program,' Malik explained. 'I'm on this team and I'm going through the code looking for bugs.'

'I didn't know Calderhill had a robotics team,' Greg admitted. 'To be honest, Malik, I didn't even know robotics teams were a thing.'

'They're totally for real, sir. But we don't have one.' He tapped the tablet. 'It's an after-school program. At Generica House.'

'On the North Side?' The name rang a vague bell. Charity, good works, that kind of thing.

'Yes, sir.'

'And have you found any?'

'Found any what?'

'Bugs.'

'Oh. Uh . . .' Malik's gaze lost focus.

'It wasn't meant to be a stumper, Malik,' Greg said, smiling indulgently.

The boy looked faintly irritated.

'Bugs aren't the problem,' he said shortly. 'I mean, there *are* bugs. There's a sh— ton of them. But that's not . . . Even if I fix them, the code won't work. The robot won't do what we want it to.'

'Well, a bright kid like you? Just keep plugging away. I'm sure you'll figure it out in no time.'

Greg's words didn't have the effect he was expecting. All of a sudden, the child was on the verge of tears.

'I already have,' he said.

And then, with the startling acceleration of teenage boys, he shot to his feet and scrambled up the steps. The door to the second-floor corridor banged open, its sound echoing and hollow against the paint and concrete of the stairwell.

Greg stood where he was for a moment, flabbergasted. Shaking his head at the incomprehensibilities of the teenage mind, he followed Malik's route at a more stately pace. Concrete gave way to highly polished parquet flooring as he stepped out of the stairwell and headed for his classroom. He sat down at his desk with nothing but empty seats for company.

Which was all to the good.

Opening one of the drawers, he reached in and pulled out a burner phone. After a moment's hesitation, he dialed the number. It rang out several times before the person at the other end picked up. Safe in his classroom, he didn't bother to check for surveillance or worry about someone overhearing should they happen to pass by.

Because the only people who might be able to understand what he intended to say were a couple of his Russian IV students. And the kids of Russian IV were stuck in someone else's class.

Greg gathered his thoughts, took a deep breath and began to speak.

7:15 P.M.

Greg sat down at a recently wiped table, the pressed-wood surface still gleaming with damp, and stared without enthusiasm at the contents of his tray. Burger. Fries. Soda. He took a small sip of the soda and looked around.

Unlike many of its brethren, the food court at the Ross Park Mall was not buried away in the basement. Up a level, it was possible to sit by a railing and look down on the floor below; to watch people wander in and out of the shops and up and down the escalators, some with huge, logo-splattered bags announcing a recent purchase, most unencumbered, either because they hadn't found what they were looking for or, most likely, because they were just looking. Above them all, the wide tessellated skylight was black with night, shielding all and sundry from the heavy burst of spring rain falling outside. No one, apart from Greg, bothered to look up.

The mall wasn't overly busy, so it was easy to see Dobrygin arrive. He was dressed in jeans, sneakers and a lightweight coat, the latter dampened dark by rain. In Europe, his imposing bulk would have attracted attention perhaps, but here he was pretty much par for the course. No one, apart from a couple of teenage girls, gave him a second glance. He picked up Chinese food and sat down at a neighboring table, paying no outward attention to Greg and apparently transfixed by the contents of his cellphone. He was simply a big, athletic guy reading the sports pages. Maybe waiting for the wife and kids, with a gleaming, full-size pickup in the parking lot outside.

'I'm here,' he said. 'What do you want?'

Greg badly wanted to examine his unwilling companion more closely but resisted the temptation. Given his unfortunate experience with the man and Polukhin's characterization of him, he was inclined to view Dobrygin as an oaf. A GRU heavy, good for little but beating people up and carrying heavy objects. But Dobrygin's English, like his own, was pitch perfect. American, though, rather than British, the accent vaguely Midwestern. Dobrygin could easily pass as coming from a wholesome, backwater place no one had ever heard of: in Iowa, or one of the other 'I' states, for instance. The GRU should have paid to fix his nose. Women here would find him irresistible.

At least, when he wasn't scowling, as he was now. There was no hiding the thuggishness thus revealed. Maybe that was the reason they'd left the nose untouched. Perhaps he was an oaf, after all. An idiot savant with language skills. Greg hoped so. If Dobrygin was more brain than brawn, this was never going to work.

Unaware of Greg's thoughts, Dobrygin made a point of looking at his big, ostentatious watch.

'I'm not here to have my time wasted, Abimbola.'

'Neither am I . . . Alec.' Greg stumbled a little over Dobrygin's Western alias. 'Which is what you've been doing up until now.'

'Spare me your bullshit and tell me what you want.'

'I want to know what really happened when you tailed Morosov from my apartment. The stuff you didn't tell Polukhin.'

A snort of laughter. More like a sneer, really.

'You know what happened. It was rush hour, the traffic was heavy, I lost him.'

'And how did our mutual friend take the news when you told him?'

'How do you think? He was furious.'

'I'm sure he was. Which means what really happened was much, much worse.'

Out of the corner of his eye, Greg could see Dobrygin's large hands balling into fists.

'I don't know what the fuck you're talking about.'

'Sure you do. It's very Russian. You, Alec, are Russian. Being Russian, you lie to your boss. Always. It's like breathing, really. You only tell him good news, put in the best possible light. Bad news? Never mentioned. Never. Unless, of course, there's no alternative. In which case, tell the least bad version you can get away with . . . like the made-up story you sold to our mutual friend.'

'Fuck off.' Dobrygin started to get up.

Greg leaned back in his seat and stared up at the tessellated skylight, the rain streaking across the glass. He wanted Dobrygin to see him smile.

'Leave now and you'll never know what my report to the man is going to say.'

Dobrygin sat down again.

'Which is what, exactly?'

'That you were *paid* to lose Morosov. That you're on the take.'

'For the love of God,' Dobrygin spluttered, unsure whether to laugh or snarl. 'Only a simpleton would buy into a pile of crap like that. I'm done with y—'

'Where'd you get the Rolex, Alec?'

'Wait. What?'

'The Rolex.' Keeping his head averted, Greg glanced briefly at the chunk of metal on Oleg's wrist. 'That's an Oyster Perpetual. Not top of the range but, still . . . what? High four, low five figures in American money? And well beyond the reach of a mere GRU major – even with a cost-of-living allowance.' Greg was looking straight ahead now; unlike Dobrygin, who was staring angrily in his direction. 'It was wise of you to hide it from Polukhin when you, ah, picked me up. That cheap watch you were wearing was for his benefit, wasn't it? No point advertising how corrupt you actually are, eh? Good call.'

'One more word out of you and I'm gonna beat you to a fucking pulp, you one-eyed Black b—'

'*Language*, Alec. You'll do no such thing, and you know it. There are children present. Delicate, developing minds. And their parents. And security cameras. And mall cops. Fearsome adversaries those, believe you me.'

Outwardly, Oleg Dobrygin subsided. His clenched fists, however, refused to get the message.

'Corrupt as you are, all I have to do is make the accusation and our mutual friend will start looking more closely at your finances. And once he does that, seeing as he has such a low opinion of you already, he'll have no trouble believing that some of your ill-gotten gains were a reward for "losing" Morosov. Being corrupt is one thing. But if it compromises operations . . .' Greg made a tutting sound. 'It will not end well for you, Alec. Not well at all. No matter how much he fancies your mother.'

For a long, stretched-out moment, Greg thought he'd pushed it too far. Dobrygin's massive body began to rise from its chair, the table in front of him squeaking as he shoved it to one side.

A few yards away, heads turned.

Dobrygin sat down again. Readjusted the table. Played with his food.

Greg, for his part, took another small sip of soda.

'I'm a civilian, Alec. I don't give a rat's arse about the GRU or its *Matryoshka* politics. I don't even want to be here. Our mutual friend dragged me into this against my will, and I want as little to do with you as you with me. Tell me what you know and your secret's safe. Then I can end this asinine assignment and we can both get on with our lives.'

In the silence that followed, it was almost as if he could hear the gears crunching in Dobrygin's head. When the GRU man finally spoke, each word was slow and deliberate. As if he was feeling his way across a minefield.

'It's not that I lost them,' he said, voice so low that Greg could barely hear him. 'It's how.' Another long pause. 'Morosov came out of your apartment building in the custody of two US marshals, both men. They got into a car with official plates, and I followed them downtown. I figured they were headed to their offices on Grant Street. Except they weren't. They went right by that sucker and parked up outside the Omni Hotel instead. On William Penn Place.' Dobrygin stared at him, his expression speculative. 'How well do you know downtown?'

'Well enough to know where William Penn Place is,' Greg replied. He was nettled that an active Russian agent thought they knew downtown Pittsburgh better than he did, which was almost certainly true. 'The Omni's an old building. It was designed with the "front" facing Grant Street, but the *real* front, where the cabs drop you off, is at the "back". William Penn Place.'

'Exactly. And if you're not a US marshal, parking is a bitch. I pulled over for long enough to see the three of them enter the building. Then someone shouted at me for parking in a rideshare space. I didn't need the attention, so I had to move on. I parked just around the corner, still illegally but without the self-righteous yelling. I left my vehicle and made it to the lobby. And now there's five of them, not three. Four marshals – three men, one woman – and Morosov. And Morosov is complaining like fuck about something, but real quiet like, and the marshals are trying to keep him onside.' Dobrygin's face twisted in contempt. 'He was their fucking prisoner, not a goddamn Arab sheikh. They should have kneed him in the balls and told him to shut the fuck up. And then. Then . . .' Dobrygin's voice trailed off. His gaze drifted down to the floor below, to the shoppers on the escalators.

'Then?' Greg prompted.

'I got fucking made. Gave myself away somehow.' Dobrygin grimaced at the memory. 'Two of them, the two men from the apartment, came for me waving their badges. Well, I couldn't fucking run, could I? I had to tough it out. They wanted to know what I was about. Asked to see some goddamn ID.'

'Which you had, I hope.'

'Of course I fucking did: Alec Peters from Lawrenceville. Just dropping in for breakfast at the hotel restaurant. They weren't really interested, figured me for a nosy bystander. They just kind of held me there while the other two, a man and the woman, took Morosov out the Grant Street side of the building. I never saw him again.'

Greg, after taking a moment or two to process what he'd just been told, found himself nodding. It took a special kind of stupid to draw attention to yourself in a space as public and busy as the lobby of the Omni William Penn. You couldn't blame Dobrygin for losing his mark. He was one guy in one vehicle running a seat-of-the-pants op at short notice. But to be *caught* like that? That was something else entirely.

No wonder the man had lied. Polukhin would have sent him home on the spot.

'You have photos, I take it? More than our mutual friend showed me?' He tried not to think of his mother.

Who thought he was dead.

'I have photos,' Dobrygin said. 'I'll leave them at the agreed—'

Greg waved him down, suddenly tired.

'Don't bother. Just mail them to me or something. You know where I live.'

'But—'

'But nothing. I'm a civilian, I'm too old for this shit, and our mutual friend has gone back east. Put 'em in the mail.'

After a moment's hesitation, the GRU man nodded, picked up his tray and left.

Greg watched his progress until he disappeared from sight. Then, with a sigh of resignation, he bit into his burger. It lay heavy on his stomach all the way home, weighing down his thoughts.

Flushing out the truth from Dobrygin was all very well, but it was unlikely to get him much further forward. That Dobrygin's additional surveillance contained useful information was a long shot at best. In all probability, it wasn't going to help him fathom out what happened to Morosov, or whether the body in the morgue was his. And if he couldn't do that . . .

Greg's grip on the steering wheel tightened as he parked outside his building. Climbing the stairs to his apartment, he wondered if it was time to get his hands on a gun.

Not for Dobrygin, or anyone else that Polukhin sent after him. For himself. When it came to the general's threatened 'conversation', it was probably best to be already dead.

Except that what waited for him on the other side would be so much worse.

Grateful for the sanctuary of home, he removed his shoes and coat, put them neatly in their appointed places and slumped on the sofa with the TV remote.

He didn't stay slumped for very long.

The TV sprang to life, albeit muted, showing the local news. The screen was dominated by the picture of a man: Caucasian, upper middle-aged, smartly dressed. His tanned face was smiling and creased with laugh lines under a shock of gleaming, gray-white hair.

An Edgeworth School trustee. He looked very different from the last time Greg had seen him. That had been on the previous evening's news show, his unbridled fury captured by the long lens of a TV camera.

ALAN MESTER, the chyron read. BANKER AND PHILANTHROPIST DEAD AT 61.

FRIDAY, THE TENTH

Noon

Class had gone better today, Greg decided, as his students started to file out, nothing but lunch on their minds. No awkward stumbles, or garbled explanations, or puzzled faces. There'd been some well-executed work, and a few laughs at the expense of Gogol, whose Russian was . . . idiosyncratic. All good.

Of course, this was Russian IV. They were decent students, who were genuinely motivated, genuinely interested in the subject. The real test would come later in the day, with Russian I. But he was ready. Smiling to himself, he turned his back on the departing children and started to wipe down his whiteboard. It needed a proper clean, he thought. He'd see to it at the end of the day. Something to look forward to. Cleanliness. Order.

Observations on *The Government Inspector* vanished forever beneath the firm swipe of his eraser.

'Sir?'

Caitlin Bell was standing on his blind side, which is why he hadn't noticed her. She looked uncomfortable, which was not like Caitlin at all. Her weight shifted from one foot to the other and then back again, purple hair wrapped and unwrapped itself around her fingers. She opened her mouth to speak and then closed it again.

'Out with it,' Greg said, smiling indulgently. 'I don't bite.'

'It's personal, sir. I'm not sure I should even be asking.'

Greg turned back to his whiteboard and began wiping again. Long, easy strokes.

'It's up to you, of course. But once I've finished what I'm doing, I'll be off to lunch, and you'll never see me again.'

'How did your parents handle being in an interracial relationship?' The words came out in a rush.

Greg almost dropped the eraser. Almost. He managed to put it down gently, still facing the whiteboard, gathering his thoughts. He turned around.

'Why are you asking?'

Caitlin's face had turned beet red.

'It's nothing, sir. Forget I asked.' She practically ran for the door.

The door opened in front of her as if by magic. Caitlin shot out, Demetrius Freedman, PhD MIT, walked in. Mildly curious, the chemistry teacher glanced after her before getting straight to the point.

'Did you hear about Alan Mester?'

'Your friend at Edgeworth? Yes. I'm sorry for your loss.'

'Did you hear how he died?'

Greg shook his head.

'Fell from a balcony at his apartment. That's what they're saying. Fell from a goddamn balcony.' Demetrius's eyes smoldered with anger. 'What bullshit.'

'I beg your pardon?' Greg could feel his eye blink in surprise.

'It's bullshit,' Demetrius repeated. 'You can't "fall" off a balcony, these days. The guard rail is too high. He'd have had to have jumped.'

'Suicide?'

'Yeah. Except he wasn't the suicidal type. And even if he was, he would never have offed himself like that. Man was terrified of heights. You ask me, he was murdered. Someone followed him home from that OK Corral of a trustee meeting at the Edgeworth School and helped him on his way.'

Greg was about to scoff – gently, of course, seeing as how Demetrius was so upset – when he remembered the unguarded moment caught by the news camera. The raw, naked hatred so brutally exposed behind the Edgeworth School's staid, mock-Georgian facade.

'Have you been to the police?'

'As if they'd listen to the likes of me. I've spoken to his ex, though. *She* went to see them. Says the police are treating it as a suicide.'

Greg nodded.

'Did they find a note?'

'No. Not that I've heard, anyway. And they won't. 'Cause it wasn't suicide.'

'Not all suicides leave notes,' Greg cautioned.

'Neither do murder victims.'

'Fair point.' Figuring that the subject of Alan Mester's death had been exhausted, Greg made for the door. 'I'm headed out for a sandwich. Care to join me?'

'Nope.' Standing between Greg and the exit to the corridor, Demetrius made no attempt to get out of the way. Greg came to a halt.

'I take it you're not hungry?'

'Why don't *you* look into Alan's death?' Demetrius said. 'Figure out what happened.'

The sound that escaped from Greg's lips fell somewhere between a squeal and a gasp.

One murder at a time, please. Form a fucking line.

'You're kidding, right?'

Demetrius laid a hand on Greg's shoulder. The touch was meant to be warm, Greg figured, maybe even imploring, but the grip was too powerful for that. He found it oppressive.

'I know what you did for the Velasquez kid. Everyone does. You done gone saved her skin practically singlehanded. Made the police look like idiots.'

'You shouldn't believe everything you hear,' Greg said, sighing. He slipped his shoulder out of Demetrius's grasp. 'Most of it is fake news. The police finally put everything together and made two plus two equal four rather than five. Simple as that.'

'"Simple", my ass,' Demetrius scoffed. 'All I know is that if you can do what you did for an assistant custodian, you can at least look into the suspicious death of one of the few white guys who ever gave me a break. Even if you think it's bullshit, help me out here.' Demetrius, whose approach to the world was what the English might call 'spiky', looked suddenly vulnerable. A man genuinely worried that something awful had happened and who was scared for what it might mean. 'Please, man. As a friend.'

That final word smashed through Greg's defenses with the unerring rapacity of a missile. Andrea Velasquez was the only other person who had ever fired it in Greg's direction, and with similar effect. Greg was used to dealing with people. He was good at it. They were assets, or allies, or targets, or adversaries, sometimes all at once.

But never friends. He'd never had one. Never been one. Never even considered the possibility.

Until now.

But, even so, there were limits.

'I'm not a private eye, Demetrius. I teach Russian, and sometimes French. I can't just march into your friend Alan's life and start turning over rocks to see what's underneath. I wouldn't know where to begin. He's a *banker*, for fuck's sake. It's not like we move in the same circles, is it?' Greg shook his head emphatically. 'Even if I wanted to help, Demetrius, I can't. I don't have access. There's no way to even get started.'

The last thing Greg expected from Demetrius was a broad smile.

'Now *that*, good sir, I can help you with. We have an in. Better than the police, even.'

'We do?'

'For sure, man. For sure. Lynn Spargo, Alan's ex? She's real keen to find out what's going on without making a fool of herself with either the police or a private detective. I've spent all morning singing your goddamn praises. If there's anything there, I told her, Greg Abimbola will find it.'

Greg emitted a groan of exasperation.

'Did anyone ever introduce you to the concept of overpromising?' Part of him, though, was thinking, *Why not? It'll be more fun than Russian I – and less dangerous, too.*

Something of what he was thinking must have leaked on to his face, the faintest hint of a smile, perhaps. Demetrius grinned wickedly.

'I'm going to take that as a yes, brother. Sewickley, seven o'clock tonight. Lynn's place. I'll send you the address.'

'Fuck off, Demetrius.'

'Seven o'clock, man. Don't be late.'

3:35 P.M.

'I should kick that ladder out from under you right this minute,' Greg said.

Andrea Velasquez, exonerated murder suspect and Calderhill Academy's assistant custodian, looked down at him from beneath a recalcitrant ceiling light. She appeared distinctly unimpressed.

'I hope you're ready to pay the workers' comp bill, dude. It's gonna be a big one.' Her expression morphed into one of mild curiosity. 'What's got you so, like, agitational anyway? At your age, you need to be careful. We don't want you stroking out or nothing. Not that I give a rat's ass, you understand; I just don't want to be cleaning up the mess.'

'Your concern is duly noted,' Greg said dryly. 'As for the source of my agitation, it's really quite simple. You've been selling me to Doctor Freedman as some kind of vigilante for justice.'

'I've been selling you to *everyone* as some kind of vigilante for justice. And why not? You saved my ass, big time.' Greg caught a glimpse of a far more serious, more emotional expression as she turned quickly away and fiddled with the ceiling light.

'Can you flick that switch for me?' she asked, still careful not to look at him.

Greg did so. Light streamed down from the ceiling. Andrea descended the ladder.

'Honestly, Andrea,' Greg said as she reached the ground, 'I'd rather you kept quiet about my involvement in your recent troubles. I can do without the extra attention.'

'Too late, Mr Bimbo; you're already famous around here.' Andrea looked up at him curiously. 'You track me down for a reason, or are you only here to give me a hard time?'

'Thanks to you, Doctor Freedman has got me involved in a bit of nonsense. Nothing, really. But if it turns out to be something, I may need your help. You know how I am with computers.' Greg spread his hands helplessly. 'And life.'

Andrea clapped her own hands in delight.

'Man, I'd love to,' she said. She began folding up the ladder. 'Beats this job.' She paused, looking suddenly uncertain. 'Can I ask a favor?'

Greg raised the brow above his one good eye.

'Another one?'

'Not so big this time, I swear.' Andrea took a deep breath. 'I'm nearly done with my associate degree, and I've started looking for a job. No more cleaning restrooms for rich people's kids, right? So . . . there's this job I'm really, like *really*, interested in, and I think I'm just what they're looking for, but they want a cover letter, and I'm not so good at the writing thing, and I was wondering if you might maybe help me out with it?'

The request came out in such a rush that Greg missed most of it. But he got the gist.

'A cover letter? Sure. What's the job?'

'Writing code for a startup called Medi8or.'

'And what does this Mediator startup do?'

'Data reconciliation. That's the idea, anyway.' Given that his face was undoubtedly a mask of puzzlement, Andrea felt compelled to add, 'Say you have two companies and one of them buys the other. They both do more or less the same thing, but their software is different. Two payroll systems, two different ways of tracking payments received, different HR tools. Right now, you got two choices: carry on with two systems for everything, like forever, or manually convert one set of records into whichever software you think is best.'

'Sounds like a nightmare.'

'It totally is. But what if you don't have to do that? The underlying information is the same. It's the code that's different. What if you could use AI-driven pattern recognition to convert one system to the other automatically? You'd save someone a bunch of money and you'd have a product that people would sell their *abuelas* for.'

Greg didn't say anything for the longest time. To hear Andrea Velasquez, Calderhill Academy's assistant custodian, talking like this, like someone who *knew* things, complex things, was a shock to the system. Even though he'd known in his head that she was more than a dead-end job at the bottom of the food chain, to see it confirmed like this hit him in the heart with unexpected force.

It was one of the reasons he felt a connection to her. Andrea had been dealt a shitty hand in life and was playing it the very best she could. People would look at her name, her appearance, her bad school and worse neighborhood, and write her off. But for his one-woman hurricane of a mother, Greg's start in life – a bi-racial Moscow kid whose very skin was a scandal – would have been no better. Spotting people a sixty-meter advantage in life's hundred-meter sprint seldom ended well.

But here Andrea was, closing the gap as best she could. An associate degree from Pittsburgh Community College – in informatics, whatever the hell that was – and now she was talking about a job he wouldn't be able to do himself in a million years.

He fiddled with the underside of his eyepatch, ignoring the sudden pricking in the still-working equivalent.

'Cat got your tongue, Mr Bimbo?'

'That's very, ah, *impressive*, Ms Velasquez.' He took another moment to pull himself together. 'I suppose we should do this properly, then. Write something down for me – the sort of things you'd like to say – and we'll see if we can work something out. Are you free tomorrow morning? Eleven o'clock? You remember the Beans of Steel coffee shop?'

'The hipster joint in East Liberty? Sure. I'll see you then. Bring your best words.'

Andrea picked up the ladder and walked off. Greg watched her go, the ladder giving her no apparent difficulty, even though it was significantly bigger than the woman carrying it.

If only he could handle his own problems half so well.

6:59 P.M.

Greg seldom had cause to drive out as far as Sewickley, a roughly thirty-minute journey north and west along the Ohio. The river's looming presence was marked only by the complete absence of light as he drove through the early-evening darkness. Following the GPS, he turned into Lerwick Street and parked up, thinking, as he always did on the rare occasions he came this way, that if you shot it at just the right angle, Sewickley could easily substitute as an English village in some Agatha Christie TV movie. The rose bushes, the tidy fences, the profusion of perfectly proportioned trees made for an ambience which, if not exactly English, did not jibe neatly with the blue-collar grit of western Pennsylvania, either.

Twenty-three Lerwick Street, his destination for the evening, turned out to be a white stucco cottage of modest proportions. It was nestled behind a front garden that was as much carefully tended flowerbed as it was immaculately manicured lawn. Warm lights shone out of rustic, paned-glass windows on the first floor, but their unlit dormer brethren, jutting out of the slate roof above, contrived to give the building a slightly brooding appearance. There was a modern video doorbell next to the aging oak-plank door, but Greg felt that ringing it would somehow ruin the countrified feel of the place. He announced his arrival by rapping out a rhythm on the heavy cast-iron knocker.

The door creaked open.

'You must be Greg,' Lynn Spargo said. 'Come on in. Demetrius is already here.' She had the face of a woman who liked to smile, although there was no sign of one at the moment. Her body was stiff with tension. Unsurprising, given the circumstances.

She led the way into a comfortable, rustic-themed living room. Demetrius's lanky frame was stretched out in an overstuffed, floral-patterned armchair, in the easy manner of someone who was familiar with the space. Greg swallowed back a frisson of surprise.

Lynn Spargo – fifties, suburban, white – was not someone he would have expected Demetrius to know well.

'Coffee? Something stronger?' Lynn offered.

Greg declined, taking a chair that matched Demetrius's, his upright posture very different from that of the chemistry teacher. The cushions threatened to swallow him up, but he managed to stay on top of them. Lynn, still tense, tried to make herself at home on the sofa.

'Greg, thanks for coming out here,' Demetrius began, his voice sonorous and rich in the confined space. 'I know Lynn appreciates you taking the time. As do I. But like I said before, Alan killing himself by jumping from his balcony just doesn't sit right with us, does it, Lynn?'

'No it doesn't.' She fixed Greg with a firm stare. 'Al was terrified of heights, Greg. *Terrified.* He wouldn't even stand on that balcony. It freaked him out like you wouldn't believe. If he wanted to end it all – and he wasn't that type of man – climbing over a high rail and . . .' She paused, fighting back tears. 'He just wouldn't, that's all.'

Greg's gaze flicked from Lynn Spargo to Demetrius and back again. How on earth do you even start on something like this, he wondered. If he were a spy, he'd just, well, *spy*, and hope no one saw him coming. If he were a cop, he'd ask the tough questions and throw his badge around. But he was neither of those things. Not anymore. He was just a private citizen in another private citizen's home, about to make a complete fool of himself.

Bollocks, he thought angrily. *And bollocks to you, Demetrius, for getting me into this.*

But then again, if he was being honest with himself, it wasn't really Demetrius's fault, was it? No one had put a gun to his head. Greg Abimbola had driven to Sewickley all on his own. Because it was more interesting than Russian I.

'Sometimes we don't know people as well as we think we do,' he said gently. 'Is it—'

Lynn Spargo cut him off with a bitter laugh.

'Oh, I *knew* my husband pretty damn well, believe you me. Why do you think we divorced?'

'Irreconcilable differences?' Greg ventured, with a smile.

Lynn laughed again, more humorously this time.

'You could say that. For sure.' Her expression turned earnest. 'I loved that man with all my heart. Always will, I guess. But I couldn't live with him. Not after . . . After . . .' She took a deep breath, steeling herself to share with a stranger. 'Al always had an eye for the ladies and, unfortunately for me, the ladies had an eye for him. He was just so damn *nice*, you know? But with an edge. Something a little dangerous if you pushed him too far. It made him very attractive.'

She reached for a tissue. Not for the first time, Greg was sure. Alan's death was still raw in its newness. Maybe not quite believable to those who knew him.

'Anyway, when we were first married, he kept it in check. He'd take it up to the line – *right* up to the line, believe me – but he never crossed it. Not at first. But as we grew older – as *I* grew older – he found it more and more difficult. Until eventually he gave in to it at some point.' She dabbed at her eyes with the tissue. 'They were always young, always beautiful, always intelligent. And always, he promised, the last. Never again. Well, "never again" never came true and I ended it. Worst thing I've ever had to do. Best thing, too. We managed to stay friends. But at a safe distance.'

'And how long has it been since you divorced?'

'Five years?' She looked to Demetrius for confirmation. He nodded. 'Yeah. Five years just gone. It feels longer than that. Like a lifetime.'

'So no reason for you to be killing him now.'

'Absolutely not.' Lynn looked at him uncertainly, not sure if he was joking. Demetrius frowned.

'And where were you Tuesday night?'

Demetrius's frown deepened.

'Harrisburg,' Lynn said. 'At a convention. An insurance industry shindig at the Hilton Hotel.'

'You work in insurance, then?'

Lynn nodded.

'And did Alan have life insurance? Someone who'd benefit from his death?'

'Greg!' Demetrius exclaimed, no longer able to contain himself. Lynn waved him down with an amused chuckle.

'I'd be shocked if he didn't. It's part of his benefits package. Last time we discussed it, I was his only beneficiary. Two and a half million dollars.'

'I see.' Greg fought to keep a straight face. Even Demetrius looked stunned.

How the one percent live.

'I know it's a lot of money,' Lynn went on. 'I do. But I don't need it. Alan was a very successful man, and the divorce, even the money, wasn't bitter as these things go. I got this house and a bunch of other stuff. Alan kept the apartment and everything else. There was plenty to go around. And I have my own career.' Steel entered her voice as she said it. 'I can look after myself. Always have, always will.' To prove the point, she reached into her purse and produced a business card: plain white and reeking of understated quality. Greg made sure to look impressed.

'Can I contact you on this number?' he asked.

'Yes. Of course.'

'In that case,' Greg said apologetically, 'can I have a couple more? In case I lose one. I'd lose my head if it wasn't screwed on.'

'Sure.'

'Thanks so much,' Greg said, sliding them into his wallet. 'Other than he fell from a balcony, what do we know about your ex-husband's death?'

'The police and the FBI guy didn't say much. Only that he was found early Wednesday morning in the parking lot at the back of his apartment building. That he appeared to have fallen and that he was . . .'

Greg waited for the crying to subside.

'Did Alan have any enemies?'

Lynn managed a wan smile.

'He was a successful man, like I said. And a banker. You don't get to be that way without stepping on a few toes. I'm sure there were dozens of people who loathed him. But enough to kill him?' She shook her head emphatically. 'I don't think so.'

Demetrius stirred in his seat.

'Well, what about the Edgeworth School?' Greg asked. Demetrius settled back down, leaving Greg strangely gratified at having anticipated him. 'From what little I could see on the news, the dynamics there look pretty grim. Can you talk to me about that?'

Lynn pursed her lips, considering.

'First off,' she said, 'the news people always get this stuff wrong. It's not the board of trustees you need to worry about. That's a pretty big group and they mostly just formalize decisions. If it's bad feelings you're interested in, then you need to be focused on the board's exco: the executive committee. They're the ones that actually make the decisions, and that's the group you'd have seen on the news the other night, not the whole board. They're also the ones who hate each other's guts.'

'How so?'

'Mostly over falling enrollment and, er, racial stuff.' Lynn, conscious of her audience, looked slightly uncomfortable but plowed on. 'Al was always very progressive about things like that. He felt that creating a more inclusive school was not only the right thing to do but would also attract more students. Brian Delcade and Clyde Leclerc thought it was all woke nonsense – this was before Brian had to resign, obviously.'

'Yeah! Because my man Greg—'

'Demetrius, please. Not now.' Greg had no desire to relive the Brian Delcade matter. Demetrius reluctantly let it go.

'Anyway,' Lynn continued. 'It made for a lot of ill feelings, but Alan won more of those battles than you'd expect, mostly because he and Iain Ferguson, the principal, were on the same page.' Lynn cast a sympathetic glance in Demetrius's direction. 'Though he did lose some. He was real sorry you didn't get the head of science post first time around.'

Demetrius gave a curt nod, his lips pressed thin at the memory.

'Did Principal Ferguson have a vote on the executive committee? The, er, *exco*?'

'Iain? Oh, no.'

'So how could Alan win any of these battles? From what you're saying, it sounds like he'd be outvoted two to one.'

Lynn's response was a peal of laughter, startling in its lightheartedness.

'Then thank God for the women, eh? Before Brian's resignation, the exco was five people, not three. And the other two, being women, were a hell of a lot more sensible – and persuadable – than either Brian or Clyde.' Lynn sat back a little, steepling her fingers. 'The fourth vote on the exco belonged to JoAnn Harwood. She would occasionally side with Al. Mainly because she really liked Iain, so if *he* wanted it badly enough, Jo would vote for it, even though she's a pretty conservative gal for the most part.'

'I see. And the fifth vote?'

A shadow fell across Lynn Spargo's face. It was clear she didn't care for the subject.

'Fatima Haddad Davis. Her family was a big deal under the Shah of Iran, I think, so they fled to the US after he fell. God knows how she ended up in Pittsburgh. She and Alan were always pretty tight. If anything, she was even more progressive than he was, which must have driven her husband, Randy, absolutely crazy.' Lynn rolled her eyes, looking suddenly like a teenage girl. '*That* guy makes Brian and Clyde look like weak-kneed liberals.' She pointed vaguely out the window. 'They live not far from here, actually, in Sewickley Heights. Anyway, after Brian resigned from the exco, she and Al could pretty much do what they wanted. Even if it was a tied liberal–conservative vote – Al and Fatima against Clyde and Jo – Al had the casting vote as chair. Jo knew that, so she either abstained or voted with the majority to give some semblance of unity. That's how Al and Iain were able to get the DEI thing moving forward in the first place. It would never have had a chance if Brian had still been there. Clyde was *beyond* livid, let me tell you. *Be. Yond.*' She looked suddenly thoughtful. 'He and Al have history. Clyde hated Al, but Al didn't give a shit about Clyde, which kinda made Clyde hate him even more.'

'But not enough to kill him?'

Lynn paused for a moment, biting gently on her lower lip.

'I guess, thinking about it, that Clyde maybe hated Al badly enough to do him harm. But not physically. He's not built for it, believe me. And even if he was, he'd not have the guts. And there's no way Al would have allowed that man into his apartment.' She grinned, albeit briefly, at the thought. 'You'd be ice skating in hell first.'

Greg rubbed absentmindedly at his eyepatch, trying to make sense of what she was telling him, to file the information in the right boxes.

'Is there any chance you can get me into Alan's apartment?' he asked after a moment. 'I'd like to look around if that's at all possible.'

'Of course.' She flashed him a quick, easy smile. 'Being the ex in a more or less amicable divorce has its privileges. I'll speak to the doorman. It shouldn't be problem.'

'Speaking of Alan's apartment, how secure would you say it was? How easy would it be for someone to break in?'

'To break in? Next to impossible. Seaford Court – that's the name of the Al's building – is pretty secure. They have a doorman service during the day, and at night you need a key card to get in or out. On top of that, Al had the penthouse, which has its own secure elevator. It won't go up without either a keycard or a release from inside the penthouse itself.' Lynn's voice soured into bitterness. 'No one broke into that apartment, Greg. They wouldn't need to.'

'Why not?'

'Because whoever did this had access. Which can mean only one thing.'

'Which is?'

'That if you find whatever twenty-something bitch-whore he was sleeping with, she's the one who tipped him over the edge.'

SATURDAY, THE ELEVENTH
11:00 A.M.

Greg was not at all sure why Andrea had referred to Beans of Steel, the coffee shop down the hill and around the corner from Greg's apartment, as a hipster place. Sure, not all coffee shops had a warm, roaring fireplace mocked up to look like a smelter, and the clientele skewed toward the highly educated – techies and students for the most part – the male contingent of which tended to sport beards. But hipster? What did that even mean? And was *he* a hipster, or were Black and hipster mutually exclusive?

Thoughts drifting, Greg closed out the *Pittsburgh Post-Gazette* on his laptop and opened something more fun. The paper had contained little that held his interest. There'd been a small section following up on the death of Alan Mester, confirming what Demetrius had already told him: that the police did not view the banker's death as suspicious.

And regardless of what Demetrius and Lynn Spargo had to say on the matter, chances were the police were probably right.

Greg glanced up as the door to the coffee shop swung open. Andrea Velasquez had arrived exactly on time, olive face slightly nervous beneath its mane of dark hair. Her expression lightened considerably, however, when she caught sight of the glow from his computer screen.

'Vogue?' she said, genuinely incredulous. 'You know that's a women's magazine, right? Even in England.'

'It's a magazine for people with taste,' Greg corrected her, with a sigh. 'It just so happens that I like nice things.'

'Uh-huh.' Andrea was grinning from ear to ear. She took a seat beside him so they could share the screen.

'I read what you sent me,' Greg said, banishing *Vogue* to the ether and bringing up Andrea's draft letter.

'I know it's crap,' she said. 'I couldn't think of anything.'

'It's not crap,' Greg said, voice firm. 'And so long as you tried your best, don't talk that way about your work, ever. Even if you think it's rubbish. There are plenty of people out there just looking for an excuse to hold you back. Don't hand them one on a plate by allowing them to agree with you.' He highlighted some large chunks of text. 'The only thing that needs improvement here is that it's far too diffident.' He favored her with a warm smile. 'You are an accomplished young lady, Maybelline Andrea Velasquez. We need to make sure these guys understand that.' He gave her a playful punch on the arm. 'So. Let's see what we can do.'

Andrea punched him back.

'*Don't* call me Maybelline.'

It didn't take long in the end. The main thing that slowed them down was Andrea's constant need to educate Greg about computer jargon. For a few brief and glorious moments, he would understand a concept well enough to craft a better sentence, only to have it wiped away by the next set of bizarre, not-quite-English words. Which was probably for the best, he decided. Leave the nerd stuff to the nerds.

'How's the thing for Doctor Freedman going?' Andrea asked as they were finishing up. She curled her fingers into air quotes. 'Have you "cracked the case"?'

'Smartarse. Do you even know what "the case" is?'

'Nope. Do you?'

Greg found himself laughing.

'Not really,' he confessed. 'A friend of Dem— Doctor Freedman's, a guy by the name of Alan Mester, fell from his balcony and died. Doctor Freedman is worried it might be more than suicide. He wants me to take a look at it.'

Andrea was clearly intrigued.

'How do you tell if someone jumped or got pushed?' she asked.

'With a great deal of difficulty, I imagine.' Greg sighed and reached for his empty coffee cup, getting ready to clear it away. 'I'm heading out to the man's apartment. To see what there is to see.'

'Can I come?'

'Well—'

'My truck's right outside,' Andrea coaxed. 'Save you a trek up the hill to get your car.'

'Uh . . . why not?' Truth was, he didn't need a lot of persuading. The thought of blundering about a dead man's apartment with no clue as to what he was doing was not a cheerful one. He could do with the company.

If he had remembered that Andrea's truck had a cracked muffler, he might have been more hesitant. The vehicle roared and coughed by turns as they edged along Fifth Avenue in stop-go traffic, heading for downtown. Greg slumped in his seat, as if by doing so he could avoid the disapproving stares of pedestrians on the sidewalk.

'That's new,' he said, in an attempt to distract himself. 'What is it? A dashcam?'

'You bet your ass it is,' Andrea said. 'You see that great dent in the fender?'

'Yes,' Greg lied, wondering how he was meant to notice one dent in particular.

'Yeah, well, some old blind dude pulled out in front of me without looking. And now he's telling his insurance company I crashed into him, which is a goddamn lie. So, from now on,' she patted the dashboard, 'I'm going to have proof.'

It being a Saturday, traffic thinned out as they reached downtown. Following the GPS on Greg's cellphone, Andrea turned into a narrow, barely visible alley that allowed them access to a parking lot.

SEAFORD COURT, the sign said. RESIDENTS AND VISITORS ONLY.

Jumping down from the truck, it was easy enough for Greg to pick out the penthouse. Seaford Court, Alan Mester's apartment building, was a modern design, no more than ten years old and five or six stories tall; a chunky, no-nonsense cube, faced in polished brown sandstone. Compared to the 1930s-style architecture of its neighbors, it looked distinctly out of place. The penthouse made the contrast even more obvious, being a mostly glass-walled construction atop the building's roof. The so-called balcony was essentially the expanse of roof not covered by the penthouse. 'Terrace' would be a better description, Greg thought. Whatever word you chose to describe it, the balcony was big.

'Nice,' said Andrea, following his gaze. 'Dude was murdered.'

'What makes you say that?'

'You have enough dough to afford all that, what possible reason could you have to jump?'

As Lynn Spargo had promised, Seaford Court's head doorman, Dan Wurth, was expecting him. Andrea Velasquez, wearing her usual

Doc Martens, ripped jeans and a Steelers jacket that had seen better days, he chose to ignore.

'So you're the insurance investigator,' he said, by way of greeting.

'Yes.' Andrea glanced at him in surprise but had the good sense to keep quiet. Greg, equally surprised, found himself smiling in approval. Mester's ex-wife had spared no effort in smoothing his path.

The doorman came out from behind his desk and pumped Greg's hand enthusiastically.

'Anything you need, sir, you just ask, OK? Ms Spargo is good people and Alan is – was – a terrific guy. No airs and graces, that one, if you know what I mean. It didn't matter who you were, he treated everyone the same, even if he did live in the penthouse.' The doorman lowered his voice. 'Do you think it's murder like Ms Spargo says?'

Greg pretended to consider the question.

'Best not to jump to conclusions at this stage, Dan. Early days and all that.'

'Of course, sir, of course,' Wurth said, looking suitably serious. 'So. What can I do for you?'

Greg took a quick look around the lobby. It was all stark stainless steel and white marble, impressive but not overly large. Anyone coming in from the main entrance on Fifth Avenue would find themselves standing across from the reception desk. Off to the right, there was a small bank of elevators, and to the left, a narrow passageway that appeared to lead to a bike storage area and, almost certainly, the rear exit to the parking lot, an exit that, as Greg and Andrea had discovered the hard way, could only be accessed from outside with a resident's keycard. There were two CCTV cameras covering the entrance, the reception desk and the elevator bank. There would almost certainly be another one covering the rear exit.

'I think,' he said slowly, 'that if you could just let us into Mr Mester's apartment, that will do for now.'

As Lynn had explained, the penthouse did, indeed, have its own private elevator, the one farthest from the reception desk. Wurth used an electronic keycard to get it to open and then pressed the button marked PH to sweep them smoothly to the top floor. The elevator opened on to a small vestibule. Light flooded in from an overhead skylight, striking a rich brown from the paneled wood walls.

With much rattling of keys, the doorman let them in.

'I'll leave you to it,' he said.

'How do we get back down?' Andrea asked, a little anxiously. 'Do we need a keycard?'

'No, ma'am. You only need a keycard to get up here. Just press the button to call the elevator and it'll bring you down no problem at all.'

Like the vestibule, Alan Mester's apartment was flooded with light. Not only did it have a profusion of skylights, but two of the exterior walls, facing Fifth Avenue at the front and the parking lot at the back, were made entirely of glass. Sliding glass doors, subtly etched with an abstract pattern, opened from the opulent living room on to the front terrace. A similar, but smaller door led from the master bedroom to the balcony at the rear. The rear balcony was just as wide but significantly less deep than its Fifth Avenue equivalent.

It was from here that Alan Mester had fallen.

'That is a long way down,' Andrea said. Petite as she was, she had to stand on tiptoe to lean over the balcony's varnished hardwood rail. Greg joined her in looking down, the rail pressing against his waist.

Demetrius and Lynn were right about that, at least, he decided. The railing was built to code. It was too high for anyone to stumble over the top of it by accident.

And, assuming you *did* have a fear of heights, it wasn't a comfortable place to sit. The balcony was only about six feet deep, and the barrier beneath the wooden railing was painfully transparent glass. To the truly fearful, it might as well not be there, providing as it did all the psychological protection of gossamer.

There was no outdoor furniture.

'What a shitty place to die,' Andrea said. 'All this money and you end up . . . down there.'

Greg grunted an agreement. The parking lot was a grimy expanse of oil-stained black asphalt, surrounded on all sides by the unattractive rear ends of downtown buildings, the bits the architects hoped you'd never see. Bricked-over remains of 1930s windows vied with elevator housings and industrial-sized aircon fans for the title of biggest eyesore.

The balcony might be nicely tiled, but no one in their right mind would want to spend time here. It didn't require a fear of heights to keep people away. Simple good taste ought to be enough.

The master bedroom, the one that led to the balcony, was

dominated by a huge bed, the frame ornately wooden; the sheets, high-thread-count linen. Greg didn't need to touch them to know they'd be creamy smooth beneath his fingers, but he did so anyway, enjoying the sensation. The bed itself was made up. Between leaving the exco meeting and falling to his death, the man had found no time for sleep.

Mester, Greg noted with approval, was a tidy man. In contrast to the bed, the remaining furniture tended to the minimalist – light wood and metal – with very little in the way of clutter.

There was no sign of a struggle.

'Ooh! Look at this. This is bigger than my bedroom. Maybe even my entire house.'

Andrea was standing in the middle of a walk-in closet, arms outstretched.

'I can't even touch the sides.'

The closet was huge, but empty. There was nothing in the various drawers. Clothes-less hangers hung forlornly on their racks, a handful of their brethren scattered carelessly on the floor.

'This'll have been the wife's,' Andrea said. 'She'd have cleaned it out when she was finally done with his ass.'

'Uh-huh.' It made sense, Greg figured. The bedroom furniture, chests and whatnot, contained clothes that clearly belonged to the apartment's owner, as did a couple of built-in wardrobes. He clearly had no need of his wife's former closet.

What a waste.

Tiring of his surroundings, he made his way back to the living room. Here, too, the furniture was sleek and modern. White leather with glass end tables. The coffee table, also glass, was etched in the same abstract pattern as the sliding door to the front terrace.

One armchair faced directly toward a vast television, its screen curved like a cinema's. On the table beside the armchair, nestling against the TV remote, was a bottle of single-malt scotch and a half-full glass of yellowish liquid. Melting ice had long since washed away the original, peaty brown. Greg looked around for a second glass, without success.

The front terrace also lacked outdoor furniture. On stepping on to it from the living room, however, what it did have, he discovered, was an additional sets of doors. Greg stepped through them into Alan Mester's home office.

The décor here was very different from the rest of the apartment, being plush and old school. Everything was dark wood atop a sea of green carpet. Tasteful prints, chosen, Greg suspected, for how they complemented the room rather than artistic merit, clung to the walls between tiers of neatly arranged bookshelves. The office's leather-topped desk contained the room's only touch of modernity: two computer screens and a closed laptop.

He flicked it on. The screens shone out at him, asking for a password.

Of course they did. He let loose a quietly muttered imprecation.

'Let's take it with us,' Andrea said, causing him to start. He'd had no idea she was behind him. 'I'll see if I can get it open for you.'

'Is this what they teach you at Pittsburgh Community College? How to hack computers?'

'Mr Bimbo! How could you say such a thing? It's more like an unfortunate side effect.'

Greg could feel a smile tugging at his lips.

'Fine, we'll take it.' Silently cursing himself for his amateurishness, he added. 'See if you can find a bag or something we can put it in. No point advertising what we've been up to.' He thought of the white-collar police raids he'd seen on the television news. Stern-faced officers marching out of some corporate skyscraper carrying cardboard boxes of full of evidence.

Rachel Lev would have had a box.

Mildly irritated by this oversight, he mooched around the apartment. Andrea's bag quest had taken her to the kitchen, where she was opening and closing drawers with little regard for their long-term survival.

He ended up in the living room, staring at the undrunk glass of scotch, at the otherwise neat and orderly surfaces. A place for everything and everything in its place. He played back what he'd seen in the bedroom, the closet, the luxurious home office.

There was no sign of a cellphone. He tapped the inside pocket of his jacket, felt the flat bulk of his own device.

It could quite easily have fallen with the body.

A shame he didn't have time to dial nine-one-one on the way down.

'What are you smiling at?' Andrea asked. A paper grocery sack from Whole Foods dangled from one hand, laptop inside.

'Something totally inappropriate.'

'And you a teacher, too.' She crooked a finger at him. 'Come see what I found.'

'What do you make of this?' she asked, having taken the two of them to the kitchen. She presented him with a large, fake-leather jewelry box. 'I found it next to the trash.' The box itself was flat and square, the sort of box in which he'd expect to find a necklace. ARECAS DESIGN was embossed across the top in curvy gold lettering.

Greg opened it up. It was empty, apart from a small handwritten card.

'"To a wonderful woman",' he said, reading aloud.

'Now look at this.' Andrea handed him another box. It was identical in every way to the first, right down to a handwritten card, in the same handwriting, with the same wording. 'You'd have thought the guy would switch up the messaging, huh? I mean, how hard can it be? Show some imagination, man.'

'I don't think bankers are famous for having imaginations, Andrea. Besides, it's the thought that counts, right?'

'And the dough, Mr Bimbo. Don't forget the dough.'

Greg nodded. A sixty-one-year-old man with a taste in much younger women might find that charm alone wasn't enough.

Find whatever twenty-something bitch-whore he was sleeping with; she's the one who tipped him over the edge.

Suddenly uneasy, he dropped the jewelry boxes into the grocery bag before heading back to the walk-in closet. He stood in the middle of it, looking from the hangers on their racks to the handful scattered on the floor.

Andrea leaned against the closet's doorframe, watching. Her dark eyes twinkled with amusement.

'Well, Sherlock, what's the big deal?'

Greg poked one of the hangers on the floor with the toe of his shoe.

'Alan Mester, we can agree, is a tidy guy. Apart from an unfinished glass of scotch, there's not a thing in this apartment that's out of place. Except for these. Why would he leave a bunch of hangers lying on the floor?'

'This was his wife's place. Maybe he doesn't come in here.'

'His wife divorced him five years ago. A bit extreme, don't you think?'

He slipped past a newly pensive Andrea and into the bedroom, opening and closing drawers, looking again at the built-in wardrobes. He dropped to his hands and knees, sinking into soft, luxurious carpet.

He peered under the bed, heavy and wooden and ornate. It took his eye a moment or two to adjust to the darkness.

And then he saw it. A frail, spidery silhouette. He retrieved it with a grunt of effort.

'Wow,' Andrea breathed. 'Who'd a thunk it?'

He was holding a spike-heeled shoe. Black patent leather gleamed in sharp contrast to a red interior and liquid-smooth scarlet sole.

'How could someone even stand in that?' Andrea asked. 'That heel's gotta be like, what? Four inches?' She glanced down at the patent leather of her own Doc Martens. 'I'd break my ankles.'

'And your bank account,' Greg added, reading the elegant script stamped into the insole. 'Christian Louboutin, Paris. A Kate, if I'm not mistaken. A pair of these'll set you back a little under a grand.'

Andrea's eyes were twinkling again.

'How come you know so much about women's shoes, Mr Bimbo?'

'I like nice things.'

'I guess *Vogue* is good for something, huh.' She grinned mischievously. 'Go on then.'

'Go on what?'

'Pull out the other one. Maybe they'll fit me.'

'I thought they'd break your ankles.'

'Beauty knows no pain, man.'

Greg laughed at that. He ducked under the bed again, just to be sure.

'There isn't one,' he said. The grin faded. He looked around the untouched bedroom, thought once more about the hangers on the closet floor. 'I guess the owner left it behind by accident.'

'Expensive shit to be leaving behind is what I'm thinking.'

'Absolutely.' Greg turned the shoe over in his hands. Felt the richness of it under his fingers. 'Unless, of course, you were in a hurry.'

'Like I-just-tipped-an-old-guy-off-a-balcony kind of hurry?'

'Exactly like that.' He dropped the shoe into the Whole Foods grocery bag, beside the laptop and the jewelry boxes.

'Let's go talk to the doorman.'

1:06 P.M.

'Why aren't we asking him about the man's lady friend?' Andrea whispered, as they followed Dan Wurth along the narrow corridor leading to the back of the building.

'Because he might not answer,' Greg whispered back. 'And once he stops talking, he won't start again. Easy stuff first, young lady. Easy stuff first.'

Andrea huffed at that but let it go.

The rear door was heavy and resistant, but the doorman forced it open with a wheeze of effort. They walked slowly into the parking lot. The day was growing warm. Probably not the best time, Greg thought, to be wearing a jacket.

'This is it,' Dan said. 'This is where I found him.'

'Are you sure?' Greg asked. He didn't want to sound dubious, but he couldn't help himself. He looked up toward the penthouse terrace, squinting against the bright blue of the sky.

'I know what you're thinking,' the doorman said. 'But I'm sure.' His voice dropped in the manner of someone imparting a confidence. 'The way I figure, the fall didn't kill him. Not right away, I mean. He had time to crawl a ways before he, er, passed. There was a blood trail, actually, but we washed it away as soon as the cops and the FBI gave the all-clear.'

'Gross,' Andrea muttered.

Greg, after a moment's hesitation, found himself nodding. Assuming the doorman was right, it was the only thing that made sense. Because the spot Dan Wurth had indicated wasn't beneath the penthouse terrace at all. It was several yards off to one side. As the man didn't have wings to fly through the air, he had to have pulled himself along on the ground.

In the direction of the rear entrance. Whatever state he'd been in after a six-story fall, he knew enough to move toward the only possible source of help.

Had expired along the way.

Standing there, he could almost feel it. Pitch black and no one around, no one close enough to hear a weak cry from flooding lungs. Pain, panic, an instinctive crawl toward safety. A crawl that might have taken a broken body hours. And all for nothing.

Did you pray? he wondered. *And, if so, what for? To go on living, or for the agony to end?*

'What time did you find him?' Greg asked.

'About five thirty, when I arrived for work. I called nine-one-one, but it was obvious he was dead. Poor guy.'

'What about CCTV? Did that catch anything?'

'No.' The doorman looked embarrassed. 'Our CCTV doesn't always work. It'll be fine for weeks and months and then, suddenly, *pfft*. Tuesday night was one of those nights. All we've got is static from around nine p.m. until four in the morning.'

Greg raised an eyebrow.

'And there was no one around to pick up on that?'

Dan Wurth folded his arms across his chest, his expression halfway between apology and glare.

'Sorry, but no. We run doorman service in the building from six till six. But even if we'd been here, there'd have been nothing we could do.' A shrug of the shoulders. 'It always clears up before the contractor gets here. What they call an intermittent fault. There's nothing they can do unless they actually catch it glitching.'

'It must be very frustrating,' Greg said, trying to keep the doorman on side.

'It can be,' Wurth agreed, relaxing a little. 'But it doesn't happen very often. It's never been a problem before. I mean, it's been a problem. But not, you know, like *this*.'

'I suppose not. What's the name of your contractor?'

'Arkless Security; they're based in Cranberry.'

'Great. And would it be possible to see the video from either side of the malfunction? From, let's say, nine p.m. on Monday until this morning?'

'Sure, I'll pull something together and email it to you.'

Yeah, send it to my school address. That won't look weird at all, seeing you think I'm an insurance investigator.

'Can you email it to Lynn Spargo instead?' He leaned in and touched the man on the shoulder, dropping his voice as he did so. 'She's taking an interest, as I'm sure you can imagine, and I'd like to help her out as much as I can. I can't properly send it to her myself, you understand. But if *you* were to do it and she forwarded it on to me . . . Well, where's the harm?'

Dan Wurth responded with a smile and a wink.

'Understood, sir. Let's say no more about it.'

'Also, while we're at it, can we see the keycard logs for the same time frame? Just the ones related to Mr Mester, obviously. I'd like to know who was using that elevator of his.'

Dan's brow crinkled.

'To be honest, I'm not sure how to do that. It goes to the security company. Give me a few days and I'll mail them out to you just as soon as I have them. If you could let me have your email address? I don't imagine Ms Spargo would want to see a bunch of times and serial numbers.'

Greg forced a smile.

'No, I don't imagine she would. Tell you what, though. Why don't I come and watch them here? Files like that can be clunky and go straight to spam. It'll be safer all round, I think, and besides, I have a very strong suspicion you'll have to translate them for me.'

Wurth broke into a grin at the thought.

'Sounds good, sir.'

They headed back inside. Greg, for one, was happy to be out of the heat. The Whole Foods grocery bag brushed against his knee as they walked along the narrow corridor and back to the lobby.

'Dan, did Mr Mester have any lady friends? Anyone who visited him frequently? This person might be quite young and—'

'Be able to rock a pair of high heels. Like, totally,' Andrea added. Greg fought back a grimace.

The doorman came to an abrupt halt.

'I'm not sure that's something I should be talking about.'

'The man's dead,' Greg pointed out. 'We owe it to him to make sure, absolutely sure, that nothing untoward happened. Or, if it did, to make sure he gets justice. He was wealthy, and single, and good-looking. It would have been odd if he *didn't* have a girlfriend.' He flashed what he hoped was an understanding smile. 'And it's not like anything you have to say will be a surprise to Ms Spargo. Not really. She did divorce him, you know.'

Much to Greg's relief, Dan chuckled.

'You're right about that, I guess.' He paused, gathering his thoughts. 'There've been a few over the years, some more serious than others. And mostly young, like you say. The serious ones get a keycard. The not-so-serious?' A round laugh followed. 'Well, let's just say we turned a blind eye. If he'd vouched for them, we pretty much let them come and go as they pleased. I don't think he wanted them in the visitors' book if you get my meaning.'

'And did he have anyone serious at the moment?'

'Yeah. There'd been a girl he'd been seeing for maybe eighteen months. Carmen, I think her name was. But she kind of faded away and there was a new one on the scene he'd not been seeing that long, maybe the last six months or so. Jill? June? Something like that. Blonde gal, maybe yay high.' He indicated a level somewhat above Andrea's head, which Greg took to be around five-four, five-five. 'I'm not a hundred percent certain that she'd got a card yet, but maybe?'

'And when did you last see her?'

'Tuesday. But before any of this happened. It would have been late in the shift, around five o'clock. I remember because she was across the street, looking like she was about to head this way, when she got stopped by some guy. Jealous boyfriend or ex most likely. Anyway, they started getting into it. I couldn't hear what they were saying, but it got pretty heated. Not shouting heated but *intense*, you know? She got real upset and stormed off.' With a slightly guilty look at Andrea, he added, 'I thought about going out there to see if she needed help, but she seemed to be handling herself OK.'

'Until she got real upset and stormed off,' Andrea said drily.

'Yeah,' Dan said, oblivious to the barb. 'Like I said, she didn't seem to be in danger, not really. Just boyfriend–girlfriend stuff.'

Greg glanced up at the CCTV.

'The camera that covers the entrance. Does it reach across the street?'

''Fraid not.'

'And you didn't see her come back?'

'No, sir. And she didn't come back after my shift, either. At least, not before nine. I've checked the tape and she's not on it.'

'And what about the boyfriend. Did he come in?'

'Absolutely not. I've never seen him before. I reckon he was only in the area because he was waiting for her. He left almost as soon as she did.'

'I see.' He reached out and shook Dan Wurth's hand. 'In that case, I think we'll get out of your hair. Thanks so much for your help.'

He and Andrea took their leave, exposing themselves once again to the heat of the parking lot.

'Andrea,' Greg asked, 'can you get in touch with those contractors the doorman mentioned?'

'Arkless Security? Sure.' Her eyes narrowed shrewdly. 'You think the doorman did it? That he futzed with the cameras before going up there and killing him?'

'It's possible. I've no idea *why* a doorman would want to kill Alan Mester, but I'm really uncomfortable with the idea that the camera system just happened to go haywire on the night our man went and got himself killed. It'd be easy enough for the person in charge of on-site security to disconnect the feed, I'd have thought.'

'I'll check it out, see if there's an intermittent fault like he said. Oh, and if it *was* the doorman, I know *exactly* why he did it.'

'You do?' Greg was genuinely intrigued.

'I do.' Andrea let it hang there for a moment. 'The guy was a lousy tipper. The doorman's originally from New York and he was expecting life-changing amounts of money for his Christmas bonus.'

Greg couldn't help himself. He burst out laughing.

'On the other hand, it sure looks like our young gal is out of the picture,' Andrea continued. 'She was long gone before anything happened.' She grunted a little as she opened the truck's heavy door. One ding too many had damaged the hinges.

'Maybe,' Greg said. 'Maybe not.'

'What does that mean?'

'Maybe she came back. After nine p.m.' He could feel his face knitting into a frown. '*Someone* cleared their stuff out of that apartment, Andrea. Someone who's now missing a very expensive Louboutin pump. If it wasn't our mysterious young woman, then who the hell was it?'

2:23 P.M.

Greg, not wanting to take Andrea out of her way, had himself dropped off at the North Side Asbury, a half dozen blocks or so from the crowded apartment Andrea called home.

'It's Saturday,' he'd explained. 'I need to do some grocery shopping and it might as well be here. I'll grab a rideshare back.'

Not being a Northsider, he'd never had cause to visit Asbury supermarket before, although several members of the faculty had spoken of it in vague but disparaging terms, like 'not nice' or 'bad atmosphere'. Now he understood why.

Black people shopped here. In numbers. They moved down the aisles past visibly wealthier white patrons, the latter a product of the neighborhood's ongoing gentrification. Both sides were polite but wary, careful to keep their distance. Value-for-money products nestled beside high-end groceries in juxtapositions that would never have been found in his usual haunts. The sparklingly clean spaces seemed unnaturally quiet.

With an inward sigh of exasperation, Greg pushed the weirdness to one side and concentrated on the acquisition of supplies. Somewhere between Canned Goods and Condiments, however, something started to gnaw at him.

Jewelry boxes. What were they doing in the kitchen next to the trash? The notes, unoriginal though they were, implied that Alan Mester had intended them as a present for someone. Perhaps the mysterious Jill/June that Dan Wurth had spoken about. But if Jill/June had received them, wouldn't she have taken them home before throwing the boxes away? Unless, contrary to Dan's understanding, she was already living there. But if she *was* living there, wasn't it kind of rude to dump the boxes – and the notes – next to Mester's trash? Presumably right in front of him.

'Greg! Fancy meeting you here.'

Startled, Greg looked up to see a beaming Principal Eisner, accompanied by an unhappy-looking man whom Greg also recognized:

from the photo in Eisner's office. The principal was, as ever, stylishly dressed; on this occasion, in an expensive-looking cashmere sweater and slacks. Greg's gaze slipped past Eisner's broad shoulders and through the store's plate-glass windows to the parking lot outside. The sun was still beating down. It could be no more comfortable for a principal in a cashmere sweater, he thought, than a teacher in a jacket. Eisner was clearly a man who dressed for the season rather than the actual weather.

Then again, the principal hadn't hung around in the Asbury parking lot to talk about dead bodies. Air-conditioned car to air-conditioned supermarket would have been a less broiling experience.

'Do you live nearby?' Eisner was asking.

'Er . . . no. I just happened to be in the area and thought I'd do some shopping. You?'

'Yes. We're locals now. We rented a place in the Mexican War Streets, didn't we, Josh?'

'Well, *you* did.' Eisner looked briefly uncomfortable.

'Anyway, best leave you to it,' he said. He clapped Greg on the shoulder and the two of them moved off.

Greg watched them leave. More accurately, he watched Josh leave. He hated the way the man walked, his feeble, reedy build, the way he stood too close to his partner. Everything about him, in fact.

Only when they turned into the neighboring aisle did the realization finally dawn.

He was jealous.

Somewhere behind the high-stacked cans of ready-made chili, the Devil was laughing at him. He fled through checkout like a man possessed, Satan on his heels.

3:11 P.M.

If he hadn't been a hot, buttery mix of libido and self-hatred weighed down by shopping, Greg would probably have noticed Rachel Lev before he stepped out of the rideshare. The detective was standing at the front door of his apartment building, looking for all the world like she'd just arrived there.

Greg doubted that very much. He pasted on a smile.

'Good afternoon, Rachel. What a pleasant surprise.'

'It is, isn't it?' she smiled back. There was something a touch too professional about it, though. Enough to make Greg even more wary. 'I was hoping to catch you. I have good news.'

'Really?'

'Yes, really. Thanks to you, we've identified our John Doe.'

'That's great! Who is he?'

'A man by the name of Viktor-with-a-K Lavrov. We canvassed the car rental companies like you suggested, asking about missing vehicles. Turns out that he rented a Chevy Silverado the day before he died and, for obvious reasons, never handed it in. We also know that he flew into town a few days earlier on a flexible return ticket from London and, for the same obvious reasons, never flew the return leg. The rental company reported the truck as stolen and, by happy coincidence, it was recovered a couple of weeks ago, having been reported as an abandoned vehicle by someone in the neighborhood.' She favored him with a knowing smile. 'People get pissed like you wouldn't believe when vehicles get left outside their front door.

'Turned out the vehicle was still in the pound, as the rental company hadn't taken delivery of it yet. We found a passport and a few other bits and pieces, which seems to match what we know of our guy in every detail.'

She reached into her jacket pocket and held out a photo.

'This is him.'

She was watching him closely as he took the photograph from

her fingers. He held his expression steady against the shock of recognition.

Morosov.

It must have been taken from the passport they'd found, the one in the name of Lavrov. It was a little blurry from enlargement but not enough to cause any doubt.

'Does he look familiar to you?'

'No. Should he?'

Lev was wearing a tight little smile.

'Do you know where we found Lavrov's car, Greg?'

'The pound?' He tried to keep his voice light, ignoring the sinking feeling in his stomach.

'Right over there.' She was pointing past his shoulder. 'Just down the street from this apartment building of yours.' She fixed him with a hard stare. 'Some coincidence, huh?'

Greg wanted to kick himself for his stupidity. Morosov had been driving a Hyundai when Greg had spotted him, but Morosov knew he'd been spotted. *Of course* he'd changed vehicles. Who wouldn't?

Something he should have thought of before blithely suggesting to a detective lieutenant, whether acting or otherwise, that she go looking for rental cars.

'Some coincidence indeed.'

'And you never saw him, even briefly?'

'Afraid not.'

'And the Chevy Silverado. You never noticed a strange truck that didn't belong here and didn't move?'

'No. I mean, I'm sure I *saw* it if it was there like you say. I just didn't notice it.' He ventured a smile. 'This is the Burgh, Rachel. The place is not what you'd call "truck challenged".'

He might have imagined it, but he thought he saw a twitch of a smile.

'Well,' she said. 'I'll be seeing you. Enjoy your weekend.'

He watched her leave, sliding into a gray Ford Taurus that had seen better days.

Safely back in his apartment, he opened up his laptop and googled 'Viktor Lavrov Pittsburgh police.' Sure enough, Morosov's alias and picture had been released to the media, along with a request for information.

He sat back with a sigh.

So that was it, then. Mikhail Sergeevich Morosov was dead. All doubt, all hope of a different outcome swept away by a blurred rendition of a fake passport. He grimaced at the thought. There was no easy way out. Not now. Now there must be justice.

Lev's justice. Polukhin's justice.

He pictured his mother walking along Lomonosovsky Prospekt on her way to work, imagined it was he taking the surveillance pictures instead of some faceless GRU operative. She'd be hatless now, maybe, as spring finally reached Moscow, blissfully unaware of the long lens, of the fork in the road that her son was all too rapidly approaching.

Morosov's photograph glowered up at him from the laptop.

He slammed the lid shut with unnecessary force.

SUNDAY, THE TWELFTH
12:15 P.M.

Church had done nothing to quiet a troubled mind. Not the incense, not the cantor, not the icon-laden weight of an entire house of God. Perhaps for the first time, Greg wished St Andrew's had been Russian Orthodox rather than Greek. The Greeks had pews.

He, on the other hand, wanted the comfort of standing. Of rocking back and forth on his heels, of banishing the churning froth of thought.

Instead, here he was, sitting on his arse as the service drew to a close, trying not to squirm on the plush seating.

Envy was a sin. Envy of a man in an openly homosexual relationship was a sin geometrically compounded. He hadn't given in to the Devil. Not really. Not recently. Not since that one time in London, start of the long, twisted road that had ended up here, his weakness exploited by British Intelligence. Traitor and sinner both.

He re-enacted the short, innocuous interaction between himself and Evan Eisner in the North Side Asbury. Except, in this version, Josh whatever-the-fuck-his-name-was wasn't there. He remembered the feel of Eisner's hand on his shoulder, the heat of it, the underlying strength. The sense of, well, *safety*. Something he hadn't felt since childhood.

Would it really be so wrong?

He almost gasped at the brazenness of the thought. The clarity of it. He glanced around for the Devil, but there was no sign of him; none of the prickling of guilt and shame and other things that indicated his presence. This, after all, was the one place the Devil dare not enter. There was just the usual throng of parishioners approaching Father Kyriakos at the end of the service; others, less pious, heading for the exits.

The thought was his and his alone.

Which made it so much worse.

His cellphone vibrated, soft but insistent. Grateful for the distraction, he reached into his pocket and pulled it out.

A text from Andrea.

You still in church?

Just finishing. What's up?

Wanted to let you know I spent Saturday working my ass off for you. Chased down arkless security. Found them on the internet and called up pretending to be mesters building. Theyre totes legit. Seaford court cams are all theres landlords complaining for years about fault that comes and goes but can never find it. looks like doorman dude is off the hook and didn't kill over lousy tips

Thanks, andrea, for all the hard work.
Your reward will be in heaven.

Greg put the phone away with a smile. Andrea was right. As unlikely a suspect as he'd been in the first place, Dan Wurth was off the list now for sure.

Which left Alan Mester's mystery woman. The Louboutin shoe he'd retrieved from under the bed was a size seven US, which seemed consistent with the doorman's description of a woman of around five-four, five-five in height. He had trouble picturing someone of that size tipping a full-grown man over the top of a balcony rail, but perhaps circumstances conspired to help her. Maybe he was drunk, or was already leaning too far over, or both.

Or maybe the guy just killed himself.

An abandoned and extremely expensive shoe, plus hangers on the floor, indicated someone who'd left in a hurry – and in the middle of the night if one accepted, as Dan Wurth claimed, that she never appeared on video while the system was working. But she could have left for reasons that had nothing to do with murder. Maybe she valued her privacy, maybe she didn't want her contemporaries to know she was dating a man old enough to be her grandfather.

And then again, maybe not.

And then there were the jewelry boxes. Why—

Someone was tugging at his sleeve. A small child. He couldn't have been more than four or five years old. Sunday school must be out.

'I can't find my mommy.'

The boy, trying to be brave, was on the verge of tears.

I hope this is as frightening as it ever gets for you, kiddo.

Greg smiled gently.

'Well, then,' he said. 'Let's see what we can do about that. Father Kyriakos will know where your mum is. Shall we go and ask him?'

He held out a hand. The boy took it. Together, they marched up the aisle toward the priest and an orbiting cloud of admirers. As they approached, one of the cloud detached themselves, became a real, concrete person.

'Dean,' she said to the boy, 'I told you to wait in the classroom.'

'Everyone left, Mom. I got scared.' The boy loosened his grip on Greg's hand and held on to his mother, leaving Greg with a small pang of regret and a suddenly cold palm. The fading imprint of a different type of life.

'Thank you,' the woman said, looking slightly embarrassed.

'It was my pleasure.' He turned to go: things to do, people to see in the world temporal.

'Greg! Can I speak to you for a moment?' The voice was male, and deep, with a noticeable Greek accent. Father Kyriakos was pursuing him down the aisle but unable to catch up. Greg slowed to a halt. The priest nodded in the direction of reunited mother and son. 'You're good with children, I see. Constantinos is a shy child. He wouldn't have walked up here with just anyone.'

It took Greg a second or two to realize that Constantinos and Dean must be one and the same.

'I'm quite sure he would have, Father. The boy was lost.'

'As are we all from time to time.' He stared at Greg from beneath thick, luxuriant eyebrows, a perfect match for his equally luxuriant beard. 'I've been meaning to ask: how would you feel about teaching Sunday school? You'd be a great addition to the team.'

Greg shook his head with a smile.

'I teach all week, Father. I need a break.' The smile turned wry. 'Besides, I'm not sure I'd be a reliable teacher of Church doctrine.'

The bushy eyebrows rose.

'How so?'

'Well, take the parable of the good Samaritan, for instance. A man went down to Jericho—'

'—and fell among thieves.'

'Exactly. But in my version, someone is passing by with his own well-armed bodyguards while the poor guy is being mugged. The Church says that we should be non-violent, which would mean standing idly by while someone is being beaten to within an inch of their life. I'm not comfortable with that, Father. I'd rather intervene. With extreme violence.' The cold certainty in his voice surprised even him. He brushed it off with a rueful shake of the head. 'I'm not a good enough, pure enough person to be teaching your young kids, even assuming I had the inclination, which I do not.'

Father Kyriakos looked thoughtful.

'You are good enough, Greg. I'm sure of it. As for your parable . . .' He hesitated a moment, as if searching for the right words. 'The Orthodox Church is not unthinkingly pacifist, you know. Violence, to be sure, does great harm to the soul. That does not mean it is not sometimes necessary. The answer for those who must use violence in the necessary pursuit of justice lies in repentance and continually seeking to be one with God.' Seeing the skepticism that Greg felt leaking all over his face, the priest added, 'The Orthodox Church has been around a long time. A *long* time. We, like our Father above, do not require perfection in all things – or *any* thing. Just faith. We are, literally and metaphorically, a broad church.'

The words produced a twist in Greg's stomach. A glimpse of a road that might not end in hellfire.

Father Kyriakos was patting his arm.

'How is your mother? I hope she is not in too much pain.'

Whatever it was Greg had been feeling gave way to something else.

Anger. At himself.

He'd forgotten what Father Kyriakos knew. Or thought he knew.

And knowing Rachel Lev, consequences would follow.

'She's as well as can be expected,' he said. He examined the priest closely, checking to see if there was more here than an innocent inquiry. There didn't seem to be.

Not yet, anyway.

Greg took his leave and headed for home, carrying the faint aroma of incense in his nostrils. Once there, he broke open the packaging of one of his burner phones.

'Crevice Rye Suits, bespoke tailoring. How can I help you?'

'I'd like to speak to Mr Rye about a fitting, please. It's for my sister, Geraldine Abbott and her two children. I told her to expect a call from you to arrange the details.'

There was a distinct pause at the other end of the line. Greg fancied he could hear the *clickety-click* of a keyboard.

'I understand, sir. Although there was really no need to remind us. We already have it in hand.' There was a hint of reproach in the speaker's voice.

Screw you, mate. Like I'd leave something like this to chance.

'When should this call be made?' the voice asked.

'Anytime in the next week or so. After that, it may not matter.'

He hung up. Then he retrieved a ball-peen hammer from underneath the kitchen sink and smashed the phone to pieces.

Stupid, he raged, bringing the hammer down again and again and again. *Stupid, stupid, stupid.*

2:11 P.M.

Greg loved Walnut Street. His only complaint was that there wasn't enough of it: a couple of blocks of high-end shopping – art, fashion, design, you name it – and then it was gone, a brief interlude in an expanse of affluent, redbrick housing. A couple of blocks in which to pretend you were in a chic, out-of-the-way corner of a far larger city. He indulged in a few minutes of window shopping before opening a wrought-iron gate. Treading lightly on the steps, he climbed the narrow stairs to Arecas Design and Jewelry.

'Can I help you?' The speaker was a Black woman, easily as tall as Greg, with a shaved head, gold hoop earrings and a languid way of moving. Her accent carried lilting hints of sub-Saharan Africa.

'I'm looking for the owner,' Greg said, reaching into his wallet and pulling out a business card.

'That would be me. Ruth Chisenga: jeweler and designer, and the owner of this fine establishment.' She said it with a smile and a sense of humor, but there was steel, too. The voice of someone tired of being mistaken for the help.

'Delighted to meet you, Ms Chisenga.' Greg handed over the business card. 'Lynn Spargo. I'm an insurance investigator. I'm looking into the death of Alan Mester and—'

'Alan's dead?' The woman's hands flew to her mouth, then dropped down again. 'Sorry. Sorry. Oh dear. He was such a *lovely* man. Just lovely.' She took a moment to compose herself, then shot him a look full of curiosity. 'How did he die?'

'A fall. Nothing suspicious, but we're worried that items of his may have gone missing in the aftermath. Valuable items.' He handed over the jewelry boxes from Mester's apartment; the gold lettering spelling out ARECAS DESIGN glinted under the ceiling lights. 'We found the boxes but not the contents, which we presume to be necklaces of some kind. We were hoping you might be able to tell us exactly what was in them.'

Ruth Chisenga pursed her lips.

'I can't be a hundred percent certain, because Alan bought a number of items from me over the years.' A quick smile. 'But I'm *ninety* percent certain they'd have held designer pieces we made for him a couple of weeks ago.' Ruth led him across the store to a large glass desk, on top of which lay a number of binders. She opened one, leafing through page after page of glossy photographs. 'Here we are.' She flipped back and forth between two consecutive pages. 'Two necklaces, identical in every respect, except this one is ruby and this one, sapphire. Now that I think about it . . .' She reached for another binder, flipping it open about a third of the way through. 'Yes. This is them.' She tapped the page with an intricately decorated fingernail. 'He was very insistent that I made the necklaces to match pieces he bought from me a few months ago. Ruby earrings, you see?' She flipped the page. 'And sapphire.'

'These are beautiful,' Greg said, meaning every word. Ruth Chisenga beamed with delight. 'Can I take pictures of your pictures?' He held out his phone.

'So long as you're not in the jewelry business, feel free.'

Greg smiled at that.

'Do you have any idea whom he bought these pieces for?'

'I would never think to ask,' Ruth said, placing a hand on her chest in mock outrage. 'Whoever she is, she's a lucky, lucky woman.'

Or a murderer.

'Did he ever come in with a, er, *companion* of any kind.'

Ruth shook her head.

'Never. Alan always came in alone. Whatever he was buying, he always wanted it to be a surprise.'

A minute or two later, Greg was back on Walnut Street, staring at photos on his phone. The necklaces and their matching earrings were stunning, no doubt about it. But there was something wrong about them, too. Greg stared for a long time, trying to figure out what was bugging him.

To no avail. With a long sigh, he put the phone in his pocket and headed for home.

When he got there, there was a package waiting.

MONDAY, THE THIRTEENTH

1:04 P.M.

It was louder than the last time, or he'd never have heard it out in the corridor.

Crying from the boy's restroom. That it was the same person as the week before, Greg was certain. People cry like they talk, with their own accents and intonations. He cracked open the restroom door, torn between a desire to help and a belief that, if he tried, he'd end up doing more harm than good.

Apart from one conspicuously locked cubicle, the restroom was empty.

After several seconds of agonizing indecision, belief won out over desire. He closed the restroom door and walked away, not stopping until he reached the entrance to his classroom.

He did not, however, go in. He had no one to teach this period, and curiosity had gotten the better of him. He waited.

Sure enough, a figure emerged from the boy's restroom and hurried away. Greg's eyebrows arched toward his scalp.

Malik Freedman.

Filing him away as a matter for another time, Greg entered his classroom, closed the door behind him and returned to work, prepping for Russian III later in the day. He could not, however, concentrate. He had other things on his mind. Things that had nothing to do with either Russian language teaching or Demetrius Freedman's youngest child.

With a sigh of resignation, he opened his desk drawer and pulled out a thick padded envelope.

Dobrygin's package.

The man hadn't been subtle about it. The delivery had been left on Greg's coffee table, Dobrygin having picked the locks to both the apartment building and the apartment itself. The GRU's way of saying you are not safe here. Not from us. Whether he'd noticed the nanny cam Andrea had installed for him, the one that had snared Morosov, Greg couldn't be sure. He thought not. If he had, Greg guessed, he'd have either disabled it or made some obvious – and obscene – gesture of acknowledgement. Greg, whose muted phone had failed to warn him in real time, had watched the entire home invasion play out after the event, phone in one hand, a glass of vodka in the other.

He'd swept the apartment for bugs, just as a precaution and, as expected, found nothing. If Dobrygin had wanted to plant one, he'd not have advertised the fact that he'd been there in the first place.

The envelope contained surveillance photographs, dated and time stamped. Morosov coming out of the gate at Pittsburgh airport; Morosov picking up a Chevy Silverado at the rental lot; Morosov entering Greg's apartment building, followed by Greg himself a few minutes later. Hairs prickled on the back of his neck as he contemplated how badly the GRU had outflanked him. He'd had no inkling. He'd been thinking only about Morosov, which was evidence of even more stupidity on his part. The GRU generally operated in pairs. He'd had no idea that Morosov had – officially, at least – resigned from the service, or that the GRU was grappling with budget cuts. The Greg in the photograph, looking tense and out of breath from almost sprinting up the hill, should have *expected* a second person, should have been on the lookout for one.

Idiot.

He put the photos down and leaned back in his chair.

What if I'm being an idiot now? Polukhin will have lied about something. *Why not the budget? What if Dobrygin* does *have a partner? Where are they, and what are they up to?*

There were a number of unpleasant answers to that last question, most of them revolving around Greg Abimbola being double-crossed, tortured and killed. He needed to get ahead of the game. If there was a partner, they'd be physically proximate to Dobrygin, keeping an eye on him and vice versa.

His mouth tightened into a grimly determined line.

Dobrygin wasn't the only one who could screw around with people's houses.

He picked up the photos again. Werner and Aldis arriving. A pair of heavily built US marshals. Greg wondered whether Dobrygin had taken the pictures simply because they happened to be entering the building, or whether some sixth sense was already telling him that something was wrong.

He flicked through the rest of the pile. Morosov emerging under guard, entering a vehicle with the marshals. Those same marshals escorting a confused-looking Morosov into the lobby of the Omni William Penn. Morosov being handed over to a man and a woman, both dressed in smart business attire. The three of them heading toward the Grant Street exit. The two marshals looking relaxed as the others departed, perhaps even sharing a joke.

His classroom door swung open. Greg casually tidied up the photographs, tapping them on the desk as he shaped them back into a neat stack.

'Anything interesting?' Andrea asked.

'Only if you like student photography,' Greg said. He slipped the photos back into their envelope. 'What can I do for you?'

'Nothing.' Andrea just stood there, one hand clasped in the other and looking slightly anxious. 'I just wanted to tell you: I sent in my application for that job.'

'That's great,' Greg said, smiling. He was inordinately proud of what he said next. 'They'll be lucky to have you.' It sounded almost American. What he'd come dangerously close to saying, though, being Russian, was 'Don't get your hopes up. They're probably going to fuck you over.'

'I got an acknowledgement, so I know they got it.'

'When will you hear back for real, do you think? From an actual human being.'

'I don't know.' Andrea continued to look anxious. 'Someone told me these companies only get back to you if you get an interview; otherwise, they just leave you hanging.'

'Really?'

'I think so. It's pretty shitty, if you ask me.'

Andrea might not be Russian, but it was clear from her expression that she was following the same pessimistic train of thought.

Which, not being Russian, would do her no good whatsoever. Andrea simply wasn't built for it. As much to distract her as from ulterior motives, Greg asked, 'How would you like to earn a bit of spare change?'

Andrea looked at him curiously.

'Is it legal?'

'Absolutely.' Greg was not entirely sure this was true. 'The dashcam in that truck of yours. Can you point it in any direction you want?'

'Pretty much, yeah. But why?'

'I'm worried one of my students may be getting themselves into trouble. Not privileged-white-teenager trouble. *Real* trouble. It's probably nothing, but if I give you the address, could you park your truck close by and have the dashcam look at the front door for twenty-four hours?' Seeing that Andrea was shaping up to mouth an obvious objection, he added, 'I'll pay you for any rideshares you need to take, plus seventy-five dollars.'

'What's the address?'

5:05 P.M.

Lynn Spargo's office was downtown, in the tall, modernist heights of the US Steel Building. Which is why Greg found himself sitting on weird, curvy furniture that looked like it had escaped from a 1960s acid trip on the building's second floor, Starbucks coffee in hand. Looking down on the plaza outside, it was easy to see the dark current of people leaking out of the tower and heading for home, each and every one of them wrapped up against the biting wind.

'I hope you're not suggesting that's one of mine,' Lynn said, eyeing the Louboutin pump with distaste. 'I wouldn't be seen dead in that thing.' She gave vent to a slightly unhappy smile. 'I'm well past the age when I could carry it off.'

Conscious that a number of customers were looking at him curiously, Greg slipped the shoe back into the Whole Foods grocery bag.

'Do you think it belongs to someone he was seeing?'

'How could it not be?' The smile turned full-on bitter. 'The older he got, the younger he liked them. I think he thought he was some kind of benevolent sugar daddy. That way, he could kid himself that he wasn't paying for whores.' She paused for a moment, shaking with anger. 'I don't know when it started, but I sure know when I found out. This would have been eleven, no, twelve years ago now. Halloween, if you can believe that. He'd set up some entitled little redhead in an off-the-books apartment. He'd sneak over there when he was "working late", or she'd come to him at our Fifth Avenue place, when he thought I wasn't around – which is how he got caught, by the way.' Lynn's eyes sparkled with tears. 'Whatever. He was ashamed and remorseful and begged for forgiveness. And like a fool, I tried to overlook it. He got rid of her, let the lease run out on her apartment – which she had the nerve to complain about, if you can believe that – and it was almost like old times again. I even got to thinking it was *going* to be like old times again.' She looked past Greg and out to the plaza below. The tower's cathedral-like windows were spattered with spots of rain. 'But, of course, it never was. He did it again, and again, and again until . . . well. You know the rest.' She nodded at the grocery bag. 'Do you think she did it? Whoever owned that shoe? What a stupid, *stupid* man!'

She was crying now. Quietly. With dignity. No one but Greg noticed. She waved away his proffered handkerchief, producing a tissue from the depth of her purse.

'It must be awful,' he said gently. 'To love someone who doesn't love you back.'

'That's not it at all.' Lynn looked at him with an expression bordering on surprise. 'He loved me. I'm sure of it. It's just I couldn't . . . fulfill his needs anymore.' She smiled sadly. 'I couldn't age backwards, is all.

'That shoe,' she added briskly. 'You can't walk on it. Not outside. Louboutins are all about the red sole, and the sole's too soft for walking on pavement. It'll wear away in nothing flat, and then it's just a shoe, not a Louboutin. Unless you pay to get it re-soled, I guess.' She pointed at Greg's grocery bag for emphasis. 'The sole on that shoe is spotless. Whoever it belongs to, she carried it around with her or, more likely if you ask me, she kept it where you found it, so she could play dress-up.' Lynn's face ignited with savage pleasure. 'She must be kicking herself that she left it behind. You can't sell an unmatched shoe on eBay. Two, and she'd have made next month's rent. Which'll be an issue for her now that Al's no longer paying.'

Greg found himself looking at Lynn Spargo in a different light. She was intelligent, and accomplished, and still besotted with a man who'd tossed her aside for being too old. Easy enough for feelings like that to metastasize into something toxic. Intelligence and accomplishment harnessed in aid of murder.

With a $2.5 million payoff.

But if that were the case, why had she asked him to look into things? She'd already gotten away with it. The police were calling it suicide. All he could do was either confirm what the police were saying, which she didn't need, or find evidence of murder, which she *really* didn't need.

Demetrius? Motivated by suspicions of his own, had he somehow forced Lynn's hand? Pushed her to a place where she had no choice but to reach out, lest Demetrius turn his attentions to her?

Maybe. Lynn Spargo was a woman of means, well able to afford the best private investigators money could buy. If she'd been forced to ask someone to look into a murder she herself had committed, who better to ask than a foreign languages teacher with no obvious qualifications for the job? True, he'd solved a murder on his own doorstep. But how likely was lightning to strike twice?

An expensive Louboutin shoe, so expensive as to be worth a month's rent, could conceivably have been left by the woman who owned it if she was lighting out of Mester's apartment in a hurry. But it could also be missed by a vengeful woman who'd no idea it was there in the first place. Who'd swept up her rival's belongings in a rage, heaped them into a pile in the back yard of her cottage and set them alight.

'Tell me,' he asked mildly. 'Alan's belongings. The stuff he had on him when he fell. Do you have any idea whom the police would return it to? I don't imagine they'd want to keep it if there was no crime.'

'I have them. I'm the executor of his will. Not to mention the closest thing he has to a next of kin.'

'I see. Do you have his cellphone? It's not in his apartment.'

'No.' Lynn looked puzzled. 'But maybe he didn't need one anymore. He was wearing a smart watch, which was not like him at all. Or, at least, I'd never seen him wearing one. It's smashed, of course, but it looks like it might have a lot of bells and whistles. Maybe that was his new phone.'

'Maybe. Any chance I could have a look at it?'

'Of course.' She glanced quickly at her own watch, conventional and expensive. 'Now, if you'll excuse me.' She rose to leave, heading not to the exit and the evening rush hour but toward the elevators and more work.

Greg watched her go, wondering if he was looking at a concerned ex-wife or a murderer.

8:39 P.M.

One look at Rachel Lev's face as she stalked into his apartment was enough. The consequences he'd feared since Sunday service were upon him.

He'd hoped for more time.

'I need you to be straight with me, Greg.'

'Always.'

'Uh-huh.' She tossed her bag on the sofa, reached into it and pulled out Morosov's photograph. 'Tell me again whether you know this man.'

'I don't.'

'What about this one?'

'Of course I know this one.' Greg forced himself to smile. 'That's Father Kyriakos. He's the senior priest at St Andrew's.' He forced the smile wider. 'This is from the website, though. He doesn't usually look that, er, *groomed*.'

The detective remained steadfastly unamused.

'OK. Now tell me what the connection is between the two of them.'

'I haven't the foggiest.' Greg worked on his heartbeat, keeping it steady and slow.

Rachel fixed him with a long stare. Dark, intelligent eyes, probing for the slightest flicker of uncertainty.

Greg stared back. After a seeming eternity, the detective relented.

'So, here's the thing. Thanks to you, we have a photograph of our vic, Viktor Lavrov. And we put it out there, looking for someone, anyone, who could give us some insight into what a Russian-born Brit was doing in Pittsburgh, Pennsylvania. And do you know what happened?'

'People got in touch?'

'Correct. Including Father Kyriakos.'

'Intriguing.'

Rachel shot him a sour look.

'We now know that Viktor Lavrov flew into Pittsburgh on a Sunday afternoon, having cleared US Customs in Charlotte, North Carolina. The very first thing he did, *the very first thing* he did when he got here, was take a cab ride to St Andrew's church. Not to his hotel, or a business meeting, or even the scenic Duquesne Incline. And do you know what he did when he got there?'

'Spoke to Father Kyriakos, I imagine, seeing as you've gone to the trouble of printing off his photo from the website.'

'Exactly. To talk about, of all people, *you*.'

'Me?' Greg fixed his face into a mask of surprise. 'That can't be right. I mean, if Father Kyriakos says they talked about me, then I suppose they talked about me. But I don't know why.' He placed a light finger on Morosov's photograph. 'I haven't the slightest idea who this man is.'

'According to Father Kyriakos, he's your cousin.'

'I don't have a cousin.'

'That's not what you told him, though, is it? You said you had *two*.' She thrust the same number of fingers in his face, the nails uneven. '*Both* called Viktor. So I'm going to ask you one more time, *Mr* Abimbola. What's your connection to Viktor Lavrov?'

Shit, shit, shit.

He hoped to God the dismay hadn't leaked on to his face. He knew that Morosov had tracked him down through Kyriakos, pretending to be a relative. Kyriakos had told him as much during what, for the priest, had been a delicate, pastoral call. For Greg, though, it had been a complete bombshell. Morosov had gotten to Kyriakos by claiming the family had lost touch and Greg's mother was terminally ill. So far, so accounted for. But he'd completely forgotten the minutiae of the phone call itself. Not knowing who was after him, and as a means of extracting a physical description, he'd not only lied to the priest by agreeing that 'Viktor' was indeed his cousin, but claimed to have two of the same name, forcing Kyriakos to reveal that this particular cousin could be none other than Mikhail Sergeevich Morosov.

Hoist by his own petard.

'Well?'

'Look,' Greg sighed. 'I did get a call from Father Kyriakos about someone wanting to get in touch with me. And he said it was a cousin, which, given I don't *have* a cousin, could only mean a couple of things: either Father Kyriakos had got completely the wrong end of the stick or some chancer was trying to pull a fast one.' He managed a decent imitation of an embarrassed chuckle. 'I didn't want to tell my priest that he'd screwed up, and I didn't want to worry him if it was someone trying it on. I told him I had two cousins so as to get a description without upsetting him. Which worked, by the way. It didn't sound like anyone I knew, so I figured it was a scam of some kind and wrote the whole thing off.'

'You didn't think to call the police?'

'About what? It was all so vague. Would your colleagues have done anything if I had?'

Lev gave a reluctant shake of the head. But it didn't stop her returning to the attack.

'And it didn't occur to you that Father Kyriakos's description matched that of our vic?'

'I don't remember the father's description, Rachel. Still don't. I just knew it wasn't anyone I recognized and forgot about it.'

'Really?'

'Really. I did have other things on my mind, you know.'

'Like what?'

'Like I'd just figured out who killed Lindsay Delcade. Now, that I *do* remember.'

It was as if he'd slapped her in the face. He'd helped her solve a murder, after all, and here she was, practically accusing him of committing one. He tried to press home the advantage.

'Look,' he said cajolingly. 'Let's accept that this Viktor Lavrov had an interest in me for some reason, and that he was using Father Kyriakos to track me down. Let's also accept that he'd been watching me – or intending to watch me – because his rental truck was parked outside in the street. But the fact remains, I have no clue who this guy is. Whatever he was up to, it never got as far as me because I never spoke to him. I didn't even see him.

'And before you ask again, he is *not* my cousin. I have almost no family, Rachel. My parents died years ago, and my only living relatives are my sister and her two kids. She's called Geraldine Abbott and she lives in—'

'Bromsgrove, England. Thirty-eight years old. Her two kids are called Alison and Nicholas. I already checked.' Lev favored him with a small smile. 'She talks just like you, by the way.'

Thank you, Crevice Rye Suits.

The detective finally sat down, on the sofa, next to her purse.

'Do you have any idea what Viktor Lavrov would have wanted with you?'

'Not a clue. Except . . .'

'Except what?'

'Well, I speak Russian, don't I? And I'm British. Lavrov is British, but not by birth. He too speaks Russian. Maybe he needed my language skills for something and was waiting for the right time to approach me.'

'For what, though?' Rachel looked thoughtful. 'Nothing good, seeing he ended up dead.' She gave Greg an earnest stare. 'And no one's been in touch with you about anything Russia-connected? No one's promised you a ton of money or threatened you in any way?'

'Absolutely not. Why do you ask?'

'Because we've been making inquiries of our own through Interpol and the London Metropolitan Police. Turns out we know next to nothing about Viktor Lavrov. He presents as a London-based businessman who sources industrial machines for Russia and Eastern Europe. But the deeper we dig, the more he looks like a front. He might be involved in organized crime.'

Greg didn't have to pretend to look surprised. Replace 'organized crime' with 'the GRU' and Acting Lieutenant Rachel Lev would be right on the money.

'You be careful,' she said. 'Maybe this was a falling-out among thieves. Whoever killed Lavrov may still have an interest in you.'

TUESDAY, THE FOURTEENTH
8:19 A.M.

Demetrius was sitting in his usual seat by the faculty lounge window, long fingers curled around the sports pages of the *Pittsburgh Post-Gazette*. He was not, however, reading it. His head would dip briefly toward the paper, only to turn to the window seconds later. He would stare through the glass for minutes at a time, as if entranced by the brand-new roadworks on Joseph Avenue. He declined Greg's offer of coffee.

Greg helped himself from the wheezing machine and sat down opposite the chemistry teacher. The rest of the newspaper lay scattered and unread on the coffee table between them.

Finding the backed-up traffic less riveting than Demetrius did, he asked, 'Are you OK?'

'Me?' Demetrius looked surprised. 'Sure. Why wouldn't I be?'

'If you say so.'

'I'm good.'

'OK.'

A minute or two passed. With a sigh, Demetrius tossed the sports pages away. They landed with a resentful rustle on top of their brethren.

'I'm wondering,' he said at last, 'whether taking the Edgeworth job was such a good idea. It won't be the same place without Principal Ferguson.'

'Any chance you could back out?'

'Nope. I've already handed in my notice. And now the school knows I've been looking around, it'd be too awkward to stay, even if they agreed to it.' He shook his head emphatically. 'Bad vibes, man. Bad vibes. I've seen it before. It never works out.' He leaned forward, long, bony elbows propped on bony knees. 'What I don't understand, Greg, is why Ferguson had to resign. No way Alan Mester should be losing a vote about DEI.'

'I'm not following.'

'To hear Lynn tell it, how the exco votes is locked in. Fatima

Davis is a reliable progressive and Alan was the chair. At worst, it should have been a two-two split between Alan and Fatima on one side, and Clyde Leclerc and JoAnn Harwood on the other. Alan, as chair, had the casting vote. Guaranteed win for the good guys, yeah? But he lost anyhow.' Demetrius's folded-over frame rippled with anger. 'Something happened at that meeting, man, I'm telling you. Something that lost him the vote and got him killed.' Greg could feel the intensity of the chemistry teacher's stare. It was like heat on his skin. 'You making any progress getting to the bottom of this?'

'A little, maybe. There's still a few people I need to talk to.'

Demetrius unfolded himself and stood, ready to face the day.

'Yeah, well, make sure that includes the trustees. DEI? Critical race theory? Keeping up "standards"?' Demetrius's fingers curled into air quotes. 'This is a race thing. You hear me? One of those PEACE bastards killed him.'

He stalked out of the room, not quite slamming the door behind him.

3:34 P.M.

'Can I come in?'

'It's not like you to ask but, sure, why not?'

Andrea Velasquez pulled a face and slipped into Greg's classroom. Behind her, the corridor echoed with noise. Kids rushing for the exits or jostling each other on the way to after-school programs.

'So,' she said. 'I did like you asked and left my truck on Forty-Fourth Street. There was freaking permit parking all over, but I got you your twenty-four hours of video.' She looked suddenly anxious. 'I had to buy a way bigger SD card on credit. I hope that was OK?'

'Of course. I'll make sure you're not out of pocket.' He had no idea what SD cards cost, or why Andrea needed one, but he was on the hook for it and that was that.

'Yeah, great.' Andrea tried not to look relieved. 'So I put the video in the cloud and sent you a link.'

'You did?'

'Dude, do you *ever* check your email?'

'Only as a last resort.' He gestured toward the rows of empty desks. 'Besides, you know. *Teaching*.'

'You do that in here? Who knew?'

'Funny. Did you check the video to see what was on it?'

'Just a little. Boooooooring. I don't know what kinda trouble your student is in or what you think is going on at that house, but I can tell you this: it ain't much. Although, if there *is* something going on in there, do you want me to find out who owns it? Or do you already know that?'

'You know how to research real estate?'

'Don't look so surprised, man. This here woman is a-full of talent.' She leaned forward conspiratorially. 'Truth is, one of my aunts is studying to be a realtor. But like you, she ain't so good with computers. I picked up a thing or two helping her out, if you know what I mean.'

Greg nodded, impressed.

'Well, if you can, please do,' he said. 'All I know about it is that it's on Airbnb.' A small, distasteful hesitation. 'So I've been told, anyway.' He skipped on to another subject. 'You have any luck with Alan Mester's laptop?'

Andrea frowned.

'Yes and no. Yes in the sense that I got past the password. No because there's no data on his hard drive.'

'Oh. Well, that's too bad.'

'I don't think you understand.' The frown had been replaced with a wry smile.

'I don't?'

'Nope. There's *no data*. If Mester had reformatted his hard drive for some reason, it would *look* empty, but the data would still be there. It's just that the address – the information the computer uses to find the data – would have been removed. You with me?'

'Not really.'

'The point is, there's something sketchy about the man's hard drive. I'm still trying to figure it out. Give me another day or two and I'll get back to you.'

'Fine by me. And while you're at it, have a look at this.' Greg reached into his desk drawer and pulled out Alan Mester's damaged smart watch. 'Lynn Spargo dropped it off this morning. Let me know if you find anything.'

'Sure thing.' Andrea turned to go, smart watch in hand. She stopped at the door, looking mischievous.

'You know, Mr Bimbo, I didn't look too close at that video of yours for a reason.'

Greg raised an eyebrow.

'The reason was a good and noble one, of course.'

'Of course.' Andrea executed a sweeping, if mocking, bow. 'I know you didn't tell me the kid's name to protect them. I get it. Like, teacher confidentiality. But if they're on that video, I'd only have to look and I'd know who they were, wouldn't I? So I didn't.'

'Er . . . thank you.' Greg was strangely impressed. Not least because it was the exact opposite of what he would have done.

'You're welcome. Someone has to help you out. Because you know what?'

'What?'

'You should have thought about that before you asked me. You'd make a shit spy.'

6:16 P.M.

The local news, muted, flickered unheeded on Greg's TV. This deep into the broadcast, it was all ads, anyway. He was more interested in his laptop. The dashcam footage.

Greg was surprised by the quality. He'd been expecting something like a security cam feed: grainy, jerky, black-and-white pictures, too blurry around the edges for fine detail. Andrea's dashcam video, in contrast, was pin sharp. It made sense, now that he thought about it. If you were going to argue the toss with an insurance company, you'd want to show every single particular of how the incident went down.

Andrea had done him proud. She'd arranged truck and dashcam so that he had an almost unobstructed view of the 44th Street safe house and a good chunk of the surrounding sidewalk. He sped through the footage as quickly as he dared. Boring, it might be. But it still provided food for thought.

No one but Dobrygin entered or left the building. In one shot, he parked right outside the front door, his large frame emerging from a silver Nissan Sentra. Greg's lips twitched into an almost-smile. It was a lot less noticeable than a large gray van, although nowhere near as convenient for snatching people off the street. At night, when he was out doing God knew what, the windows were completely dark. There was absolutely no evidence of some unseen partner remaining in the house while Dobrygin was away.

Dobrygin himself, Greg thought, was every bit as sloppy as Polukhin had implied. He seemed unconcerned about surveillance, and the safe house appeared to have no alarm system – not even a doorbell camera. So far as Greg could make out, the man had left himself with no means of telling whether the house had been entered in his absence or not. Like a match wedged into the doorjamb, say. Something inconspicuous that a home invader would be unlikely to notice as they dislodged it.

Greg, at least, had his nanny cam. He doubted Dobrygin had

anything similar. If he had, he would have looked for much the same thing when he'd burglarized Greg's apartment, but there was no indication on the video that the thought had even occurred to him.

His cellphone rang.

'Hello?'

'Mr Abimbola? It's Dan Wurth, the doorman at Seaford Court. I've got that keycard information you were looking for.'

WEDNESDAY, THE FIFTEENTH

11:57 A.M.

Despite the nearness of the lunch hour, Russian IV remained deathly quiet, working through a question from a NEWL Russian exam. A prototype for the hoped-for AP in Russian Language and Culture, the question assigned had struck Greg as unfairly difficult, but he was curious to see what his students would make of it.

They would thank him later.

Or not. Heads were bent over desks, scribbling furiously. One of them, hair dyed purple and, for this week at least, heavily beaded, was so low as to be almost touching the formica.

Occupied as she was, Caitlin Bell was unaware that she had become the subject of Greg's attention. There was unfinished business there, he felt. Last week's after-class question had to have come from *somewhere*, after all, and he wondered if he'd ever get to the bottom of it.

Of course, getting to the bottom of it would probably require an answer to her question, so maybe it was best left alone.

The bell rang. Notebooks were handed in, accompanied by groans, and grimaces, and softly voiced complaints.

Caitlin Bell said nothing, merely giving him a tight little smile as she handed in her work.

Classroom empty, he sat at his desk for a while, mulling over the mysteries of the teenage mind. He'd been one once, he knew, but he couldn't really remember, not the way he wanted to. He recalled some of the things he'd done – the fights, the petty crimes that his mother had paid to go away – and he sometimes had a vague recollection as to why. But, for the life of him, he couldn't really remember what it *felt* like, why some of his dumber exploits had made sense at the time.

All he knew was that you couldn't pay him to go back there.

The yay-it's-lunch-break chaos had died down by the time he stepped into the corridor and headed to the faculty lounge.

Teenagers. What was it Ms Tsai was fond of saying? Oh yes. Can't live with 'em. Can't drown 'em in the bath.

On impulse, he changed direction and opened the door to the back stairs, as if seized by a sudden desire to go down to the playing field.

Sure enough, there he was, sitting at the top of the lower flight and buried in a tablet.

'Good afternoon, Malik. Not hungry today?'

'Er . . . no sir.'

'Robotics?' Greg asked, pointing at the tablet.

Malik gave an abrupt nod, clearly hoping to discourage him from further chatter.

Futile, of course.

'And the solution you were telling me about last week? The one you'd figured out on your own? Are you the hero of the team now?'

'No,' Malik mumbled, his voice so choked that Greg could barely hear the answer. The boy's eyes glittered dangerously. He scrambled to his feet, intending to flee to the comparative safety of the second-floor corridor. That, however, would mean squeezing past Greg, who'd placed himself in such a way as to be as obstructive as possible.

The boy hesitated, hopping from foot to foot like a cat on the proverbial roof.

'Look,' Greg said gently. 'I don't know what the problem is, but I do know it's bad enough that you've been crying your eyes out in the boys' restroom.' He pushed on, ignoring the dawning horror on Malik's face. 'You don't have to talk to me – or any teacher, for that matter – but I think you should talk to *someone*, don't you? So. How about it?'

For a moment, it looked like Malik was going to brush him off. He took a step up, moist eyes yearning for the freedom beyond Greg's shoulder. Then he stopped, slumping against the stairwell wall, tablet across his chest.

'They won't load my solution,' he said. But for the silence of the stairwell, Malik's soft voice would have been impossible to hear. 'They won't even look at it.'

'Why ever not?'

'They say I'm an idiot, that I don't know anything.' Malik's head was bowed now, staring at his feet. 'They won't even give me a chance.'

'Who's "they"? Your robotics team?'

Malik nodded. Somewhere in the deep, unexamined recesses of Greg's mind, old feelings tossed and turned in their sleep, struggling to wake.

'Have you complained to anybody?'

'Like the adults in the room? No.' Malik's laugh was short and bitter. 'They're just parents. They'd never believe me. 'Cause then they'd have to deal with their kids, wouldn't they?'

'Well, what about your dad?'

'You can *not* tell my dad. Please, sir.' Malik looked absolutely horrified. 'He'll make a scene and pull me from the program.'

'Would that be so bad?'

'It's the best robotics competition in the state. And I'm *good* at this, sir. I want to take part. Really. I just need a chance.'

Sure you do. But if you're not twice as good as everyone else, they'll say you're crap. And then you'll be worse off than when you started.

The thought caught Greg by surprise, sending his pulse racing in anger.

The road to madness. The dysfunctional rage that robbed you of the ability to get where you needed to go.

He took a deep, cleansing breath.

'This team of yours. Is it all of them or just one or two?' Malik was looking at him blankly, so he tried again. 'Is there a ringleader? Someone keeping the others in line when you try and do stuff.'

Malik was staring at his shoes. Mumbling.

'I'm sorry. I didn't catch that.'

The head came up. Slowly. Reluctantly.

'Brad,' the boy said. 'Brad Leclerc. He says I'm only on the team so they look good. For diversity. That if I touch anything, it'll turn to shit, and they'll lose.'

For some reason, the name sounded familiar.

Oh.

'There's a Clyde Leclerc who's a trustee at the Edgeworth School. Any connection?'

'I think that's the dad. Brad's a junior there. We'll be in the same school next year, when Dad changes jobs.'

And then, suddenly, Malik was sliding down the wall, bawling his eyes out as he sat on the floor, face buried in his knees.

'I don't want to go there, sir. To the Edgeworth School. I'm scared.'

5:40 P.M.

Malik Freedman's problems cast a pall over the rest of Greg's day. So much so that it was a positive relief to work his way downtown through increasingly heavy traffic. Mission accomplished, he turned into the Seaford Court parking lot. The setting sun bathed the top of the building in pink.

'That chair OK for you, Mr Abimbola?' Dan Wurth asked. 'I know it's kinda rickety.'

'It's fine,' Greg said. And it was. Squeezed in beside the doorman at a desk in the back room behind reception, he was much more interested in the glowing pixels of Dan Wurth's computer screen.

'This is the keycard record for Mr Mester's elevator,' the doorman was saying. 'See this serial number? That's for Mr Mester's keycard. You can see that he accesses the elevator at twenty-three-oh-seven on Tuesday night. Twenty-three-oh-seven is—'

'Seven past eleven,' Greg said, with a smile.

'Exactly.' The doorman ventured a smile of his own. 'Of course you'd know that, wouldn't you, sir, being English.' The screen shifted slightly under the whirl of a mouse wheel. 'Mr Mester comes home at seven after eleven. Nothing happens after that, pretty much as you'd expect, until oh-one-oh-two, when a *different* keycard swipes in.'

Greg sat up in his seat, making it creak.

'And who's keycard is that?'

'Ms Spargo's.'

'Are you sure?'

'All the cards are registered in the system, sir. This one' – he reached out and tapped the screen with a thick finger – 'is registered to Ms Spargo.' Seeing the expression on Greg's face, Dan burst out laughing. 'No need to worry, Mr Abimbola. There's no way she killed him. Not literally, anyway.'

'Because?'

'Because Mr Mester was still alive at oh-two-sixteen. He swiped in *again*, see? Dead men can't do that.'

'I don't understand.' Greg could feel himself frowning. 'He's already home. Why would he need to come in twice?'

'Oh, it's pretty common, sir. Ms Spargo came to see him at one in the morning. Unusual, but, as you know, they're still pretty friendly, despite the divorce. They chat – or whatever – and Ms Spargo leaves a little after two o'clock.'

'But that's not in the system, is it? She wouldn't have needed to swipe when she came down.'

'And neither would Mr Mester. But it's two in the morning. The parking lot is dark and Mr Mester is old school. He'd have walked her to her car.' A click of the mouse and the screen shifted. 'See? This is the log from the rear entrance, the one that leads to the parking lot. He swiped back in at oh-two-fourteen, two minutes before he swiped the elevator. Simple really.'

The doorman looked suddenly sad.

'You never know what's going on inside someone's head, do you, sir?'

'How do you mean?'

'He was alone in his apartment. Had to have been. No one uses that elevator again before five thirty when . . . when I found him. No one laid a finger on him up there. That poor guy, he checked out all on his own.'

The doorman had a point, Greg thought, as he opened the door to his car. It was already fully dark, and the parking lot was lit just well enough to be creepy. It made perfect sense that Alan Mester would escort his ex-wife to her vehicle.

Which did not explain what Lynn Spargo was doing there in the first place.

He belted in and pressed the ignition button. Headlights sprang to life in synchrony with the soft cough of the engine. He moved off, turning into the narrow alley that led back to Fifth Avenue.

Behind him, another car started up, its lights a dazzling flare in the rearview mirror. Greg reached up, intending to adjust the mirror for nighttime. As he did so, the lights behind him turned off again.

Even though the car they belonged to had started to move.

Despite the fact that traffic was no longer a problem, Greg took his time on Fifth Avenue. He moved slowly between one set of streetlights and the next, each one making the road almost daylight bright. His progress was so lackadaisical, in fact, that the impatient driver stuck behind him managed to swerve past with an angry honk. Which gave him a clear, well-lit view of the car that had been two vehicles back. The car that still had its lights off.

A silver Nissan Sentra.

Driven, no doubt, by one Oleg Dobrygin.

THURSDAY, THE SIXTEENTH
9:40 A.M.

In his dreams, Oleg Dobrygin and Malik Freedman had gotten mixed up so that it was Dobrygin crying on the stairs and Malik driving the Nissan Sentra. Greg was tailing Malik, with Dobrygin, still crying on the stairs, somehow sitting in the passenger seat and giving directions.

It had made for a disturbing start to the morning, made worse by a grammar-heavy first period with Russian I, a class neither destined nor designed to lift the spirits. Almost none of them appeared to want to be there or manifested the slightest interest in the subject. Fraud that he was, trying to teach this particular group anything, anything at all, felt like casting false pearls before real swine.

Tired of marking papers in an empty classroom, he headed toward the faculty lounge. There would be coffee there and, if he was lucky, a conversation about something other than professional sports.

He failed to reach his destination. Polished parquet changed to painted concrete as he turned on to the back stairs instead, in search of Malik Freedman. He'd been there around this time on the previous Thursday, so there was a decent chance of acquiring him again today.

So far, so logical. What was significantly less logical, though, was the fact that Greg Abimbola, ex-GRU agent, hadn't the slightest idea what he'd do if he actually ran into him. Check the kid was all right, probably, which made no sense at all. He was uncomfortably aware that, whatever Malik might actually say, the kid was most definitely *not* all right.

So what the heck did he think he was doing?

Perhaps it was fortunate, then, that Malik Freedman wasn't there. Not on the first landing, anyway. Greg continued down, failing to find him on the subsequent steps, either. Reaching the lower level, he heard shouts of encouragement and the rubbery thump of a basketball emanating from the gym. Greg, happy to be distracted, went to take a look. He slipped inside and stood inconspicuously in the nearest corner, his presence mostly masked by the bleachers.

This, it turned out, was PE rather than a Cougars practice. Two rag-tag teams, heavily outnumbered by the substitutes waiting on the sidelines, were scrambling from one end of the court to the other. The ball, however, refused to go into the basket. Even to Greg's untrained eye, it was clear this was amateur hour. One of the amateurs, hair tied back in a ponytail, was Caitlin Bell. She grinned shamelessly as her shot not only missed the net but the backboard as well.

The gym teacher, perhaps fearing that things could only go downhill from here, called time. Greg shifted to one side as children streamed past him, heading for the showers.

Except for Caitlin Bell, who was lingering on the court, fiddling with one of her sneakers. After a minute or so, she was the only one left. Greg, too, turned to leave. But as he stepped through the exit and into the corridor, he collided with Caleb Freedman, who was running pell-mell in the opposite direction. Greg staggered under the impact and was forced back into the gym. It was touch and go for a moment before he regained his balance, one hand gripping the nearest bleacher.

'Oh my God! I'm so sorry, sir. I didn't see you.' The poor boy looked guilt-stricken.

'Not to worry, Caleb. Worse things hap . . .' His voice trailed off as it dawned on him that Caleb's expression was only partly connected to the collision. Caleb wasn't even looking at him. He was staring beseechingly into the middle of gym. Where Caitlin Bell, hand over mouth, was wearing an expression remarkably similar to Caleb's own.

Teenagers. The girl's anguished inquiry suddenly made sense.

Greg suppressed a smile. Tried to. If they'd just behaved even halfway normally, he'd never even have noticed.

'Well,' he said. 'I suppose I should be on my way.' He stepped out into the corridor. 'Don't be late for—'

'Sir?' Caleb stepped out with him.

'About . . . you know. You're not going to tell my— Doctor Freedman about this, are you?'

'About what, Caleb?'

'Me and Caitlin. He'll flip his lid.'

'I have absolutely no idea what you're talking about.'

The teenager looked puzzled.

'I mean about—'

'Stop digging, Caleb.' Caitlin Bell had caught up to them, a relieved smile on her face. 'If Mr Abimbola doesn't know what you're talking about, it means he didn't *see* anything worth talking about, capeesh?'

'Oh.' Realization slowly dawned. '*Oh.* Thank you, sir.'

'Nothing to thank me for, Caleb. Although . . . Do you mind if I ask you something?'

'Shoot.'

'Your brother. Is he as good at robotics as he thinks he is?'

'Better, sir. Kid couldn't execute a jump shot if his life depended on it. But that sh— stuff? He's kind of a genius.'

'Thanks, Caleb. Well, er, carry on.'

As he stepped back into the corridor, Greg became aware he was under surveillance. A pair of baleful green eyes stared at him from the entrance to the custodian's room.

Señor Sanchez, the school's semi-feral cat. The creature turned its back on him and walked off in the opposite direction, coal-black tail held high in disdain.

A reminder. Of many things. But, in this case, of the need to speak with Andrea Velasquez. Once the cat and its hideous dander were at a safe enough distance, he stuck his head into the custodian's room.

There was no one there. Empty mugs stood upturned beside the paint-stained sink. A lurid paperback lay abandoned on the sagging cushions of the sofa. The vast metal bulk of the school's boiler, rising out of the concrete floor like a sea monster breaking the surface, rumbled away unattended.

The heavy metal door on the far side of the room, the one that led out into the loading bay, was ajar. Greg strode across, closing his mind to the memories, and shoved it open.

'Ah, there you are,' he said. 'Lazing about on the school's dime. You ought to be ashamed of yourself.'

Andrea refused to rise to the bait. She was sitting on the edge of the loading dock, transfixed by the contents of her cellphone.

'I got one,' she said. 'Freaking wow. I've got one.'

'Got what?'

'An interview: with Medi8or.' Andrea turned her head to look up at him, face beaming. 'They want me to call and schedule a time.'

'That's wonderful! I'm sure you'll blow them away at the interview.'

But don't get your hopes up.

'Do you think so?' Andrea looked suddenly anxious.

'I do. When you get in there, just tell yourself that they'll be lucky to have you and they'll end up agreeing with you. You'll do great.'

'Like, fake it till you make it, yeah?'

'Er, yes. I suppose so.'

'Fake it till you make it,' Andrea said – mostly to herself this time. 'Fake it till you make it.' She pushed herself up from the dock, dropped her phone into her pocket and brushed herself down. 'And you, Mr Bimbo? What can I do for you?'

'I need you to check up on Lynn Spargo for me.'

'You think the lady gone done and killed her ex?' Andrea's eyes sparkled with intrigue.

'I'm considering it, though I'm not sure how or why. Love gone bad, maybe, or two and a half million dollars' worth of life insurance.' Andrea gasped at the number. 'What I do know is that she was the last person to see him alive. She was in his apartment at one o'clock in the morning the night he died.'

'Sketchy.' Andrea shuddered. 'You think she was doing the nasty with him? For old times' sake?'

'Honestly, I don't know what to think. I can place her in Mester's apartment at one a.m., but she says she was at some insurance convention in Harrisburg, at the Hilton. Can you check her alibi?'

'Sure. Uh, how do I do that?'

Greg considered for a moment.

'Call the hotel. Tell them you're Lynn Spargo's assistant, and that Ms Spargo lost something – a pair of sapphire earrings, say – when she was out of town on the Tuesday and Wednesday, but she didn't tell you the hotel she was staying in, or the room number, which might be important. Could you let me know if she stayed there and whether anything was lost. Something like that. If that doesn't work, wait a while, come up with some other story and try again.'

'Sure thing, boss.' Andrea nodded sagely. She glanced up at him, face thoughtful. 'Isn't that what they say, Mr Bimbo. That it's always the spouse?'

4.30 P.M.

'Come on in,' Lynn said. The words brought on a teary smile. 'It feels weird to be saying that, after all this time.'

Greg let her usher him into the Seaford Court penthouse.

'What brings you here?' Greg asked. When he'd arranged to meet with her, he'd hardly expected her to suggest the dead ex's apartment.

'I'm the executor of the estate.' She gestured toward a tablet lying on the glass hallway table. 'I'm here to take inventory. Thank God he was so organized. Otherwise, I'm not sure I'd be able to deal.' She led him through to the living room, the *click-clack* of her heels on the hallway's glossy marble floor snuffed out by the transition to deep-piled carpet. Beyond the room's floor-to-ceiling windows, the sky over downtown was a turbulent-looking gray, pregnant with unfallen rain. Greg waited for her to position herself on the white-and-steel couch before taking a seat. She looked out of place here, he thought. Her comfortable edges more suited to the soft furnishings of her own home, rather than this perfectly arranged, starkly angular habitat.

'What was it you wanted to see me about?' she asked.

'I'm still trying to piece together Alan's interactions. Whom did he speak to and when, that sort of thing. I was hoping you could tell me when you last saw him.'

'Me? Uh . . . let's see . . . the week before last. He'd been up at the school, and he dropped by on his way home. Took me out to dinner.' Her eyes were misty with recollection. 'He was his usual charming self. Full of plans.'

'You're quite sure you didn't see him later than that?'

'Positive. Why?'

'Because your keycard says you were here in the early hours of Wednesday morning. The morning he died.'

Silence. Lynn stared at him. The tears in her eyes had drained away, leaving behind a cold, hard surface that matched the furniture.

Greg stared back.

'I have no idea what you're talking about. I don't have a keycard.'

'The building is very clear that you do.'

Lynn Spargo broke eye contact, blinking furiously as her gaze darted about the room.

The blinking ceased.

'I used to have a keycard. From when we were married. But I gave it up in the divorce.' Her expression hardened again. 'It'll be one of his gold-digging little bitches. So she could make herself at *home.*' The last word was uttered with a vituperative ferocity, sending a small drop of spittle arcing through the air. She stood up suddenly, as if sitting on a sofa used by some other woman was too much to bear. She stalked toward the windows and their subtly etched glass. 'This proves it. She was here the night he died. It's like I said. She killed him, didn't she? *Didn't she?*'

'How did *you* get up here? Today, I mean.'

The question brought Lynn Spargo up short, anger replaced by bemusement.

'Dan brought me. Ask him. I don't have a *goddamned keycard*.' The anger was back again. 'Are you going to find the . . . the woman that did this, or are you going to waste your time insulting me with false accusations?'

'Getting ahold of the woman in question may not be the answer.'

'Of course it is. It's staring you in the face, for God's sake. *Find her*.'

'He was alive after she left. We know this because he walked her to the parking lot at two in the morning. He used his own card to come back up. Right now, it looks like he was up here alone.'

Lynn looked horrified.

'He didn't jump, Greg. Don't you *dare* say he jumped!'

Greg rubbed at the bottom of his eye patch.

'OK,' he said. 'We'll track down this woman of his and find out what she has to say for herself. In the meantime, I'm wondering if I might ask a favor.'

Lynn fixed him with an angry stare.

'You are on goddamned thin ice with me right now.'

'Is there any way you can introduce me to someone who was at the exco meeting?'

There was a further, even angrier look.

Lynn Spargo reached for her phone.

7:00 P.M.

There were roadworks on Forbes Avenue, parking turned into a whole, convoluted thing, and the signage was confusing, so Greg counted himself lucky to have found his way to UPMC Mercy's radiology department without being late. A short, forty-something woman, who'd obviously been watching the door, stepped over to meet him. She was even shorter than Greg had originally assumed, as she was strapped into a pair of expensive, steeply heeled stilettos.

'Greg Abi . . . Ambi—?'

'I am indeed. Doctor Harwood?'

JoAnn Harwood nodded, favoring him with a pleasantly professional smile. She led him to a small, cluttered office with a couple of plastic chairs for visitors. The smell of antiseptic tickled at his nose. He settled into one of the seats, knees jammed against the metal skirt of Dr Harwood's desk.

'So, Greg, how can I help you? Lynn said you wanted to ask a few questions about the exco meeting?'

'That's right.'

'I don't see how a school meeting can have anything to do with Alan's death.' She shook her head, the gesture laden with regret. 'Depression is an insidious disease, you know. It doesn't really need a trigger. It's more like a state of being.'

'Lynn is convinced that there's more to this than suicide.'

'Of course she is. These things can be very hard to accept. Particularly if it's someone you're still besotted with.' She reached out and touched Greg on the wrist, brief and feather light. 'You need to wake up and smell the coffee, Greg. A bunch of middle-aged parents and alumni arguing about school policy is a reason for . . . what? Homicide? Gimme a break. Still . . .' Dr Harwood leaned back in her chair, hands loosely clasped in her lap. 'Lynn is a wonderful, wonderful person. If exploring the alternatives will help her get to a better place, I'm happy to do my bit. What do you want to know?'

'Was the exco meeting as bitter as it looked on TV?'

JoAnn grimaced.

'You saw that?'

'I'm afraid so.'

'It was never going to be an easy meeting. The exco has been increasingly fraught the last few years and this one really spiraled out of control. There was no need for Iain to resign, though. None at all.' She ran an absent-minded hand through her hair. 'But maybe it's for the best.'

'What made this meeting worse than the others?'

Dr Harwood didn't answer. Not at first, anyway. She looked at him carefully, weighing him up. Greg, for his part, allowed a slight but respectful smile to appear on his lips. He needed to appear as charming and non-threatening as possible.

'You're English?'

'For my sins.'

'I love that accent. So refined.'

'Thank you. Years of boarding school and bad food.'

JoAnn chuckled at that. She leaned back in her seat, having evidently come to some kind of decision.

'I'm a radiologist, Greg. It's my job *not* to see color. To look under the skin. Like my machines. They don't care if you're Black, or white, or purple with pink spots. They just want to get to the truth of things. To find out what, if anything, is wrong. They're like Martin Luther King. You've heard of Martin Luther King?'

'A little.' It was a struggle to keep his expression neutral.

'Yes. So, like Martin Luther King, they want to judge you by the content of your character, not the color of the package it comes in. And I'm the same way in life as I am in my job. I don't see color, Greg. I see character.'

'That's very laudable.'

JoAnn tilted her head in demure acknowledgement.

'So when I tell you I'm opposed to critical race theory, it's not because I'm racist, it's because I care. I care about the Edgeworth School, I care about the quality of the education, and I worry about the radical left taking control of our children. We can't have our kids' minds poisoned by social justice warriors.' She let loose a heartfelt sigh. 'I cannot tell you how exhausting, how *demoralizing* it is to come home from this place, with all its troubles, only to find your child sitting at the kitchen table spouting Marxist nonsense.

I'm trying to raise an independently minded, forward-thinking human being: an *American*. Not some foaming-at-the-mouth socialist drone.'

She leaned forward in her chair, lending emphasis to her words.

'Look. Iain did great things for the school. He made it fully co-ed, modernized the curriculum, inspired some terrific fund-raising. But over the last few years, he's gotten more and more woke, and enrollment started to drop off as a result. And as for fundraising . . .' The grimace that followed was statement enough. 'Brian and Clyde had managed to curb his worst instincts, but when Brian had to resign, Iain, with Alan's support, pushed through a bunch of initiatives that went too far. Frankly, this Diversity, Equity and Inclusion office was the last straw. I always tried to give Iain the benefit of the doubt because, apart from the wokeness, he's an incredible leader for the school. But this thing . . . it's just a vehicle for making perfectly good kids feel bad about themselves, for turning them into second-class citizens. Frankly, I'd had it. If it had gone through, I'd have resigned and pulled my kids out at the end of the semester.'

'But it didn't go through, did it?'

'No. And I guess that's why this one got so bitter. Neither Iain nor Alan expected it to go the way it did. Not with Brian out of the way.'

'So what happened?'

'Iain made his presentation to the committee. You know the drill: PowerPoints with lots of smiley photographs; some lefty-woke talk about making our students feel valued, welcomed and respected, as if they weren't already; a claim it would make the school a leader in the marketplace, increase enrollment, that kind of thing. I could tell just by looking at him that Clyde was already livid. And then Alan weighed in, in support of the whole thing, which, for Clyde, made it even worse.'

'Alan and Clyde didn't get on, I take it?'

'Hated each other. Always have, I think.

'Anyway, Alan finishes whatever it was he was saying and then Clyde starts in. This time, though, he'd brought a letter with him from PEACE. We all knew about it, of course. It had been circulating around the school for a couple of days by then.'

'I heard about that on the radio. Strong stuff.'

'It sure was. But necessary. It pointed out the dangers posed by critical race theory very well, I thought. And what you won't have heard, because Clyde only produced it at the meeting, is that there was an addendum. It was an anonymized list of PEACE members and the total contributions they'd made to the school in the last five years, which was a *big* number. If the DEI initiative went through, Clyde said, every person on the list would withdraw future funding. And some, he said, were even prepared to sue for the return of donations they'd already made. Because they'd been misled as to what their money would be used for.'

'And that had an impact?'

'I didn't think so, not at first. Iain said that because no one knew who PEACE was, it was impossible to gauge how well it reflected parental views. Particularly when, apart from Clyde and a couple of others, no one had ever expressed similar concerns to him. It didn't make sense to have school policy driven by what was probably a small fringe group with a lot less clout than they claimed.

'Well, Clyde took that *very* personally. He said he knew who the PEACE parents were, they were *not* a lunatic fringe, and that the numbers in the addendum were real. At which point Alan said he wouldn't trust Clyde to take out the trash, never mind produce accurate numbers. Anyway, you can imagine how *that* went down. The two of them would have come to blows if Fatima hadn't intervened.'

'She intervened physically?'

'Oh, yes. I was kind of rooted to the spot. She managed to get between the two of them before anything bad happened. But then, when they'd both calmed down a bit, she said that maybe Clyde had a point. That even if PEACE wasn't exactly what it claimed to be, a number of the parents were genuinely worried – not simply about the direction the school was headed in, but also the speed of change. "Wouldn't it be better," she said, "if we all just took a beat and tabled the DEI proposal till next year?" That way, she figured, the school would have time to think things through more deeply and maybe reach a consensus.'

Dr Harwood touched his wrist again, eyes wide in recollection.

'Oh my God, you could have knocked me down with a feather. The room was just, well, stunned. Everyone assumed Fatima would vote with Alan because she *always* votes with Alan. She's even more liberal than he is – was, I mean. Than he . . . er, *was*. Sorry. I'm sorry.' JoAnn's eyes brimmed with tears. She blinked them away by sheer force of will. 'I didn't agree with him about politics, but he was a lovely, lovely man. Kind, for the most part. And charming. Except with Clyde. And except for what happened next.'

'Which was?'

'Well, he just rounded on Fatima, wanting to know if it felt good to stab him in the back like that, and demanding she tell us who'd paid her – *paid* her, for God's sake. He called her – and I quote – "a two-faced bitch". The poor woman burst into tears, at which point Clyde stepped in to defend her.'

'And how did that go?'

'About as well as you'd expect. Alan and Clyde were calling each other every name under the sun, and then Alan said something to Clyde like, "You've crossed a bleeping line, you bleeping bleep. You seem to have forgotten that I know things about you that no one else does." Clyde kind of stepped back a bit and then said, "So what? I know things, too. Like the OJ. Did you know that? I know about the bleeping OJ."'

'Any idea what either of them was talking about?'

'Shouting about, you mean.' JoAnn's face broke into a sudden, impish smile. A glimpse of the woman behind the radiologist. 'No, not really. I mean it's clear to me the two of them have a history outside of the school, though I don't know what that is, exactly. They're both in finance, so I'm guessing that's how they know each other. But as to the details, I haven't the faintest.

'So, anyway, the meeting is even more of a disaster than usual. And I stick my head above the parapet just long enough to suggest that we end the proceedings without a vote. Maybe come back to the DEI question once things were . . . calmer. I figured it was about the only thing we might be able to agree on. But before we can do even that, Doctor Ferguson, who, like me, had just sat there totally shell-shocked, very quietly says that he can't go on like this, and the school clearly needs a leader the committee can trust, which isn't him. And then he announces his resignation. Just like that. Which causes even more recrimination and chaos, because nobody wanted that. OK, maybe Clyde didn't look too unhappy, but the rest of us were gutted. Iain had clearly had enough, though, so we had no choice really but to accept. And having had time to think about it, I'm beginning to think he was right. It was time. He'd been great for the school but there needed to be a parting of the ways.'

'You lost me in the procedure. Did a vote actually take place, then, three to one against the DEI office?'

'No. Fatima, remember, had suggested tabling the whole thing to the following year instead, but we didn't vote on even that. After Iain said what he had to say, the meeting basically ended in chaos. It was clear, though, given Fatima's change of heart, that if Alan *had* forced a vote on DEI, it would have failed: three to one, like you say.'

'And how was Alan after the meeting ended?'

'Livid, of course. Even though he was the chair, he refused to say anything but the bare minimum to all the press hanging about outside. Told Clyde that this was all his bleeping fault, so he could do it, and stalked off. But not before having a final dig at Fatima.'

'Which was?'

'He told her he would never forgive her for betraying him like this. And that by the time he was finished with them, she and Randy – that's her husband, by the way – she and Randy would be on the street.'

'Did he say how he was going to do that?'

JoAnn shook her head.

'Not really. All he said was "I know how Randy makes his money."'

FRIDAY, THE SEVENTEENTH
10:31 A.M.

For the umpteenth time that morning, Greg checked his phone. Fatima Davis, despite being contacted by Lynn Spargo beforehand, had not returned his call. He was about to go back to the task in hand, tweaking some Gogol talking points for his upcoming Russian IV, when the screen lit up with incoming text.

See me after class (or during!) ☺ I have stuff

Figuring he had time and that he could wing it a bit with the Gogol, he left his classroom and headed down to the basement in search of Calderhill's assistant custodian. The custodian's room, as on the previous occasion, was empty. A low roar rumbled out of the boiler, and two sport-themed mugs stood upside down on the draining board. The heavy metal door that led out to the loading bay was ajar. He pushed it open.

'Oh. Sorry, I didn't mean to disturb you.'

Instead of Andrea, or even Vernon Szymanski, her boss, the person Greg found sitting on the rough concrete ledge, legs dangling over the side, was none other than Principal Eisner. He looked up at Greg, startled, eyes red with tears behind his stylish, rimless glasses.

'Are you all right?'

It was only then that Greg noticed the letter in Eisner's hands. Heavy notepaper covered from edge to edge with sweeping, beautifully even calligraphy.

'I'll leave you in peace,' he said quietly.

Eisner scrambled to his feet.

'No. Wait. Please.'

Greg stepped out on to the loading bay, closing the door behind him. Although the sun was shining, the loading bay, surrounded as it was on three sides by tall, redbrick walls, remained in shadow. Greg's skin prickled with the chill. And memories.

'I'd be grateful if you could keep this, er, between us,' Eisner said.

'Of course.'

The principal looked down at the notepaper.

'Josh . . . my partner, Josh, is leaving me. Doesn't want to live in Pittsburgh, he says. By letter. Can you believe that? Better than a text, I guess.'

'I'm sure.'

Eisner cracked a watery smile.

'At least it's nice paper. Classy. I'm worth that much at least.'

Greg's stomach knotted with discomfort. Men shouldn't be receiving breakup letters from other men. It was wrong. Sinful. The Church said so.

And yet. Here was a man – a good man, as far as Greg could tell – in very real pain. What did it matter if the cause of that pain was of the same sex? Did that make it any less painful, any less valid?

'I'm sure you're better off without him.' If the words that limped off his tongue felt trite and devoid of warmth, Eisner didn't seem to notice.

'Says Pittsburgh is too small of a town. That I shouldn't have rushed into this without talking it through. But I thought we *had* talked it through. I thought he was on board, you know?'

Greg felt strangely lightheaded, as if nothing was quite real. That he wasn't really standing on the side of a concrete-lined loading bay. That he wasn't really listening to his school principal, a man he barely knew, unburden himself. That Eisner was talking to him like this had nothing to do with Greg Abimbola, he decided. It was an accident of timing. *Anyone* who had stumbled across Evan Eisner at that precise moment, the moment the man's heart had cracked and broken, would have been treated the same way.

And yet. Greg found himself staring into Evan's eyes. Not as dark as his own, but warm, and deep, and glittering with too much moisture.

'And it's not like Pittsburgh is *small* small. I grew up in a small town, Greg. I know what small is, believe me.'

'You make it sound unpleasant.'

'If you don't fit in? Yeah.' Eisner took a deep, tremulous breath. 'I grew up a few hours north and west of here, not that far from Clarion, Pennsylvania. Ever been out that way?'

Greg shook his head.

'Well, it's beautiful, beautiful country. Great people. Friendly. Would give you the shirt off their back if you were in trouble. But not so great if you were . . . different. And I was. I knew it from when I was maybe four years old. I hid it, tried to hide it, of course. I fitted in. Played football, sang in the church choir, made passes at girls in eighth grade. But it was all a lie. By my sophomore year in high school, I couldn't stand it anymore. So I came out. Told the youth pastor at my church. Someone I thought I could trust.'

'And it turned out you couldn't?'

'He looked at me like I'd just crawled out from under a rock. Said that I would burn in hell if I didn't repent and change my ways, that there was no place in God's house for deviants. That was the word he used, by the way: "deviants". He sent me away to think about what I was saying, to pray to the Almighty and find a way back to Jesus.

'So I tried. For one whole day. That's how long it took for the news to travel across town. No more football, no church choir, no school friends. Two of my former teammates beat the bejesus out of me behind the gas-station restrooms. Thank God for Mom.'

'Mum?' Something tight was pulling at the inside of his chest. He was back on Lomonosovsky Prospekt, on imaginary surveillance.

'Yeah. Mom.' Eisner's face filled with warmth. 'Mom is a force of nature. Big on church stuff, one of the few people in America who can actually play the organ. I was terrified, and I mean *terrified* of what she'd do when she found out, given how religious she is. But . . . yeah. Parents can surprise you sometimes. I think, as a child, you just don't understand how much they love you.

'She told the pastors exactly what she thought of them, left the church, dragged Dad with her and moved us to a more understanding one, an hour from home.' Evan's expression turned wry. 'Sundays were *loooong*, let me tell you. But I knew, no matter how tough it got at school, that the moment I got home, I would be safe. And that was enough to get me through. Besides, things did get better after a while. Most people can only hate you for so long, it turns out. They get used to the gay kid next door. So long as he's properly polite and respectful.'

Greg found himself thinking of the road not taken. What if he'd toughed it out when MI5 came calling? Even now, he could remember every sickening moment of the honeytrap closing around him. The falsely sympathetic agents; the obscene, hi-res photographs of him and Robert Godfrey. What if he'd done what he should have done and told them to go fuck themselves? He'd have lost his job for sure, but his job was lost the moment he'd caved in to those polite, two-faced bastards. What if he'd fessed up to his mother? *Trusted* her. Would she have disowned him like he feared? If so, it was better she think him dead. But maybe, *maybe* she would have understood and held him closer, like some fiery old lady in the Pennsylvania wilderness.

Evan was looking at him, worried.

'Excuse me?'

'I said "TMI"? Too much information? I shouldn't have run off at the mouth like that. I don't know what go into me.'

'Heartbreak is what got into you,' Greg said, surprised by the gentleness in his tone. 'It will be bad for a while, but this, too, shall pass.'

Evan smiled at that. Grateful for the kindness.

The smile vanished at the sound of someone entering the custodian's room.

Greg gestured along the potholed stretch of asphalt that led from the loading bay to Joseph Avenue.

'Go round the outside to the main entrance. No need to be seen moping around here, eh?'

Eisner headed off, looking unnecessarily grateful. As soon as he was clear of the building, Greg opened the big metal door and stepped into the custodian's room. Andrea, who was spooning coffee crystals into a mug while waiting for the kettle to boil, looked around in surprise.

'Where the heck did you come from?'

'The loading bay.'

'I can see that. What I mean is: what were you doing out there?'

'Can a man not get a breath of fresh air, now? I'm here because you sent me a text.'

Andrea's expression brightened.

'So I did. Yeah, dude. I got things to tell. Take a seat.'

Somewhat reluctantly, Greg lowered himself into one of the grubby, sagging armchairs. It creaked under his weight.

'You know I was saying there was something sketchy about your man Mester's laptop?'

'Yes. Formatting. Data. Blah, blah, blah.'

Andrea rolled her eyes.

'So. I figured it out. The hard drive is brand new.'

'He bought himself a new computer?'

'No. The hard drive is new. The computer is a couple of years old.'

Greg felt himself frowning, his low-tech brain trying to think through the implications.

'Where's the original hard drive?'

'Exactamundo.'

Greg mulled that over for a moment.

'How big is a hard drive? Physically, I mean.'

'Let's see. Mester's would be about four inches long, by two and three-quarters wide, by maybe three-quarters of an inch thick.' Andrea's hands danced in front of her, illustrating the measurements. 'They're not very big.'

'Easy to hide, then.'

'Totally.'

Greg's frown deepened.

'But why would he bother? If he jumped, why would he care about a computer hard drive? And if he was murdered, he'd not have had time to swap it out for a new one.'

Now it was Andrea's turn to frown.

'If he did off himself, maybe he was ashamed of something and didn't want anyone to find it.' Her expression darkened. 'Rich old guys who live alone can get into some pretty weird shit. Weird shit that gets you jailed.'

Greg nodded. Andrea had a point. Particularly if Mester was alone when he died. Something that was looking increasingly likely.

As for the hard drive, simply taking it out and hiding it didn't make a lot of sense. If it was incriminating enough to take out of his laptop, it was incriminating enough to destroy it. Otherwise, someone might stumble across it after his death and ruin his legacy. The thing would be gone for good.

It's not like he'd have any use for it in the hereafter.

Greg sighed. His biggest problem wasn't solving the mystery of Alan Mester's death; it was selling the most likely solution to his 'client'.

'You get anywhere with Lynn Spargo's alibi?'

'Sure did.' Andrea gave him a wicked grin. 'Hotel people will tell a PA pretty much anything, I reckon. Anyway, looks like she was where she said she was. She didn't check out until Wednesday morning, when the convention ended. And she called for room service around nine p.m. on Tuesday evening, so she must have been there overnight.'

'They told you that?' Greg didn't bother to hide how impressed he was.

'Sure did. Like I said, if you're a PA, they'll tell you everything you want to know. Particularly if you let slip that your boss is an a-hole.'

Greg clapped his hands together in delight.

'Is there anything you *can't* do, Ms Velasquez?'

'Nope. Not really. Come take a look at this.' Andrea cracked open her battered laptop, which was lying on the coffee table. 'I did like you asked and had a look at that fancy watch of his.' The laptop's screen came alive with a series of graphs and tables. 'The casing was smashed but the tech inside was pretty much undamaged. This thing is from a company I've never heard of, a startup connected to Carnegie Mellon. I figure, start-ups needing money and Mester being a rich banking dude, it's some kind of beta model he was testing out for them before he handed over any cash.'

'Or maybe *because* he'd handed them cash.'

'Also possible. Anyway, lots of apps but real shit security, so it was easy to download the data.' Andrea's expression became unusually somber. 'The dude suffered, man. Suffered bad.'

'And you can tell all that from a watch?' Greg didn't bother to hide his skepticism.

'What *are* you? Amish? Or just really, really old?' She tapped one of the graphs on the screen. 'This gizmo was recording your man's heartbeats and other vital signs. Some of it I don't understand, not being a doctor or anything, but the heartbeats are pretty freaking graphic.' She took a deep breath before continuing. 'This is Mester's heartbeat at ten in the evening. Steady, right?'

With just one working eye, Greg had to squint. The only other option was to get on his hands and knees in front of the coffee table and press his face closer to the screen. Squinting was less humiliating. He could just about make out the thin, wavering line that Andrea had her finger on.

'But by ten-oh-three p.m., it's super elevated, like almost two hundred beats per minute. I figure that's when he decides he's going to top himself, because by ten-oh-four it's dropped way down. All calm again. Decision made, see? Die cast and all that. *Then*, at ten forty-seven p.m., it climbs again, not as high as before but high, which is when I figure he's on the balcony, because by ten forty-eight his heart rate is all over the place. It's super, super fast for a while and then it gets real erratic and then slower and slower until it stops at twelve forty-one.'

Greg did the math. Reluctantly. Pictured the distance the man had crawled toward the rear entrance of his apartment building.

'So he was alive for almost two hours after he fell?'

'You got that right.' Andrea shook her head sadly. 'What a shit way to die. Do you think he'd have jumped if he'd known it would take so long? Dude must have been in agony.'

Greg didn't know what to say to that.

'Can you tell me anything about the house on Forty-Fourth Street?'

Andrea closed her laptop, as eager to change the subject as Greg was.

'Until three years ago, it was owned by a Maura Looby, who'd lived there, like, forever. I reckon she either died or moved into a home. Anyway, after that, it got bought by some outfit called Quarry Mount Capital. I can't tell you much about them, though, except that they're registered in Delaware. I'll send you the deets.'

'Thanks. Did you happen to figure out if it was ever rented on Airbnb?'

'It wasn't. I did some web scraping—'

'What the hell is that when it's at home?'

'Don't you worry your pretty little head, Mr Bimbo. All you need to know is that the house has never been on Airbnb. Though it *was* listed for rent in the real-estate pages a couple of years ago. Six weeks after that, it was flagged as no longer available, which is when, I figure, it was rented. No sign of it since, so my guess is that whoever rented it then is the same person renting it now. Couldn't find anything on the tenant, though, which is definitely odd.'

'Uh-huh.' Polukhin had been rattling his chain about Airbnb, then. For fun. Or out of habit. Something the two of them had in common.

Andrea, he noticed, was looking at him curiously.

'What?'

'I was just wondering when you're going to tell Lynn Spargo her ex topped himself.'

'"Not just yet" is the answer to that one. I've still got a couple of things to run down. One of which requires a slightly different approach.'

12:09 P.M.

Greg tried to ignore the swirl of memory that invariably accompanied him to the admin suite. It wasn't just the unpleasantness of his various interactions with the previous principal. Some of it had to do with the way the place had changed. Admin was always empty at lunchtime now. Not like before. Not when—

He crushed the thought before it could fully form. He sat down at a workstation, instead, and picked up a landline. This was the different approach he'd mentioned to Andrea. The caller ID at the other end would read as CALDERHILL ACADEMY. What it would not say was GREGORY ABIMBOLA, AMATEUR DETECTIVE, TO WHOM I DO NOT WISH TO SPEAK. If the target picked up, she would talk, even after realizing it was him. Because people, in Greg's experience, would almost invariably speak to you if you could just get ahold of them in the first place. It was human nature.

'Hello.'

'Fatima Davis?'

'This is she.'

'Hi. My name's Greg Abimbola. I—'

'I know who you are. Lynn wants me to talk to you. About Alan.'

'That's right.'

'But you're not the police?'

'Correct.'

'Or a private detective?'

'Also correct.'

'Which means I don't have to talk to you, right?'

'Correct again. But—'

'Goodbye, Greg.' The line went dead.

Greg leaned back against the black mesh of the office chair and pushed out a sigh of disappointment. Reluctant to move, he logged on to the computer in front of him and ran a search for Fatima Haddad Davis of Pittsburgh, Pennsylvania.

He was surprised by the number of hits that came back.

Fatima Davis, it turned out, was quite the socialite. A number of local magazines had published lifestyle-type stories about her. There were numerous pictures of her at charity galas, exhibition openings and the like.

Lynn had been right about the woman's family. Her parents had fled Iran after the fall of the Shah and ended up in California, which is where Fatima had been born. The family had fallen on hard times, so much so that her father had driven a taxi for a number of years before getting a job more suited to his qualifications. Fatima, meantime, was a straight-A student at high school and ended up within the Ivy League confines of the University of Pennsylvania, which is where she met Randy Davis, her husband-to-be. The couple had settled down in suburban Pittsburgh, close to Randy's parents. The Davis family being far from poor, her career as a charitable benefactor and high society butterfly had begun almost immediately. Having two children at the Edgeworth School, Randy's alma mater, meant that membership of the board of trustees, and then the exco, had been almost inevitable.

The web's various pictures showed a svelte, glamorous woman who had aged gracefully over the years. To Greg's eye, the forty-something socialite of the present day was far more poised, far more attractive than the twenty-something version that had preceded her. Her husband, by contrast, struck him as quite the opposite. A passable specimen in his youth, the various images of the two of them together showed a steady degeneration. These days, he was little more than a well-fed fat guy in a tuxedo. Whether pictured with her husband or not, Fatima Davis appeared to have a penchant for red. The warm tones of her skin were able to carry the color in a variety of shades, tastefully accessorized, of course. A lot of women would have looked pale and washed out. Fatima looked vibrant.

She was certainly living the good life, he decided. The sort of life with which he was entirely unfamiliar. Except, perhaps, for its hardscrabble beginning.

Greg, studying a picture of her taken at the Carnegie Museum of Natural History, found himself frowning. He blew up the picture as far as it could sensibly go. The frown turned to a smile of recognition.

Done with web-stalking but still smiling, Greg logged off. The lunch hour would soon be over. It was time to get back to the business of teaching. He left the admin suite and headed out into the corridor.

'Oh. Hello, sir.'

'Do you need a hand with that?'

Caitlin Bell stumbled by, weighed down by a chaotic assortment of cameras, mics and ancillary equipment.

'Thanks, but no.' Purple hair shivered as she nodded toward the end of the passageway. 'I'm almost there, sir. I just have to get these babies into the AV room.'

'As you wish.' Greg headed toward his own classroom.

And stopped.

'Caitlin?'

'Yes, sir?'

'I wonder if I might ask a favor?'

'Sure.'

'It's about a documentary, actually. I need your expertise. I'll make sure there's extra credit in it for you and your assistant, er—?'

'Will.'

'Will. Exactly. What do you say?'

'Who says no to extra credit?' Caitlin's eyes twinkled with amusement.

Greg filled her in on the plan. Or at least as much of it as had sprung into his head in the past few seconds. Despite the fact that it involved a chunk of her weekend, she nodded enthusiastically and headed off, weaving slightly under the weight of her equipment.

Greg reached his classroom, only to discover that he was not the first one there.

'The security lady let me up,' Lynn Spargo explained. She looked ill at ease, the grip on her purse tight enough to whiten knuckles. 'I told her you were expecting me.'

'I pride myself on expecting the unexpected, so it's not like you were lying, is it?'

Lynn smiled a little at that. But her knuckles were no less white.

'Why don't we skip the "I was just passing" stage,' Greg suggested, 'and get to why you're here?'

'It's kind of delicate.'

'OK.'

Lynn said nothing. Neither did Greg. Footsteps passed to and fro in the corridor outside.

'I found this with some of Alan's things,' Lynn said at last, opening her purse. 'It's a key.' She handed it to Greg, who examined the fob attached to it with interest.

'"Seven fifty-three-A Main Street, Stayard, Ohio,"' he said, reading its label. 'An apartment, you think?'

'I don't know what to think.' Lynn put her purse down on the nearest desk. 'No. You know what? I know *exactly* what I think. I think this is where *she* lives. The gold digger who murdered him. And I . . . I can't face going there. In case I'm right. Or wrong. I just don't . . .'

Her voice died away, unable to compete with a quivering top lip.

'And you'd like me to go instead, is that it?'

Lynn nodded.

'Well, why not? I've always wanted to see the college. I'm told it's beautiful at this time of year.'

Lynn's response was something between a laugh and a sob. Greg hoped it meant he was back in her good graces. Back enough, at least, so he could follow up on another matter.

'Can I ask you something? About Clyde Leclerc?'

For a moment, Greg thought she was going to refuse, to tell him that Clyde had nothing to do with this and to focus on 753A Main Street instead.

'What do you want to know?'

Greg ignored the lack of enthusiasm in her tone and pressed on.

'When we first met, you told me that he and Alan had a history. But you didn't tell me what it was.'

'Oh, that.' Lynn looked vaguely around. 'Do you mind if I sit?'

'Go right ahead.' Greg tried not to smile at the sight of a well-dressed, professional woman sitting at a desk usually occupied by slouching teenagers. He pulled up a chair and sat down beside her.

'This was all years ago, you understand.'

'Of course.'

'So, back in the day, Clyde, who was not that long out of school, was a junior vice president at W.A. Sperling.' She favored Greg with a wry grin. 'I see the name means nothing to you.'

'I don't know much about finance,' Greg admitted. 'High or otherwise.'

'It was one of the world's biggest banks, headquartered right here in Pittsburgh. Until its last CEO sold two hundred years of history down the river and merged it with a West Coast competitor.' She shook her head sadly. 'No one remembers it now, but back then it was really something.

'Anyhow, until the merger, Alan worked at Sperling in a number of senior positions. When Clyde joined the bank, he became a member of Alan's team.'

'Clyde worked for Alan?'

'Oh, yes. Until Alan got him fired.'

'Wow.'

'"Wow" is right. There was an intern there at the time – a woman called, er, Susan Tan. She came to Alan in tears one day, saying that Clyde had been harassing her all summer. The last straw was when he said something to her in the elevator. I don't remember what, exactly, but it was something like "I'm looking at you right now and thinking about how Asian women look when they . . ." Er . . . well, you get my drift. Anyway, Alan was livid. He sent Clyde away to a branch office on some BS project and got him canned a few months later.'

'For harassment?'

'Not exactly, no.' Lynn's lips had pressed themselves into a grim line. 'I'm not sure harassment was even a word back then. It would have been "well, if she can't take a few jokes, she'd better find herself another line of work". But Alan, he hated that sort of stuff, always. He thought Clyde was a wrong 'un, so he gave the guy a below-average performance review. The bank was looking to make cuts at the time, so Clyde was easy pickings. Clyde, as you can imagine, never forgave him.'

Greg mulled that over for a moment.

'Does the phrase "the OJ" mean anything to you?'

'Like, orange juice?'

'I don't think so. Doctor Harwood – JoAnn – told me that Clyde said something to Alan at the exco meeting: "I know about the OJ." Something like that.'

'Huh.' Lynn was frowning. 'No. Can't say it rings any bells with me. It might be a code name, I guess.'

'Really?' Greg was intrigued.

'Oh, sure. Many of the deals Alan was involved in were super-super confidential. People would be concerned about market movements, SEC rules, that kind of thing. So, instead of talking about A merging with B, say, they'd talk about "Operation

Goldenfork" or some such meaningless nonsense. Your OJ might be something like that.'

The classroom door opened. A couple of girls barged in.

'Oh. Sorry, sir. We didn't know you had *company.*' Hands flew to mouths, covering barely suppressed giggles.

'Enough, you two. Take a seat and be ready to talk all things Gogol.'

'I'd best be going,' Lynn said, smiling.

'I think so.' He tugged the sleeve of her jacket as she brushed by. 'Sorry. Before you go, one more thing.'

'Yes?'

'Randy and Fatima Davis. You said they lived near you, in Sewickley Heights?'

'That's right.'

'Where, exactly?'

SATURDAY, THE EIGHTEENTH
4:11 A.M.

Silently cursing Dobrygin, Greg slipped out of his apartment building, still rubbing the sleep from his eyes. The Russian's silver Nissan Sentra had been waiting for him after school the previous day, tailing him to the gym, to Giant Eagle and, eventually, home.

Given the amount of time that had elapsed, Polukhin's patience vis-à-vis Morosov was sure to be wearing thin. At some point, and some point soon, Dobrygin would be tasked with either bringing him in or shooting him dead on the street. Tailing him was just a preliminary. A know-your-target op before the inevitable call to action.

And Dobrygin, thug that he was, would be more than eager to get on with it.

But not today. Because today Greg Abimbola, for reasons ranging from bloody-mindedness to self-preservation, was determined to give him the slip.

Dobrygin, he knew, had no backup, would have a feel for Greg's routines by now and was lazy. He would not be expecting Greg to be up and about so soon. If Greg had read the situation correctly, Oleg Dobrygin would be fast asleep in the house on 44th Street, his alarm set for maybe four thirty.

Assuming, of course, that Greg was on his to-do list for the day. The man might have other plans.

It was this latter thought that crushed the joy out of the situation. Dobrygin's vehicle was nowhere to be found among the shadowed humps of metal lining the street. But whether he'd outwitted his adversary, or simply gotten up pointlessly early, was impossible to tell.

Accompanied by the cheerful burble of National Public Radio, Greg drove north and west along PA-65 as if headed to Sewickley, the unlit expanse of the Ohio somewhere to his left. This time, though, instead of heading into downtown, his GPS took him past it and into the steep hills beyond. Hood pointed toward the sky, he drove along narrow roads that crept past well-manicured driveways and increasingly large homes. Eventually, the steep gradients leveled out and Greg turned on to a narrow, agricultural-looking road, lined on both sides by the low silhouette of hedgerows. Oil-treated gravel scrunched under his tires.

He doused the headlights, creeping forward until he found what he was looking for: the gated driveway that led to 148 Burnt Oak Road, home to Randy and Fatima Davis. He parked up and waited. After a moment's hesitation, he propped his phone up on the dash and set it to play *Alexander Nevsky*. It was a long movie but, thanks to Dobrygin, he had plenty of time.

Alexander Nevsky had ended, the sun had come up, and *Battleship Potemkin* was well under way by the time Greg acquired Fatima Davis. She was sitting behind the wheel of a mud-spattered SUV as it emerged from the driveway and turned toward him. She paid no attention to Greg's Mini Cooper as she swept past, her eyes hidden behind a pair of large, expensive-looking sunglasses.

Greg, who had an afternoon appointment, was grateful that it was still early. He tossed his phone on to the passenger seat, brought the engine to life and set off in pursuit. Following his quarry at a discreet distance while she wound through the peaks and troughs of the North Hills, it took Greg a considerable amount of time to figure out where she was headed. After a seeming age, she was pulling into the parking lot for Oakmont Bakery, a vast charcoal-and-glass edifice that looked more like a high-end outdoor pursuits store than a home for artisanal carbohydrates.

He shook his head in mock disbelief.

This place isn't a bakery, he thought to himself. *It's a cult*.

Even though it was still early in the morning, Oakmont Bakery was crammed with customers desperate for its wares: traditional baked goods that drew people, quite literally, from miles around. Sitting in his vehicle a row further back in the parking lot, he watched Fatima Davis enter the building and followed her progress through crystal-clear plate-glass windows.

She was meeting someone, it turned out: a dyed-blonde woman of similar age and as smartly dressed as she was. They grabbed a table at the bakery's café, engaging in animated conversation. Keeping half an eye on the two of them, Greg put his phone back on the dashboard and returned once more to the long-ago world of *Battleship Potemkin*.

For all of twenty minutes. Then his phone died, the continued delivery of Russian epic movies too much for its Chinese battery.

'Fuck.'

A car parked next to Fatima's reversed out of the lot, its rear seat loaded with produce. Deciding that this would be as good a time as any to make a move, he slid his Mini Cooper into the vacated space, parking in such a way that his passenger door was no more than six inches from the driver's side of Fatima's SUV.

He exited the vehicle, strolled to the edge of the parking lot and waited.

Sure enough, Fatima came out of the bakery accompanied by her friend, each of them carrying a large bag. On reaching Fatima's vehicle, the two women stopped, visibly annoyed by the impossible-to-access driver's door.

Greg ran across the parking lot, a studiedly goofy smile plastered across his face.

'Sorry, ladies, sorry. The guy next to me was parked badly and I thought I could squeeze in for just a minute. Let me move my car for you. *So* sorry.' He waved his key fob at them. A peace offering.

'No problem.' The expression on Fatima's face made an untruth of the words. Her friend rolled her eyes, grinned mischievously at Fatima and headed off, high heels clicking on asphalt.

Greg waited till she was out of earshot.

'My name's Greg Abimbola. We need to talk.'

'Wait. What?' Fatima's eyes flitted from Greg to the too-tight gap and back again. 'Did you do this *on purpose*? That's it. I'm calling the—'

'Before you do anything hasty, I know you've been having an affair with Alan Mester. Which makes you a murder suspect.'

'Murder? Affair? I have no idea what you're talking about. And I'm certainly not talking to the likes of *you*. Move your stupid little rinky-dink car *right now*.'

'You own a fine pair of ruby earrings, Ms Davis. You wore them to a gala at the Carnegie Museum not so long ago. Set off your dress perfectly, if you don't mind my saying. A bespoke setting from Arecas Design and Jewelry, wasn't it? Which I happen to know was a gift from Alan Mester. The note was quite touching, I'm sure.'

It was like watching the air go out of a beautiful, glittery balloon.

'Shall we step back inside?' Greg suggested. He moved them both quickly enough to grab a barely vacated table. The air around them echoed with chatter and high spirits. Fatima Davis, arms folded across her chest, glared at him across an expanse of light wood and crumbs.

'What do you want?'

'I want to talk about the night Alan died. The exco meeting.'

'What about it?'

'Why did you vote with Clyde Leclerc against the DEI proposal?'

Fatima's expression was incredulous.

'That's it? That's all you want to know about?'

'It seems like a good place to start.'

Fatima relaxed slightly.

'I don't think DEI is a good idea, not right now. The situation at the school is too . . . delicate.'

'And I suppose that's a view you've held for a while, is it?'

'Of course.'

'Is the situation delicate because there are a number of parents who think the idea is too, er, woke?'

'Exactly.'

'And being a parent there yourself, you've always been aware of these views?'

'Yes.'

'Which I daresay have been held by the same sorts of parents for years?'

'Absolutely.'

'And when you say you thought the situation at the school was too delicate, that's also been the case for years, hasn't it?'

'For at least a couple, sure.'

'And so it's fair to say, I imagine, given that the situation has been delicate for at least a couple of years, you've been against implementing DEI for roughly the same amount of time?'

'Yeah. More or less.'

'So how come you never told Alan?'

'I . . . I did.'

'You did not.' Greg's voice was hard and flat. In his mind's eye, he reached back in time: a hot African night, a bare light swinging from beneath a corrugated iron roof, whimpered words of confession. He let the memory reach his face.

The blood drained away from beneath Fatima Davis's makeup.

'You didn't tell Alan Mester, because Alan Mester was as surprised as everyone else when you made it clear you were voting with

Clyde. He was furious with you, accused you of *betraying him*. Not the reaction of someone who was aware of your allegedly long-held views.' He leaned across the table. Fatima flinched. 'So,' he said, voice icy soft. 'Truth now. Why did you change your vote at the last minute?'

Fatima's large eyes welled with tears. Under the smart clothes, her delicate shoulders were shaking.

Greg tried not to feel guilty.

'It was Randy.' He could barely hear her above the joyful hubbub of bakery-goers. 'Randy needed me to at least delay the vote on DEI to get him out of a jam. To get *us* out of a jam.'

'How so?'

'We have, er, cashflow problems. Randy made some investments that didn't turn out so well.'

'OK. But how does that translate into siding with Clyde?'

'Because it was Clyde who was going to get us out of the jam. He's an investment banker. He was going to pull a bunch of people together to get Randy the financing we need to move forward. But only if I either voted against the DEI thing or delayed it.'

'Clyde hated it that much?'

'So did Randy. He and Clyde are basically PEACE.'

'Just the two of them?' Greg couldn't stop himself from raising an eyebrow.

'There are a few other parents, but Randy and Clyde are the main drivers. They both think the school is changing out of all recognition, that the admissions department is diluting the brand by chasing students of color rather than students of quality.'

Something complicated flitted across Fatima's features.

'I take it you didn't agree with that?'

'No, I did not. Never have, never will.'

'But you went along with it anyway.'

'Of course I did.' Fatima's eyes blazed with defiance. 'My family were rich when they lived in Iran. Then they were poor. And it's exactly like they say: rich is better. I'm not going back there. And if the price of not going back there is being on the same side as Clyde Leclerc, so be it. You'd have done exactly the same in my position.'

'Even though the price of what you did was stabbing Alan in the back?'

Tears seeped silently through Fatima's eyelashes. She reached into her purse for a tissue. Dabbed away the moisture.

'I wanted to tell him ahead of time. I did. But I could never find the right moment. And then, when . . . He was *so* angry. I knew he'd be cross, but I had no idea he'd be like that. It was like he was a completely different person. I just wish . . .'

She dabbed at her eyes again.

'He was so angry he threatened to put you and your husband on the street.'

'Yes.'

'What was that about?'

Fatima's lips pressed together in a firm line. Greg sat calmly, waiting for her to remember which side of the table had leverage.

She let out a small sigh.

'Randy's main business is payday lending. Do you know what that is?'

Greg shook his head.

'If someone needs a loan for a few days, to tide them over to the next paycheck, a payday lender will loan them the money. The amount to be paid in interest is small – a few dollars more than the loan amount – because it's only for a few days. But the actual interest rate is high. Four hundred percent, maybe more. If you pay off the loan at the next paycheck, great. But a lot of people don't do that; they roll it into another loan, and then another. By the time they finally pay it off, you've earned a return of hundreds of percent on your original loan. It's big money.'

'So what's the problem?'

'There isn't one. Unless you happen to live in Pennsylvania, which views payday loans as a type of predatory lending. Payday loans are illegal here. Randy runs his business through a Native American reservation out in Montana. The reservation has its own laws and payday lending is just fine. They get a small cut of the business, and everything is above board.'

'But?'

'If they were to find out, some prosecutor here looking to make a name for themselves might still find a way to take Randy to court. They'd say the reservation was just a front, that the whole arrangement was a sham – which it kind of is – and that Randy was a criminal. They could shut him down, maybe.'

'And Alan knew this?'

'Yes. I . . . I must have told him once. When we . . .'

Fatima was unable to meet his gaze. She looked down at the

table and its attendant crumbs. Greg resisted the temptation to brush them away.

'Did you try and get him to change his mind?'

'I tried to catch up with him, after the meeting. But he just . . . he brushed me away like I wasn't there. Like I didn't even *matter*.'

Fatima Davis folded in on herself, sobbing and inconsolable. Passersby, unused to such sights in the happy confines of Oakmont Bakery, made no attempt to hide their displeasure. And the object of their displeasure was Greg Abimbola, the asshole guy who'd chosen a completely inappropriate venue to break up with his girlfriend.

Greg ignored them.

'Did you follow him home to his apartment?' he asked, once the sobs had subsided. 'Maybe try to have another go at him?'

'No.' Fatima took several deep breaths, composing herself.

'But you've been to his apartment?'

'Not often, but yes.'

'What size shoe do you take?'

'Excuse me?'

'Your shoe size. What is it?'

'Size seven. Why?'

'Do you own a pair of Louboutin pumps?'

'More than a pair, actually.' A faint smile made its way to her lips. 'Red is kind of my color.'

'Have you misplaced any?'

'Absolutely not.' Fatima looked scandalized. 'You don't just *lose* a pair of Louboutins.'

'I see.' Now it was Greg's turn to smile. 'Did Alan ever give you a necklace to match the ruby earrings he gave you?'

'No.'

'How about a sapphire one?'

'Oh, no.' Fatima's expression turned fond. 'Alan would know better than that. Blue doesn't work for me – it's way too cold for my skin tone.'

Greg, who had views about this sort of thing, was inclined to agree. He refrained, however, from saying so.

'And after the meeting, after Alan had brushed you off, where did you go?'

'Home. Alone. Randy was out of town and the kids were both on a school trip.'

Greg digested that for a moment. Fatima's cheeks were faintly flushed. In all probability, she and Alan had been planning to spend the night together.

'Where was Randy?'

'At a Republican fundraiser in King of Prussia.' Her expression turned wry. 'You can see him on social media.'

'Good to know. Well, thank you, Fatima, I appreciate you taking the time.' He made to rise from his seat.

Fatima reached out and grabbed his wrist.

'Look, you won't tell Randy, will you? Or Lynn? I answered your questions like you wanted.'

Greg, thinking about Lynn's expression when she'd first mentioned Fatima, said, 'I think Lynn already knows. Or suspects, at any rate. But I won't tell anyone unless I absolutely have to.'

Fatima breathed a sigh of relief.

Greg stood up, happy to be away from the crumb-littered table. Fatima left as hurriedly as he'd expected, almost running out of the building to be free of him. Not bothering to wait for Greg to move his car, she entered her vehicle from the passenger side and reversed out of her parking space, missing a passing minivan by inches.

Greg looked at his watch. There was plenty of time.

He bought a half dozen pastries before leaving.

2:07 P.M.

'You're not on the list,' the security guard said. 'What are you here for?'

'We're making a documentary,' Greg explained. 'Following the ups and downs of the youth robotics team. We're here to get footage of some of the prep work before the actual competition.' He leaned heavily into his English accent, fixed the guard with his most apologetic smile. 'My students have given up part of their weekend for this, sir. I hope I haven't wasted their time over some sort of mix-up.'

Behind him, Caitlin Bell, Will Zuckerman and their equipment waited expectantly. Caleb Freedman, whose relationship with Caitlin was clearly known to Will, had come along for the ride. As for Will himself, he was leaning in the posed manner of teenage boys against a large sign. The sign for the building to which they were trying to gain entry: GENERICA HOUSE. Greg resisted the urge to tell him to stand up straight, like a man. Even with an English accent, the whole thing would have sounded far too Russian.

The security guard looked at the kids, and the equipment, and came to a decision.

'I guess it's OK,' he said, his expression genial. 'You don't look like mass murderers. Please don't prove me wrong.'

Greg managed to mask a small sigh of relief.

'Thank you so much, sir. I really appreciate it.' And then, to his co-conspirators, 'Come on guys, we – by which I mean you – have work to do.'

Brad Leclerc was pleasantly surprised to learn that his robotics outfit, Team Resistors Are Futile, was going to be the subject of a student documentary, even if it was 'only' for Calderhill Academy. The team captain was happy to answer all the questions Caitlin asked him and waxed lyrical about the abilities of their robot. The robot, which was basically a cooler-sized box on wheels, went by the name of Ohm-Maha, for reasons that presumably made sense to someone. It did not escape Greg's notice, however, and possibly Caleb's, that Brad Leclerc somehow managed to avoid any mention of Malik Freedman. Malik, for his part, was sitting a little away from the others. He refused to make eye contact. Caleb's gaze traveled slowly from his brother to the team captain and back again.

'So what are you guys working on today?' Caitlin was asking. Will directed a camera toward an open expanse of floor. The floor was littered with multiple footballs and a single soccer ball that looked distinctly out of place.

'It's shape discrimination,' Brad explained. 'It's quite difficult to teach a robot the difference between something round, like a soccer ball, and something round-ish, like a football. Ohm-Maha needs to cross the field – that's what we call the space here – without disturbing any of the footballs, identify and pick up the soccer ball, and then get to the other side of the field, still avoiding the footballs. And he has to do that without any human intervention.'

'It sounds simple enough.'

'For a human being, sure. For Ohm-Maha? Not so much.' He let loose a theatrical sigh. 'It's a work in progress.'

Greg stood behind Caleb and murmured, 'Now would be a *really* good time for your brother to speak up.'

Malik was looking at the ground but, even from a distance, it was clear he was stressing out. The grip on his tablet was so tight his knuckles had turned pale. Greg wondered how Caleb planned on getting the boy's attention without making it too obvious.

'Hey, Malik!' Caleb shouted. 'You got a fix for this thing, or what?'

Malik, shocked that anyone would be talking to him right now, never mind his brother, jumped to his feet, startled.

'Uh . . . uh—'

'Malik's a very junior member of the team,' Brad said smoothly. 'He's still learning the ropes. You're not ready to operate on this level, are you, Mal?'

Malik looked like he was about to agree, but then his gaze slid from Brad to his brother, and then Greg.

'I can help with this,' he said, voice shaky. And then more firmly, 'I got a fix right here.' He tapped his tablet.

'I'm sure you think you do, but—'

'Why don't we see what the lad's got,' Greg said, cutting across the two of them. 'It'll be interesting footage to see how you work through things using, er, *every* member of the team, won't it, Caitlin?'

'Totes, sir.'

Caught between the stick of adult authority and the carrot of media interest, Brad gave way and beckoned Malik forward. Malik huddled around the robot with the others and engaged in urgent conversation. Caitlin, Will and their attendant equipment hovered on the outside of the group.

'Do you have any idea what they're talking about?' Caleb asked.

'Not a clue,' said Greg. 'It's all geek to me.' He was gratified to be rewarded with a small chuckle.

The group had somehow connected Malik's tablet to the robot. A couple of the team members, two boys of maybe sixteen years of age, were hunched over a nearby keyboard and screen, typing in tandem. They looked like a piano duet.

Eventually, though, Ohm-Maha was ready. With a whine of electrical motors, it set off across the field of footballs in search of something else.

To Greg's untrained eye, the whole thing was painful to watch. The little machine lurched forward and then back, spinning clumsily on its wheels to execute crude changes of direction. What Greg had assumed would be the job of a few seconds stretched into minutes.

The team seemed pleased, though. And to be fair, if your only objective was to neither hit nor attempt to pick up a football, Ohm-Maha was doing OK.

The robot had reached the center of the field. It turned itself to face the soccer ball, moved forward to pick it up with some paddle-like appendages.

And stopped dead.

'Cut,' Brad said briskly. Someone tapped on a keyboard in response. 'Well, Mal, it wasn't a bad try in the circumstances but, like I said, you're not ready for—'

'Wait,' said one of the boys at the keyboard. 'I don't think it's the code. It's just a calibration issue. Look.'

The team huddled again.

Greg, resigned to another interlude of incomprehensibility, checked his phone.

And swore under his breath. He'd forgotten it was dead. Murdered by his love of old Russian movies. He wandered off, pacing slowly around the edges of the room, admiring the landscaping on the far side of a tinted, plate-glass window.

So much so that he almost tripped over a pile of bags and teenage detritus strewn in his path.

Picking his way through, he lit upon a lanyard and ID tag protruding from an upscale holdall. With only one eye, it was hard to read the small print, but the photograph made things easier.

Brad Leclerc's high school pass.

The team was still huddled around the keyboard. Caitlin and Will were concentrating on the action. Even Caleb was taking an interest.

He picked up the pass and stuffed it in his pocket.

By the time he'd circled back to his starting point, Team Resistors Are Futile was ready to go. Ohm-Maha made its shambolic way across the field until it once again found itself facing the soccer ball. With a high-pitched whine, the robot's paddles extended, hesitated a moment on either side of the ball and picked it up. Wild cheering ensued.

'Good job, Noah,' Brad said, giving the boy who'd spoken up about calibration a fist bump.

Greg waited a beat.

'And "Good job, Malik" – yes?' Greg didn't bother to keep the ice out of his voice.

Brad looked momentarily nonplussed.

'Oh. Yes. Well done, Mal.'

Greg was glad he had the kid's ID in his pocket.

4:42 P.M.

When Greg returned home, it was to find Dobrygin's silver Nissan parked within sight of his apartment building. He hoped the fucker had been there all day.

He plugged in his phone and settled down in front of the TV. No sooner had he done so, however, than the apartment buzzer went off. He picked up the intercom.

'Hello?'

'It's Rachel Lev. I'm coming up.'

As he opened up his front door in anticipation of the police officer's arrival, he could hear her clattering up the stairs. Given the rate of ascent, she had to be climbing them two at a time.

'Good afternoon, Rach—'

'Don't you "good afternoon" me, you lying, limey bastard.' She stormed past him into the living room, hurling the large bulk of her purse on to the sofa. 'You know Viktor Lavrov.'

'I have no idea what—'

'*He was in your fucking apartment!*'

Greg tried to ignore the sinking feeling in his stomach. Morosov *had* been in his apartment, right where Rachel Lev was standing, actually, albeit restrained. The US Marshals knew that, MI5 knew that, and so did the GRU. But how did—

'I was coming over to see you, to talk about the case, because even though there's something off about you, you've been helpful, and I value your input. But as I'm driving over here, I got to thinking. Thinking about the fact that while everyone seems to like you, nobody – and I mean *nobody* – knows much of anything about who you are. Not the teachers at that fancy school of yours, or the priest at your church, or your neighbors in the building. You have no friends. Except maybe one. Maybelline Velasquez, assistant custodian at Calderhill Academy. A woman half your age, with whom you have absolutely nothing in common, except that you went to the mat for her on a murder charge and got her off. Why is that, I wonder?'

It was like watching her click Legos together in her head. Piece by piece into an inevitable, final structure.

'So I pay your good *friend*, Ms Velasquez, a visit, and you know what? It turns out she doesn't know anything about you, either. Except for the fact that you're – and I quote – "crap with computers". So crap that you had her install a nanny cam in your living room. And no sooner had she done so, it just "happened" to pick up one Viktor Lavrov *wandering about this very room*! Large as life and very definitely not dead. You—'

Greg made sure he was mumbling. It was the tone that mattered this first time around, not the words. Stunned surprise, contrition, dawning realization.

'What did you say?'

'I said I thought she was joking.' Greg's voice was little more than a whisper, loud enough to be heard, low enough that the detective had to lean in to hear him.

'I'm sorry. You thought she was what now?'

'Joking.' Hoping he wasn't overdoing it, he drew in a ragged breath, his voice louder. 'It's just like you said. I'm not as bad with computers as Andrea says, but I'm definitely not great. She installed the camera just like you say. I went for a morning run, and she calls me up, claiming there's some strange man in my apartment. So I turn right around and head back as fast as I can. But when I get here, there's no sign of anyone. The door hadn't been forced, nothing had been disturbed, and absolutely nothing had been taken. I figured it was just a prank.'

'And you confronted her about this, I guess? It's not very funny, making someone think they'd been burglarized, is it? I imagine you were pretty mad, yeah?'

Greg suppressed a smile. Rachel Lev was good.

The GRU would have loved her.

'Mad? No. Annoyed? Most definitely. I did have to talk to her about changing the account details, after which she couldn't access the alerts. But apart from that, I played it with a straight bat.'

'I don't know what that means.'

'It means I barely mentioned it at all. I didn't want to give her the satisfaction. Mischief is Andrea's other middle name, and getting excited about it would only have encouraged her. All I said was there was no one there when I got back. But, Jesus fucking Christ' – he gave a low whistle – 'I had no idea she was telling the truth.'

And thank God I shut the camera down before I got home. Otherwise, this would be so *much worse.*

'Did you not check your own copy of the video?'

'I didn't have a copy. Andrea had only just set it up and everything went to her at the time. That's why I had to change the account details.'

Acting Lieutenant Rachel Lev was staring at him hard. Greg stared back. His one good eye, he knew, would be a dark, bottomless pool, unblemished by guilt.

'And what would Viktor want with you?'

'Like I said before, Rachel, I don't know. Whatever he was looking for, he definitely didn't find it. Nothing was taken.'

Another long stare.

'Here's my problem,' she said at last. 'Viktor Lavrov, in your apartment, is the last sighting of this man alive. He must have driven here because his rental was parked in your street. But he didn't drive away again because the same rental car was towed away weeks later as an abandoned vehicle. Which tells us what, Mr Abimbola?'

'That you think he was killed or incapacitated either in my apartment or just outside.' The words left a sour taste in his mouth.

'Exactly.' She gave him a thin smile. 'I'm sorry. Do you mind if I use your restroom? I can't think straight right now.'

'Of course you can. It's through there.'

If Rachel Lev wanted to snoop about his apartment under the guise of powdering her nose, she was more than welcome to. There was nothing for her to find.

She'd left her purse on the sofa.

Two can play at that game.

Sure enough, there was a thin manila folder containing a handful of photocopied documents. He leafed rapidly through them, pausing at the ballistics report. Rachel had given a pretty accurate summary. Morosov had been shot by a nine-millimeter pistol using 'Mak PB' ammunition.

There was a flushing sound in the bathroom. Greg slammed the file shut and put it back where he found it, his heart thumping with sudden and unwanted urgency. By the time Rachel returned to the room, he was back where she left him.

'Consider yourself a person of interest,' she said, scooping up her bag and heading for the door. 'And, so help me God, if you did this thing, your days as a free man are fucking numbered.' She glanced down at her bag, at the file inside. 'Even if it costs me my job.'

She didn't quite slam the door on the way out.

Greg was surprised to find that his hands were shaking. It took a couple of shots of vodka to get them to stop. Once calmed, he reached for his now partly charged phone to check on Randy Davis's social-media alibi.

And found the first in a series of missed texts from Andrea.

> Dude just spoke to police lady from my case you told me not to lie to police ever again remember she showed me picture of dead guy that I recognized so showed her nannycam of your weird ass home invasion and she is pissed!!!! Look out!!!!! ⚠

Too late now, of course. And too late for regrets. Regrets for once telling Andrea that another lie would get her convicted for murder, regrets for watching not one but two classic Russian movies on his cellphone, regrets for failing to have a charger in his car. And, most of all, regrets for pulling a lie out of nowhere that might or might not hold up under a full-scale police investigation.

Look out, indeed.

Watching shaky, online video of Randy Davis at a Republican fundraiser, Greg's jaw tightened in grim determination.

He wasn't the only one who was going to have to look out. Not by a long shot.

SUNDAY, THE NINETEENTH
1:14 P.M.

As he drove west on US 22, across the thin strip of West Virginia separating Pennsylvania from Ohio, Greg reflected on how his Sunday morning had become one long exercise in avoidance. He had knelt in church and avoided prayer, because what he had to ask was nothing God would be interested in granting. He had avoided Father Kyriakos because he had no wish to discuss how his 'cousin' Viktor Lavrov had ended up as a murder victim. Lastly, and most definitely least, he had avoided Dobrygin by squeezing his Mini Cooper down an alleyway too narrow and congested for the latter's bulkier Nissan to keep up with him. It would look, Greg hoped, like an unfortunate shortcut rather than a deliberate strategy to ditch a tail. The longer Dobrygin remained unaware that his surveillance had been compromised, the better.

He crossed the state line, careful to keep to the speed limit.

The Whole Foods bag on the passenger seat slid into the footwell as he swung north on to a down-at-heel local road, following signs for the small town of Stayard, Ohio.

Passing the city limits, Greg rolled slowly along Main, intending to keep track of the street numbers but distracted by the fact that one side of the road was a profusion of shops and small businesses, while the other was a huge, grassy space interrupted by a handful of abstract sculptures and a band shell, beyond which lay a sprawl of mid-rise buildings, each one different in style and design from its neighbor, each one immaculately maintained. Immaculate or not, Greg found the lack of architectural cohesion vaguely disturbing.

Stayard College.

The shops and businesses petered out almost as soon as he passed the college green. They were replaced by neatly painted wooden houses fronted by wide porches overlooking modest, manicured yards. A few blocks later, similar wooden houses split themselves into one-up, one-down apartments.

Greg came to a halt outside 753 Main Street, a tidy gray-and-white building with a carport off to the side. The structure sheltered a brand-new, bright red Fiat 500. Whole Foods bag in hand, Greg strode up to the front door, peered at the names taped to the entry system and rang the lower of two buzzers.

A young woman, slim and unnaturally blonde, wearing an oversized Stayard Law School sweatshirt and not much else answered the door. It was abundantly clear that she was not long out of bed.

'Ms Julie Keigel?

'Yes. Who are you?'

Greg showed her Lynn's business card and presented the contents of the Whole Foods bag for inspection.

'Lynn Spargo, Insurance Agent. I'm the man returning your missing Louboutin pump.'

2:37 P.M.

'I've never met a male Lynn before,' Julie Keigel said.

She'd taken the time to put on jeans and sneakers, to tie her hair back into a ponytail. Surrounded by bookshelves on every wall, she was perched on the edge of a worn sofa. Lynn Spargo's business card rotated slowly in her immaculately manicured hands.

'Well, now you have,' Greg said. He found himself both nonplussed and slightly worried. Nonplussed, because it had simply not occurred to him that Lynn might be an unusual name for a man. He'd met more than one male Lyndsay, after all. But not, now that he thought about it, in America.

And slightly worried, because it was only now occurring to him that he should never have introduced himself as Lynn Spargo in the first place. If Julie Keigel was who he thought she was, the name embossed on the business card might already be familiar to her.

He held his breath, waiting for the ax to fall.

'That isn't mine,' she said, pointing at the Louboutin.

Air returned to Greg's lungs. Denials, he could deal with.

'If that were true, Ms Keigel, you'd never have let me through your door in the first place.'

Gray-blue eyes glowed at him with a shrewd intelligence, their gaze steady.

'Maybe I'm just being hospitable.'

'Maybe you are. In which case, I'll just hand it over to the police, let them swab it for DNA. See what happens next.'

His one eye, he knew, would appear relaxed and good-humored. And utterly, utterly certain.

For the tiniest fraction of a second, Julie Keigel's gaze flickered.

'I'm not here to judge, Ms Keigel. Or accuse. Or get you in trouble. I work in insurance, not law enforcement. I'm only interested in understanding the circumstances surrounding Mr Mester's death.' He paused for a moment before adding, 'Did you buy them yourself or were they a gift?'

Greg let the silence stretch and stretch.

'A gift.' The words, when they came, were so low as to be barely audible.

'And can you confirm for me how you met him?'

'On the internet. Through a website called MaySeptember dotcom.' She allowed herself a faint smile. 'The "S" in "September" is a dollar sign, so you get the picture.'

Greg didn't. Not until he remembered something Lynn Spargo – the real Lynn Spargo – had told him.

'MaySeptember dotcom is a website for, er, sugar daddies?' He was grateful to be a so-called person of color. Otherwise, his furious blushing would have been out there for the whole world to see. He was ex-GRU. Why this particular aspect of the human condition made him uncomfortable when so much else did not was a mystery for another time. He tried to concentrate on what Julie Keigel was saying.

'Sugar daddies and sugar babies, yes.' Her voice had regained its former strength. 'I wanted to meet someone solvent to ease the pain of law school and Alan fit the bill. Plus, he was really, really nice.' Julie's eyes glittered with unshed tears. 'I had no idea he was in so much pain.'

'What makes you say that?'

'You don't jump from the back balcony of your luxury penthouse if you're feeling good about yourself, do you?'

'I take it, then, he gave no outward sign of being unhappy or depressed?'

'Not when he was with me. He just liked to have a good time. Go to nice places, eat good food, have some laughs, you know? He was a great guy to be with.'

Greg nodded, imagining the two of them together. Having fun, keeping it light. Not the sort of relationship where there'd be deep, meaningful conversations about Alan Mester's ex-wife. Little wonder, then, that Lynn Spargo's business card had sparked no hint of recognition.

'When did you last see him alive?'

'The weekend before.' A tear ran down her cheek, flawless skin making it look strangely beautiful. She waved vaguely at one of her bookshelves. 'He'd been on a business trip to LA. He came out here with a bunch of files, and then we headed off to a cottage he'd rented in Mohican State Park.'

'And he didn't come across as tense, anything like that?'

Much to Greg's surprise, Julie giggled.

'Oh, he was tense all right. That's why he came to see me. He was a lot less tense when he left.'

More invisible blushing.

'And when did you learn he'd passed away?'

'The following Thursday. It was on the news.'

'What did you do then?'

'I drove into Pittsburgh and cleaned all my stuff out of his apartment.' A rueful glance at the Whole Foods bag. 'Almost all my stuff.'

'Why?'

'Why do you think? The guy was on the *news*. I didn't want anyone finding out I was his girlfriend, know what I mean? Can you imagine what people would say if it got out that a sixty-year-old man was seeing a second-year Stayard law student? It'd be the end of me.' She leaned forward on the sofa, as if willing him to understand. 'I don't come from money, Mr, er . . .'

'Call me Lynn.'

'I don't come from money, Lynn. I grew up on a small farm in rural Idaho with five siblings. I'm the only one who's gotten out, and my family needs me to be successful, to send money back home, so we don't lose the farm, and so everyone there can have a life that's not just one bad break away from Welfare.

'Getting into Stayard was the golden ticket. I'm doing well at school. I'm the chair of the Federalist Society, and I've got a summer associateship at a big New York law firm. I am *set*. My family will be OK. Unless this sugar-daddy crap gets out. Then it's over. No school honors, no big-paying job. *You* might not judge me, but the rest of the freakin' world sure as hell will. And I can't afford that. I can't.'

'Then you can't afford to lie to me, do you understand that?'

'I'm not lying.'

'Someone visited Mr Mester in the early hours of Wednesday morning. He let them up to his apartment and then he walked them down to their car.'

'It wasn't me. I wasn't even in town that day.'

'So who were you arguing with outside Seaford Court at five p.m. on the Tuesday?'

Julie was not a person of color. It was an easy thing to see the blood draining from her face.

'I don't know what you're talking about.'

'The doorman, Julie. The doorman *saw* you.' He leaned forward, elbows on knees. 'Look. I work in insurance. I'm paid to be discreet. But I don't *have* to be. Don't make me spell it out for you.'

For the first time, Julie's eyes left his face. Her gaze skittered around the room as if seeking some way out. Finding none, she slumped back on the sofa.

'Fuck you, Lynn. Fuck *you*. This is none of your business.'

'I'm afraid it is.'

'If you must know, I came into town to see Alan, Tuesday afternoon. I got a text to say he was running late and so I was waiting for him by the entrance when an ex-boyfriend caught up with me, wanting to get back together.' Julie rolled her eyes. 'As if.'

'And does this boyfriend have a name?

'William – Bill – Marbury.'

'And where can I find Mr Marbury?'

'Thailand, at a guess.' Julie was wearing a thin smile. 'He was going backpacking. Wanted me to go with him. Like I was going to drop out of law school for that guy.'

'And did you wait for Alan?'

'No. I was too upset. Alan doesn't – didn't – like drama, or sad faces. I wasn't in the mood to be the gal he wanted to spend time with, so I figured I'd make myself scarce. I made some excuse about a last-minute assignment and bailed.'

'If you'll excuse me asking, why were you waiting in the first place?'

'Sorry?'

'I mean if you were in this, er' – Greg tried not to stumble over the words – 'sugar-daddy arrangement, why didn't you have a keycard to the penthouse? It would have been more discreet, surely, than hanging around on the sidewalk?'

'He was going to get me one. He just hadn't gotten around to it.' She made a face. 'I'm not naïve, Lynn. Alan was a nice, nice man. But he was a long-time user of MaySeptember. I'm guessing it was a lot of trouble to get a brand-new card for a building like his and that maybe he'd not gotten the old one back from my, um, predecessor. Like, maybe they'd had a falling-out and he couldn't tell me about it.'

Greg mulled this over for a moment.

'Any idea who this woman might be?'

'Sorry, no.'

'And Alan really was nice to you?'

'Oh, yes.' Julie smiled with what looked like genuine affection. Jarring, in the context of such a nakedly transactional arrangement.

'He would give you gifts from time to time, no doubt?'

'Sure.'

'Including, say, a pair of sapphire earrings?'

Julie hesitated, her expression guarded.

Greg found himself smiling.

'Look, if he gave you something as a gift, it's yours. The insurance company isn't interested in trying to get it back. We just want to clear up the paperwork around Alan's death.'

A sigh of relief.

'Yeah. He gave me a pair. Months ago, not long after we started seeing each other.

'Did he ever give you anything to match – a necklace, something like that?'

'No.'

'How about a ruby necklace?'

'Definitely not.' Julie's laugh was a short, dismissive bark.

'Not your color, I take it?'

'Exactly.'

'Fair enough.' Greg looked around the room, taking in the books on the shelves, interspersed here and there with the odd box file.

'Alan paid the rent on this place, I imagine.'

'Yes. There's no way I could afford it otherwise.'

'Do you know how far in advance?' He asked the question gently, without malice.

'Through the end of next month. After that . . .'

She left the rest unsaid. Greg had little doubt that Julie Keigel would soon be back on May$eptember.com.

'OK. I think we're about done here. I'll need your number in case anything comes up.'

'All right.'

'Oh. One last thing.'

'What?'

'You said the last time he came out here to see you, he brought a bunch of files. Did he do that often?'

'Not often but occasionally.' She waved a hand at the nearest of the shelved box files.

'Do you know why?'

'Keep them away from prying eyes is what he said.'

'As they *are* his property, I'd better take them back with me.'

'Knock yourself out.'

Greg had to make a couple of trips to the car. In truth, he had no interest in any of them, except one.

The one labeled QUARRY MOUNT CAPITAL LLC.

6:48 P.M.

'Who is it?'

The voice coming out of the speaker was female and slightly wary.

'My name's Greg, from Generica House. Does Brad Leclerc live here? If so, I have his school ID tag. He left it behind yesterday.'

There was a slight pause.

'Well, in that case, you'd better come in. And thank you!'

The wrought-iron gates that guarded the driveway to the Leclerc family's palatial Sewickley Heights home swung open on silent hinges. Greg drove up to a front door that was already opening as he arrived. As it did so, it revealed a tall, slightly stout woman standing in the threshold. She wore a broad, friendly smile. The mother, Greg presumed.

The smile flickered as Greg stepped out of his car.

'Oh,' she said. 'I was expecting someone . . . never mind.' The smile returned. 'Thank you so much for bringing Brad's ID back. I swear, that boy would leave his head behind if it wasn't screwed on.' She held out an expectant hand.

Greg removed Brad Leclerc's stolen ID from his pocket.

'As I've driven all the way out here,' he said, 'would you mind terribly if I had a quick word with Clyde? It won't take a minute.'

The slightest of hesitations. Greg held his breath.

'Of course. Do come in. *Clyde! Someone to see you!*'

He was shown into a small front room that looked out on to an enormous porch. The landscape beyond was shadowed in darkness.

He caught sound of a brief, whispered conversation on the other side of the door.

'Who is it?'

'I don't know. Some Black guy called Greg.'

The door opened.

'Hello there,' Clyde said, stepping into the room. Greg rose from his seat and stifled a frisson of surprise. Subconsciously, he'd been expecting to meet the snarling creature from the newscast. But this version of Clyde Leclerc, ensconced in the comfort of his own home, wore a pleasant, mild-mannered expression. Tall, like his son, he had run slightly to fat, but not so much that most would notice. Even though it was a Sunday, he was dressed in a business casual uniform of navy-blue polo shirt and khaki slacks. 'I'm afraid you have me at a disadvantage. Do I know you?'

'Not really. I've already spoken to JoAnn Harwood and Fatima Davis. I'm here to make a few inquiries about Alan Mester.'

Clyde Leclerc's good-natured expression vanished in an instant.

'Get out of my house.'

Greg rose, as if preparing to leave.

'Of course. If that's what you wish. But I thought you might want to give your side of the story before any of this gets to the police.'

'What side of the story? What police?'

Apart from a slightly raised eyebrow, Greg was careful to keep his expression neutral. He could almost hear the gears whirring in Clyde Leclerc's head. Lubricated, Greg hoped, by a healthy degree of curiosity.

'Fine,' he said at last, with an audible sigh. He took a seat across from Greg and sat down. Greg followed suit. 'Tell me what all this is about. The man committed suicide.'

'Maybe. Maybe not. I have the benefit of some rather vivid descriptions of the exco meeting. By the end of it, Alan Mester was threatening you.'

'You got that right.'

'And you were angry enough to kill him.'

The sound that came out of Clyde Leclerc's mouth was something between a bark and a laugh.

'Total BS.'

'Not if he was threatening to bring up Susan Tan.'

Clyde's eyes narrowed.

'How the hell do you know about that?'

'Or that you were putting money into Randy Davis's dodgy payday loan business.'

'There's nothing "dodgy" about payday loans. They're perfectly legal and they provide a service to people who need it.'

'Perhaps. But they're not legal in Pennsylvania, clever games with Native American reservations notwithstanding. Sexual harassment *and* payday loans? If Alan had followed through, he could have made it pretty hot for you, I imagine. Hot enough that people wouldn't want to do business with you anymore.'

Clyde just laughed.

'Then you don't know much about business, Mr, er . . . I'm afraid I didn't catch your last name.'

'Greg will do.'

'Well, *Greg*, the sort of people I work with aren't going to be worried by liberal claptrap nonsense about high-interest lending. And no DA is going to bother going after someone like me. Randy? Maybe. *Maybe.* I'm just the money guy, and we're too much trouble for a bunch of low-rent lawyers looking for easy convictions. And as for . . . for that woman, it's all water under the bridge. No one cares anymore.'

'You've heard of Me Too, I take it?'

'Oh, for the love of . . . I did not kill that a-hole. I didn't even know where he lived until I heard on the news that he took a swan dive off his own balcony. And good riddance. Man was a goddamn Marxist-Leninist.'

Greg struggled to keep a straight face.

'I'm also thinking the DA might have an easier time going after you if Randy laid it out for them. He can't have taken kindly to you threatening to withdraw funding unless his wife changed her vote at the exco.'

'Oh, that,' Clyde chortled, his face cracking open with amusement. 'Randy won't care about that at all. He was *in* on it.'

'I'm sorry?'

'Between the two of them, Mester and Principal Ferguson were driving the Edgeworth School into the ground. Diversity this, diversity that, diluting the school's student body with low-quality admissions, watering down the curriculum so those same sub-par students could – quote, unquote – *thrive*. And with Brian gone and Fatima off the reservation, there was no way to stop them. Randy was as sick of it as I was. We were on the same side. He was always going to get his money.' More laughter. 'But Fatima didn't need to know that, did she? She likes her creature comforts, that one. All Randy had to do to get her to change her vote was tell her the gravy train was about to hit the buffers. Wish we'd thought of it earlier. Would have put an end to this woke nonsense years ago.'

Greg could feel the rapid blinking of his eye. That Randy Davis could do that to his own wife struck him as beyond the pale. The man was as unattractive on the inside as out. For Fatima Davis, Alan Mester must have come as sweet relief.

'And where were you, exactly, when Alan Mester died?'

'Where do you think? It was the middle of the night. I was here at home, with my family.'

'A house this size? It'd be easy enough to come and go without anyone noticing.'

'Sure. But no one did.'

'Fair enough. Alan threatens you; you say it wasn't enough to make you kill him, but it *was* enough for you to threaten him back, wasn't it?'

'What? No.'

'What did you mean when you told him you knew about the OJ?'

'I have no idea what . . . Oh. Wait.' Puzzlement was replaced by an amused smile. 'Not *the* OJ. *D*-OJ. The Department of Justice. Alan Mester was in trouble all the way up to his commie neck. He was going to—'

Clyde stopped talking. Glanced toward the door as if he expected someone to be standing there.

'Who did you say you were working for again?'

'I didn't.'

Greg was about to explain when he noticed the blood draining from Clyde Leclerc's face. The banker wiped the palms of his hands against his khakis, the movement awkward and abrupt.

'Look, Greg, it was just empty words, OK? I don't really know anything. Nothing that would hold up in court, you understand what I'm saying? And neither me nor my family want any sort of trouble.'

Greg would have enjoyed the man's terror if he hadn't been so puzzled by it.

Clyde jumped to his feet.

'Let me see you out,' he said. 'There'll be no trouble,' he repeated. 'No trouble at all.'

10:01 P.M.

Greg stretched out on his living-room sofa. Surrounded by books he had opened but failed to read, he turned on the television. He was expecting to watch the local news, only to find that he'd accidentally tuned in to some documentary channel. The subject looked macho and military, with lots of guns, uniforms and running around with an imposing bass voiceover. Greg turned down the volume till it was little more than background but didn't bother to change the dial. He was, he decided, too distracted for the news, anyway.

What was Clyde Leclerc so scared of all of a sudden? The question, which had been bouncing around Greg's head all evening, was freighted with annoyance. Not at Clyde: at himself. Younger Greg – *Grigoriy* – would have seen Clyde's terror for what it was: a tool to be used. He would have leaned in to Clyde's fear, would have used it to extract information, not least on what it was that had made the man so jumpy.

Instead, he'd allowed his surprise at Clyde Leclerc's sudden change in demeanor to get the better of him, to give Clyde space to usher him out of the house, albeit with a level of obsequiousness that was almost laugh-out-loud funny.

On the television, a military assault weapon was being broken down into its component parts, the commentator rumbling on about gas pressure.

Clyde had only gotten spooked when he'd started talking about the Department of Justice. Greg knew enough about the Department of Justice to be aware that it did a little bit of pretty much everything, like a ministry of internal affairs. And one of those things, the thing that seemed most likely in the circumstances, was criminal prosecutions. The DOJ could put you away for a very long time, even by American standards.

Could it be that simple? That Alan Mester was going to be prosecuted by the DOJ, and Clyde Leclerc, his sworn enemy, had somehow found out about it? Had the knowledge that it was all about to come into the open, the knowledge that his gilded life of mistresses and sugar babies and monied influence was coming to an end, driven him to jump?

It fit, mostly. Alan Mester had been alone in his apartment when he died. And he didn't strike Greg as someone who would do well in prison.

But it didn't explain why Clyde Leclerc was frightened.

And apart from Clyde Leclerc's say-so, there wasn't a shred of evidence that Alan Mester was being prosecuted for anything.

Unless you counted the documents Alan had filed away at Julie Keigel's apartment. He'd brought stuff there to keep it away from prying eyes, she'd said. And you didn't get more prying than the Department of Justice. The boxes Greg had taken from Stayard seemed to be full of spreadsheets for the most part, nothing he could easily understand. And even the box labeled QUARRY MOUNT CAPITAL LLC held little of interest. Spreadsheets relating mostly to real estate, so far as Greg could tell, including Julie Keigel's apartment, with bunches of numbers that looked like they might be rent payments, or mortgage payments, or both. There was a document called a certificate of formation for Quarry Mount Capital, and a password-protected thumb drive labeled STRUCTURES. There was nothing he could sink his teeth into.

The TV show had shifted from a computer simulation of soldiers storming a building to yet another weapon. A pistol this time.

'British elite forces,' the commentator was saying in his impressively deep voice, 'are among the best in the world. For close-in work, their weapon of choice is the Sig Sauer two-two-six pistol. This is ideal for close-quarter combat in hostage situations because the nine-millimeter round it fires will not pass through a target or a wall, minimizing the risk of unwanted casualties. The Sig—'

Greg was sitting bolt upright on the couch. Suddenly, everything made sense.

At least, if the structures on Alan Mester's thumb drive were what he thought they were.

He scrambled around looking for his phone. Dialed a number.

'Andrea?'

'This is she.'

'It's Greg Abimbola. I—'

'Mr Bimbo! I was just thinking about you. I was going to tell you tomorrow. I got the job! I got it!'

'I . . .' Greg felt his face broadening into a wide smile. 'You got the job? Congratulations! That's wonderful news. Wonderful. Which makes you fully qualified for the task I have in mind.'

'Which is what, exactly?'

'I need you to break into one of Alan Mester's thumb drives for me. It's password protected.'

'No problem. At least, I doubt it's a problem. Guy was old. He probably uses the same password for everything. When do you want it done?'

'Now would be good.' The European in Greg flinched inwardly as he said it. It was too demanding. Andrea had a life, and it was late on a Sunday evening.

'Sure,' she said, without a moment's hesitation. 'Can you bring it to the school?'

'Absolutely. Er, what are you doing at Calderhill?'

'Working. On my last ever assignment. You ever try writing something in a rowhouse full of people, Mr Bimbo? It's a freaking nightmare. It's nice and quiet over here. I can get shit done. And when this shit is done, I am done with school for good.'

'I'll be there in fifteen minutes.'

Dobrygin's Nissan Sentra was still parked in the street outside. It had been there when he had finally made it home, the GRU man's only sure way of reacquiring him. Greg wondered once again if Dobrygin understood he'd been given the slip or was simply putting it down to bad luck.

Then he decided that, one way or the other, he didn't care. This whole thing was going to be over soon enough. And when it was done, he'd either be dead or not. He got into his car, started up the engine and headed to Calderhill.

He could see Dobrygin's vehicle in his rearview mirror. Greg made no attempt to shake him. He was a teacher heading to school on a late-night errand, someone retrieving misplaced homework or prepping his classroom for the week to come. Nothing to see here.

Unless you counted the mode of entrance.

It felt weird to be standing in the school loading bay, facing the heavy steel door to the custodian's room.

So many memories.

He rapped on the cold metal. Moments later, it swung open on silent hinges. A puff of warm air wrapped itself around him.

'Come on in, Mr Bimbo. Welcome to my office.'

With the school boiler rumbling away in the background and illumination provided by an adjustable desk lamp, the custodian's room looked surprisingly cozy. Andrea had set up camp on the worn cloth sofa, where a laptop, a couple of textbooks and a battered writing pad lay waiting on the cushions.

'See what you can do with this,' Greg said, handing over the thumb drive.

Andrea plugged it into her laptop. It took no more than a few keystrokes before she broke into a broad grin.

'See? What did I tell you? Old people.'

The screen in front of her came alive with information.

'Scroll down,' Greg ordered. 'There. Stop.'

Now it was his turn to grin.

'Can I borrow your notepad?'

'Uh, sure.'

Greg scribbled frantically on a blank page. Realizing he was writing in Russian, he scratched it out and started again. He handed the finished product to Andrea, whose eyes gleamed with intrigue. She scanned Greg's scrawled, angular writing, lips quirking.

'Can you call and tell them this, *exactly* as I've written it down?' he asked.

'I can read, can't I?'

A tool sitting on one of the shelves caught his eye.

'And do you mind if I borrow that?'

Andrea followed the direction of his gaze.

'What do you want a monkey wrench for?'

MONDAY, THE TWENTIETH

4:25 A.M.

Greg played with the hood of his hoodie, checking for the third or fourth time that his face was obscured. A nervous tic. He forced himself to stop. He pretended to consult his cellphone instead, just some early-morning jogger standing on the steep slope of 44th Street, waiting for his running mate. He had no doubt he looked suspicious. But not, he hoped, suspicious enough to draw the attention of a police cruiser.

The monkey wrench lay heavy in the hoodie's front pocket.

A car rolled slowly down the hill toward Butler Street. Greg distracted himself by wondering if it belonged to a shift worker or a party animal. Mystery unsolved, the car reached the intersection with Butler and turned right, vanishing from sight. The street returned to deserted silence.

Seeking reassurance, Greg's gaze crossed the street to where Dobrygin's Nissan Sentra stood parked against the curb. All was as it should be.

He tried to breathe a little easier. Fingers drifted up toward the edge of his hood. He forced them back down with a small hiss of irritation.

He was too old for this.

Beside him, the front door of a rowhouse with no front yard became limned with light. There was a rattling of keys in the lock. The door opened. Major Oleg Dobrygin of the GRU stepped on to the sidewalk, gaze fixed on his automobile, ready to begin his morning surveillance.

Greg crashed the monkey wrench into the back of his head.

4:53 A.M.

'Dig,' Greg said, tossing Dobrygin the shovel.

Dobrygin staggered slightly as he caught the implement, his feet slipping on the graveled floor of the safehouse basement. Greg didn't think he was faking. The man looked dangerously pale. Concussed, in all probability. In other circumstances, Greg would have called an ambulance.

In other circumstances.

'Or what, you'll shoot me?' Dobrygin tried to glare at him, but the gaze was watery and unfocused.

'Yes.' Greg was conscious of the weight of Dobrygin's service weapon in his right hand. He didn't need to look at it to know that the barrel was pointed squarely at Dobrygin's chest.

He couldn't *afford* to look at it, not now that he'd handed his prisoner a sharp-edged weapon. Concussed or not, Dobrygin would slice him apart if his attention wavered for more than an instant.

It was a risk he was prepared to take.

With a sigh of resignation, Dobrygin dug the shovel's blade into the pebbly earth. The blade turned gray with concrete dust, the grating noise of the thing unnaturally loud in Greg's ears.

The basement was almost exactly as he remembered it. Scattered construction equipment; a workbench covered in either hand tools or implements of torture depending on who was using them; a video camera on a tripod.

The workbench, though, had a handful of new additions.

'Why did you kill Morosov?' Greg asked.

The grating noise stopped for a moment. Began again.

'I don't know what you're talking about.'

Greg allowed himself a small smile.

'You know, while you were out cold, I thought long and hard about removing your shoes. It would make you easier to control, but also harder for you to dig. So I left them on because I don't have all day. I did, however, remove your watch. Or should I say, *Morosov*'s watch.'

Dobrygin's only response was a hiss of anger.

'If you were going to steal it, you should have taken the trouble to get rid of the engraving on the back. Those initials aren't yours, they're his.'

'Fuck you.' Dobrygin dug deeper into the earth. Greg's finger tightened on the trigger. He thought for a moment that Dobrygin was reckless enough, angry enough, to hurl a shovelful of soil in his general direction and hope for the best.

Dobrygin emptied his load on to the small pile at the side of the hole.

'I thought it was a weird coincidence, when I saw you with it at the Ross Park Mall, that you and Morosov had the same taste in large, expensive watches. But then again, they're portable and easy to turn into cash at short notice. And for a corrupt—'

'Go screw yourself.'

'For a corrupt GRU officer, portable assets are always a good thing to have if you need to head for the exits at short notice. So then I got to thinking that it wasn't a weird coincidence at all, just a side effect of you and Morosov being crooked.'

Dobrygin's grip on the shovel's long handle tightened.

'But *then* . . . then I got to thinking about your surveillance photos.'

The grip loosened in surprise.

'The photos told you nothing. There was nothing to tell.'

'Yeah. I thought so, too. At first. But then I thought about how you got made in the Omni William Penn lobby. How the marshals kept you there until after Morosov was escorted out the Grant Street entrance.'

'So?'

'So, the photos don't show that, do they? They show Morosov being escorted out like you said, and the original two hanging about while they left.'

Dobrygin was frowning now. He leaned on the shovel.

'I don't get it.'

'Keep digging. Don't you see? If you'd been detained by the marshals like you say, then those photos wouldn't – couldn't – exist. You told me you got made in the lobby during the handover, and the marshals kept you there until *after* Morosov left. So, not only were you unable to follow, you certainly wouldn't have been so stupid as to attempt to take pictures while you were the object of their attention. But the photos show Morosov *actually leaving*, not to mention two very laid-back US marshals who clearly had no idea you were there. You're better at this job than you let on.'

'And what if I am? What business is it of yours?'

'Not so fast, Oleg. I said you were better than you let on. I didn't say you were actually any good.'

Dobrygin shifted suddenly and dangerously on his feet before pulling himself back, his face almost purple with rage. Greg's heart hammered loudly in response, gearing up for an assault from the bigger, younger man that didn't quite come. The two of them faced each other in silence. Both painfully aware that the only reason Greg Abimbola was still alive was the fact that it was Greg, not Dobrygin, holding the gun.

'Keep digging,' Greg said again, gratified that his voice sounded so much calmer than his cardiovascular system. He waited till the sound of soil scraping metal returned to something approaching a steady rhythm before continuing.

'Of course, having figured out you were lying about what happened at the Omni, the question becomes "Why?" Why lie about it and make yourself look like an even bigger idiot than Polukhin thought you to be? You'd already told him you'd lost Morosov. Then, under pressure, you "confessed" to me that you'd lost him in an even more embarrassing way than not keeping up with traffic. Why would a man like you deliberately make himself look like a fool twice over?

'Because the truth is worse, obviously. And the truth in this case is that you didn't lose Morosov at all. You followed him from the Omni William Penn and killed him.'

'This is absurd,' Dobrygin said, though Greg fancied he could detect a quaver of uncertainty in the man's voice. Dobrygin leaned heavily on the shovel, using a dusty hand to wipe the sweat beading his face. Dirt smeared itself on his forehead and cheeks.

'Here's the clincher, though. I'm lying on the couch yesterday, watching TV, and there's this stupid, macho American program about guns, all sorts of guns. Including pistols used by the special forces. That's when I knew it was you.'

'Bullshit.'

'Not at all. You've been following me for weeks, yes? You know

I've been visited on a number of occasions by a Pittsburgh homicide detective.'

'Of course I do.' Dobrygin allowed himself a coarse laugh. 'A bit plain for my taste, but whatever floats your boat.'

'I'll tell her you said that, so she can make you pay. But only if you live through *this*, obviously. Which is totally up to you.'

With a slow, deliberate insolence, Dobrygin stopped digging. He leaned over the hole at his feet and spat into it. He'd dug out a seven-foot trench, maybe a couple of feet wide and the same deep.

The dimensions of a shallow grave.

'You think I'm scared by any of this, you English fuck? You haven't got the balls.'

'Really?'

'Yeah, really. You know why we still have an empire, an empire that stretches across twelve fucking time zones, when you don't?'

'Enlighten me.'

'Because the English got soft. We did not. A Russian? Sure, a Russian – or an American, if he were the right sort – would make me dig my own grave, lie down in it, and shoot me in the forehead. He wouldn't think twice. But you?' Dobrygin shook his head contemptuously. 'You're English and spineless. Forgive me: I said the same thing twice by mistake.' He practically spat out the words. 'You'll do nothing. You won't even hand me over to the police because, if you do, if you even *think* about it, Polukhin will make what very few hours of life you have left a living hell. Digging your own grave in somebody's basement will be the very least of it.'

'Huh.' Greg was annoyed with himself for letting out the sound. And the note of surprise that went along with it.

Polukhin had lied. Of course Polukhin had lied. To everybody. Including Oleg Dobrygin. Dobrygin had no idea who he was. He thought Greg was a local asset, some ex-pat Brit with a soft spot for Russia, maybe. Or an exploitable weakness. Someone who'd been dragged off the street because he needed a scare: a reminder that once you agree to work for the GRU, saying no is not an option.

'Huh.' He said again. Deliberately this time. Thoughtfully.

Dobrygin's eyes, mistaking what they were seeing, crinkled with amusement.

'So you see,' he said, 'there's nothing you can do to me at all. This? All this is just a charade.'

'Keep digging.' The snap in Greg's voice wiped any trace of

humor from Dobrygin's face. 'We'll get to the absolute fucking enormity of your mistakes in a minute. Where was I? Oh, yes. The Pittsburgh homicide detective. She was good enough to let me have sight of the ballistics report into Morosov's death. He was shot with a nine-millimeter. What their forensics guy called a "Mak PB" round.'

Dobrygin was staring at Greg with narrowed eyes.

'You and I both know what the guy meant by "Mak PB", don't we? *Makarov* PB, the GRU's weapon of choice, either with or without a silencer. Your gun. The very gun I'm holding in my hand. If I were to give this thing to Acting Lieutenant Lev, it'd be a perfect match for the bullets you put in Morosov, wouldn't it?'

'*Pah!*' Dobrygin spat into the trench once again. And then smiled, lazily confident. 'What does it matter? You can't touch me. You can't hand me over to the police. Not if you want to live. I shot Morosov. There. I said it. Happy now? Move on already.'

Greg hadn't realized he'd been holding his breath.

'Why, though? How?'

'Really?' Dobrygin looked pained.

'Really.'

'Suit yourself.' The sigh that followed was long and theatrical. 'I didn't lose Morosov when the marshals turned him over to his new handlers. I saw them leave the hotel, skipped back to my car and was able to acquire them on Grant Street just as they pulled away. Big, black SUV: the type with armored doors, bullet-proof glass and low-profile tires. Intelligence, not law enforcement. They leave town but keep to the back roads, heading east into the Penn Hills. I've no idea how far they're going. Maybe all the way to DC, maybe to some safe house in the woods where they can work him over. And I never get to figure it out because the idiot driver runs the low-profile tires over a fucking pothole and bursts one. Obviously, they have to stop and fix it. So I drive past and park out of sight a couple of hundred meters up the road.'

Dobrygin was leaning on the shovel again, eyes staring into the unfocused distance.

'So, I'm waiting for them to fix the tire and come driving by, when all of a sudden there's a shitload of screaming and shouting. And I'm thinking something has gone wrong and maybe it's an opportunity to spring our guy. So I run back toward the SUV and see Morosov. *Somehow* the bastard had got loose and is out of the car.'

Greg could feel a smile of reluctant admiration tugging at his lips. Morosov and his big, chunky watch. The bullshit escape tool. Maybe it wasn't bullshit after all.

Or maybe the Americans had gotten sloppy.

'Anyhow, I come over the top of a rise and the female escort is on the ground, completely out of it, and Morosov is swinging a tire iron at the male. He connects, big time, so the male goes down as well. And now Morosov is leaning over the guy, looking for keys to the SUV. That's when I call out to get his attention. Something like, "Hey, man. Over here."'

A brief expression of regret flitted across Dobrygin's face.

'I've been in country too fucking long. I spoke in English, not Russian. And now it turns out Morosov thinks I'm some kind of American backup, and he's not looking for keys at all but the guy's goddamn *gun*. He pulls it out and fires at me.' Dobrygin shook his head, as if not quite believing what he was about to say. 'I didn't think, I just reacted. Pulled my gun, fired twice, hit him both times. Man is dead as a nit.'

Greg, like Morosov, would have been unable to hit anyone in the circumstances Dobrygin was describing. Certainly not with a pistol. But Polukhin had said it himself. Firearms was the one thing Dobrygin was good at.

He's an excellent shot, by the way. He might kill me too, if you try to use me as a shield, but that won't stop him pulling the trigger. Not much of a thinker that one.

What a monumental cock-up.

'And then what?'

Dobrygin scowled at him.

'What do you think? I cleaned up my own mess. The escorts were in no condition to stop me. I tossed Morosov into their SUV, drove up the road on three wheels, transferred him to the trunk of my own vehicle and hightailed it out of there. I removed his ID, waited till evening and tossed him off the side of the Sixty-Second Street bridge. Job done. Nothing to tie me to the body, even if it was found. Water would mess up the forensics and no one would ever figure out what happened. Except for you.' A wolfish grin. 'And there's fuck all you can do about it.'

'Your grave isn't deep enough,' Greg said coldly. 'Dig.'

'Oh, for fuck's sake, Abimbola, give it up already.'

'Dig!'

'All right, all right.' Dobrygin returned to his labors. Slowly.

But, slowly or not, the piles of displaced soil were starting to get quite high. The earth on the end of the shovel was dark now, and fibrous with rootlets. There was no sign of the concrete dust that had permeated the upper layers.

'Do you want to know what else is bothering me, Oleg?'

'Not really.'

'Why you're in Pittsburgh at all.'

'To bring you in for a . . . conversation. The colonel general's orders. Then, to keep an eye on you. What do you think Polukhin's going to say when I tell him about this nonsense?'

'No,' Greg said, ignoring Dobrygin's question. 'That's not right. You were already here. Polukhin said so. This house, the one you might end up buried in, has been rented out for close to two years. And Polukhin had no idea where Morosov had been until his people acquired him in DC. Even then, the GRU didn't know where Morosov was returning to until he boarded a plane to Pittsburgh. And yet, there you were, ready and waiting with your long lens the moment he reached Arrivals.

'Or did you follow Morosov to Reagan National, see him board the flight and then commandeer an American fighter jet to get here before him?'

Dobrygin's eyes narrowed at the sarcasm, but he said nothing. He continued to dig, slow and deliberate.

'And here's the other thing that's bugging me. You're here on your own. I took the trouble to stake this place out before I paid you this little, uh, *visit.* The only person who ever came in and out was you. I also took the liberty of looking around while you were out cold. There's no one else living here.

'You don't have a partner. I don't care what the budgetary situation is back home. There's no way GRU would send you on an extended mission to the States without someone to keep an eye on you – and you them. Which tells me that this little sojourn of yours is completely off the books. Just you and the colonel general, am I right?'

'Leave it alone, Abimbola. That is, if you know what's good for you.'

'It's too late for that. I already know you killed Alan Mester. You've been a very busy man, Oleg.'

The hole was deep enough now that Dobrygin had to climb

out of it. He did so, apparently unafraid of the gun still trained on him.

'You are a fucking imbecile.'

'But I'm not wrong, am I?'

Dobrygin just glared at him.

'I know you were in Mester's apartment, Oleg. I *know*. Like I told you, I've had time to wander about this house of yours. You really do have sticky fingers, don't you?' Greg stepped to one side, so that Dobrygin could get a good look at the items Greg had added to the workbench: the fruits of Greg's comprehensive inspection of the safe house. 'It's not just Morosov's watch. It's Mester's very expensive smartphone. And then there are these necklaces – two of them – from Arecas Design on Walnut Street. Necklaces that I just happen to know were intended as presents for two of the women in Mester's life. Sapphires for a lady named Julie Keigel, and rubies for one called Fatima Davis. You pocketed the stones and left the boxes behind when you murdered Mester. A nice bonus, seeing that the only thing you really had to get your hands on was Mester's hard drive. Which, as you can see, is also here.' He gave the hard drive a proprietary tap with his free hand. 'You replaced it with a brand-new one, years younger than his actual computer, and hoped no one would notice.' He shook his head ruefully. 'Young people, Oleg. *Young* people notice.' He looked at Dobrygin curiously. 'Why didn't you destroy the hard drive? That was the job, wasn't it? Kill Mester, retrieve the information on his computer and destroy it, yes?'

'You are so dead.'

'Because I know what Mester knew?'

'You know nothing.'

'Oh, no, sunshine. I know a lot. I know, for instance, that this house, the one you're going to die in if you're not very careful, is owned by a company called Quarry Mount Capital LLC. I also know that Quarry Mount Capital was run by Alan Mester, and that Quarry Mount Capital is a front for a whole bunch of shell companies – "structures", Alan called them – that are used to hide millions of dollars of dodgy money that comes from – wait for it – Russia. There's names, dates, places; everything an investigative journalist or prosecutor could possibly want. That's the information Alan had hidden away on the hard drive. The one you went to all that trouble to retrieve. Problem is, he'd copied it elsewhere, too. On to a thumb drive he'd hidden with one of his girlfriends. Probably as insurance, although, if so, it didn't work so well, did it?

'Of course, it might not have been for insurance. Maybe it was a homework assignment.'

Greg was very much enjoying the look of confusion on Dobrygin's face.

'You see, the other thing I know is that Alan Mester was being investigated by the US Department of Justice. I should have figured that out earlier, Oleg. Both Mester's wife and his doorman, when talking about the initial investigation, talked about the FBI, not just the police. Why would the Feds be interested in Mester's death? Unless, as they say here, he was a "person of interest". Or, more likely, someone who was *cooperating* with them. Not out of any sense of moral decency, you understand; he was just trying to save his own neck. I imagine the department would be very grateful for a file setting out in detail how a money-laundering scam is organized. They probably asked Mester to create one. If even I can understand it, imagine what a DOJ lawyer would do.'

Greg allowed a wry smile to appear on his face.

'You know, the person who finally put me on to this – some of this – got very scared in the telling of it. It was funny, really. If you'd been there, you'd have enjoyed it. A lot. Anyhow, I couldn't figure out what his problem was. Not until after I put two and two together.

'You see, I'd neglected to tell him who I was. I was just some Black guy who'd inveigled his way into his home on a Sunday night. I could have been anybody. And the only person who could have inspired this level of fear was the person whom Alan Mester was cooperating *against*.

'I don't know how much this person knows about Alan Mester's dealings, but he knew enough to be scared. And there's not much scarier than Russian organized crime. Unless it's Russian organized crime with off-the-books help from the GRU. This person had me tagged – can you believe this? – as Russian. Or someone working for them at least.'

'You're no Russian,' Dobrygin snorted. 'Anyone can see that just from looking at you.'

'Because I'm Black?'

Dobrygin didn't bother to reply.

'No matter. And there you have it. Two plus two. Alan Mester is laundering dodgy Russian money. Alan Mester is cooperating, or about to cooperate, with the Department of Justice. The GRU, who have been keeping an eye on him, discovered he was a rat, so you tossed him over his own balcony to shut him up. On the colonel general's orders, no doubt. And now you, Oleg Dobrygin, have a choice to make. Talk or die.'

'Talk to whom?'

'The local police.'

'Fuck off, Abimbola. I wonder how many pieces we can cut you into before you shuffle off for good. You should have quit with Morosov. It could have been our little secret. But this stuff? There's no way out for you now and you know it.'

'I could shoot you right here and pretend none of this ever happened.'

'You haven't the balls. You're a fucking schoolteacher, and an English one at that. The best you can hope to do now is run. And even if, by some fucking miracle, you managed to squeeze the trigger, you think Polukhin would be fooled for one second?'

'You need to think this through, Oleg.'

'Oh, believe me, I already have.'

Greg didn't say anything.

He started whistling, a small smile playing on his lips. Pretending to be lost in thought, he was watching Dobrygin closely. Enough to see the change in expression that flitted across his face.

'What?' he asked Dobrygin.

'Why are you whistling that stupid tune?'

'What stupid tune?'

'*V Lesu Rodilas Yolochka*. It's a holiday song for children. I can't think of anything more irritating. Or are you planning to torture me with music?'

'I'm so sorry, I didn't realize I was doing it,' Greg said apologetically. 'Although, honestly, it's the only tune I know how to whistle. My mother taught me.'

'Your mother?' Dobrygin's eyes widened in surprise. 'Your mother's Russian?'

'Oh, yes. I was born in Moscow.' Greg switched seamlessly into Russian. 'Maternity Hospital Number Twenty-Six. But we lived in Krasnogorsk at the time. You know Krasnogorsk?'

'But you're . . . Your father . . .'

Dobrygin stumbled into his native language as if he was speaking it for the first time. It never ceased to amaze Greg how hard it was for people to grasp the concept of mixed-race Russians. Or Brits, for that matter.

'Long story,' he said. The words came out more brusquely than he'd intended. 'The point I want you to understand, and understand very clearly, is that I am *not* English. I will have no hesitation in putting you in that hole you've just dug. *None.*' Russian was better for this, Greg decided. The words had an edge that English somehow lacked. 'Also, understand this. Colonel General Polukhin has *ordered* me to put you in that hole. The only question that need concern you is whether or not I'm going to follow those orders.'

Dobrygin stood frozen in shock.

'I don't understand,' he said, his voice barely above a whisper. For the first time, he looked like he should have all along. Fearful.

'Of course you don't,' Greg snapped. 'This is the part where we get to the absolute fucking enormity of your mistakes. Did it not strike you as odd that Vladimir Vladimirovich had you bring me in by force but then wouldn't let you lay a finger on me? Except for those gut punches. Which I neither forgive nor forget, by the way. Did it not worry you that he threw you out of the room when he and I had our little talk? That he just let me walk out of this place without even hiding its location?'

Dobrygin mumbled something.

'Speak up, idiot.'

'The colonel general keeps many things to himself.'

'Yes he fucking does. And one of the things he kept to himself – he didn't even bother telling *me* – is that he suspected you of killing Morosov. Otherwise, why not have you assist me in my investigations? Why keep you in the dark?

'My orders are to kill you, Oleg Petrovich. Slowly. Painfully. Then leave your dead body somewhere public.' He encompassed their surroundings with a wave of the hand: the damp, whitewashed walls, the pebbly ground, the makeshift grave. 'This will do, I think. By the time I'm finished with you, your corpse will be so mangled you'll make the major US newscasts and, from there, the world. You'll be famous, Oleg. Famous. A message to any other moron who thinks they can mess with the GR fucking U.'

The shovel in Dobrygin's hands was shaking.

'Your only sliver of hope – and believe me, a sliver is all it is right now – is that I hand you over to the cops instead.'

'Why would you do that?' There was a desperate hope in Dobrygin's tone. But skepticism, too. Sloppy or not, he was still an intelligence operative.

'Because I'm done with Polukhin. With this life. I want to be the Black English guy that teaches Russian, and sometimes French, to pampered, privileged white kids. Kids whose only experience of trauma is being given a used car for their seventeenth birthday instead of a new one. I want to get soft. And lazy. And maybe spineless.'

'The colonel general will kill you first.'

'Let me worry about the colonel general. Besides, if it turns out you're right and he does kill me, you'll still be alive to see it.'

A faint smile crossed Dobrygin's face.

'What do you want to know?'

'Not much. What triggered the decision to kill Mester?'

'You said it already. He'd started talking to the Feds. We'd bugged his phones, of course. He suspected as much and tried to be careful, but he fucked it up. He'd not told them much at the time, just a rough outline, but he was pulling together a dossier setting out all the details. We needed him dead, and the dossier removed, before he talked with them again. So.'

'And if it looked like a suicide, the Feds would simply assume he'd chosen death over cooperation and let it go?'

'Which is exactly what they did.'

'OK. I think I know how you got into Mester's apartment undetected but I'm not sure. How did you manage it?'

'That was easy. I used his mistress's keycard.'

'Which mistress?'

Dobrygin smiled.

'The young, blonde one. Julie Keigel. We knew enough about her to apply pressure when we needed to. She was terrified that her whoring with Mester would become public. The evening Mester died, I intercepted her outside his building and persuaded her to "lose" it.' Dobrygin's face twisted with contempt. 'She barely put up a fight.'

'And the video in the building? The fact it didn't work that night was no coincidence, I take it?'

'Of course not. We could jam it whenever we liked. Useful if someone from home was visiting Mester to discuss . . . business.'

'What time did you enter Mester's apartment?'

'About one a.m.'

Greg tried to keep his face expressionless as the timeline in his head finally began to make sense.

'And what happened next?'

'What do think happened next? I knocked him out cold before he could scream the place down, gagged and restrained him, searched the apartment, retrieved the hard drive, replaced it with a blank and tidied everything up. Then I *un*restrained him and tossed him into the parking lot. I was quick. He barely knew it was happening, believe me.'

Greg saw no reason to disabuse Dobrygin of his belief in his own mercy. The heartbeat monitor on Mester's watch told a very different story.

'Why'd you keep the hard drive? It should have been destroyed by now.'

'Leverage, Abimbola. Leverage. This whole op is off the books. There's no way I'm going down for this if the shit hits the fan back home. The drive makes me pretty much untouchable.'

'After you disposed of him, I take it you left the apartment?'

'Yes.'

'Immediately?'

'Pretty much. Eliminating the guy was the last order of business.'

'Did you return for any reason?'

'I'm not an idiot. Of course I didn't return. I carried out my mission. I left. The end.'

Greg was silent a moment, processing the implications.

'All right, Oleg. This is the story you're going to tell. You and Morosov, whom you know as Viktor Lavrov, are foot soldiers for the Russian mafia. You will refuse to explain whom you work for, and you don't know Lavrov or anything about him: you were put together by your anonymous bosses and sent to the States to kill Alan Mester for trying to rat them out. Of course, once Mester was dead, your bosses would need a new banker to handle the money, preferably in Pittsburgh, but they weren't sure who. They needed a middleman, someone they could use to access potential money launderers. Who better than a Russian-speaking school teacher, located by the simple expedient of using Google, with access to hundreds of rich parents, many of whom worked in finance? Lavrov's job was to poke around in the guy's life, find something compromising – or plant something compromising – and force him to cooperate. Once the teacher was on board, introductions could be made to likely targets – a banker having trouble paying the school fees, say – and the whole shady enterprise could get going again.

'That was the plan. Unfortunately, you and Lavrov had a drunken falling-out – over a woman, I imagine – and you shot him. You dumped him in the Allegheny, planning to tell your bosses that he'd done a runner. Then, using a keycard provided by those same bosses, you entered Mester's apartment and acted exactly as you've described, stealing some valuables and tossing the poor man over the balcony. With me so far?'

Dobrygin nodded. Then laughed.

'Your story has a big problem.'

'It does?'

'How are you going to get me in front of your police? I'm not going to walk in and confess, am I? And you can't possibly have caught me. You're pretending to be a schoolteacher. How did you track me down? And, even if you did, how did you subdue me?' The amusement on Dobrygin's face was real. 'I would break you like a twig.'

'Oh, Oleg. That's the very best part.' Greg's smile, he imagined, looked positively wolfish.

'Bullshit.' But there was something in Greg's demeanor that had unnerved him.

Greg walked toward his adversary, still smiling, still holding Dobrygin's pistol and still keeping a wary eye on the man's shovel.

'Having killed Lavrov, it fell to you to suborn the poor Russian teacher. Lacking Lavrov's subtlety, you bundled him off the street during his morning run and brought him here, intending to torture or otherwise terrify him into working for you. Everything was going swimmingly until you made the mistake of brandishing that gun of yours in his face.'

'What mis—'

Greg pulled the trigger. The basement exploded in fire and smoke.

6:07 A.M.

'*Nu vse, tebe pizda!*' Dobrygin screamed, hopping on one leg. He had to use the shovel for support. He switched to English. 'You shot me in the fucking foot, you moron!'

'Yes, I did,' Greg agreed calmly, in the same language. 'This is how you get caught. The teacher desperately grabs for your gun, there's a struggle, you get shot in the foot. Simple really.

'The teacher is a quick-thinking soul. He's Black, after all, and doesn't really trust the police. How's he to know they won't fuck him over in favor of the stand-up white guy?' He looked around melodramatically. 'My, my. What do we have here? A video camera? The sort the GRU uses to film confessions? What a coincidence.'

'You cannot be serious.'

'Deadly, old boy. The teacher wants you to tell your whole story on video. *Before* he calls the police. He really, really doesn't want to go to jail.'

'I'm bleeding out!'

'Don't be a baby, Oleg Petrovich. Plenty of time for a confession first.' Waving the gun, he pointed Dobrygin toward the chair that he, Greg, had once been duct-taped to. Greg adjusted the camera while the GRU man hobbled his way to the seat. 'Now, then,' he continued. 'You know the drill. It's not as if you haven't done this before, albeit from the other side. Ready?'

Dobrygin glared at him before nodding.

Greg pressed the RECORD button.

'My name is Oleg Petrovich Dobrygin. I make this confession of my own free will. Mr Gregory Abimbola has acted at all times in a totally lawful and adequate—'

'Stop. *Stop.*' Greg erased the recording. Favored Dobrygin with a gentle smile. 'This is my fault, Oleg, not yours. I told you to behave as if this was a forced confession for Russian state media. But it isn't. Our audience is American – the most sophisticated, the most demanding TV audience on the planet. It's got to look real to *them*. Understand? Less formality, please. And leave my behavior, lawful or otherwise, out of it. Just tell the story as if you were drunk in a bar, OK?'

'You are all kinds of asshole. You know that, right?'

'I do. Ready to go again?'

'Yes.'

Greg took a deep breath.

'Then once more, Oleg Petrovich. With feeling.'

4:16 P.M.

The rain was cold and hard and torrential. Greg, still in his hoodie and lacking any kind of overcoat, was soaked to the skin within seconds of leaving the police station.

He couldn't remember the last time he'd been so happy to be alive.

No one had beaten him, or made him dig his own grave, or shot him in the foot. He'd been treated with courtesy, allowed his phone call, provided with refreshments.

And it had been absolutely brutal.

Rachel Lev and her colleagues had come at him again and again, with variations of the same probing questions. Then the follow-ups, delivered kindly and with coffee. Didn't he think this was all too much of a coincidence? Could he understand why they were skeptical? Wouldn't it be better to tell them what really happened?

It had been far, far tougher – and longer – than he'd anticipated. But, somehow, the ramshackle story he'd thrown together in an unfinished basement on 44th Street held up. Or held up well enough that they'd had to let him go.

'Over here, Mr Bimbo!'

Andrea Velasquez was on the other side of the street, leaning out the window of her parked pickup truck. Dodging the early rush-hour traffic, he crossed the road and jumped into the passenger seat. Rain pounded on the roof.

'Thanks, Andrea. You're an angel. Did you do what I asked?'

'*Si, señor*. Your wish is my command.' Andrea's expression was arch. Greg pretended not to notice.

'And they're coming?'

'I think they're already there by now.' She peered curiously into the street. 'Where's your lady-cop friend?'

'I'm pretty sure lady cops and their male colleagues have access to a parking lot. She'll meet us there. Shall we go?'

Andrea started up the truck and eased into the traffic. Greg looked at her in surprise.

'What's up with your muffler?'

'I got it fixed, man. Now I got a job, I figured I could spare the expense.'

Greg nodded, reveling in the comparative absence of sound as they rumbled along Fifth Avenue and into the Seaford Court parking lot. Rachel Lev pulled up beside them. Sliding out of her vehicle, she stood under a rapidly raised umbrella and fixed him with an intense stare.

'You sure about this, Abimbola?' The tone was brusque, formal, with no hint of forgiveness.

Greg was surprised at how sad that made him feel. He pulled up the hood on his sweatshirt in a vain attempt to keep out the rain.

'Quite sure, detective. I wish I wasn't.'

If Dan Wurth, the doorman, was surprised to see Greg enter the building looking like a drowned rat and accompanied by a police officer, he gave no sign of it.

'I let her in like you asked,' he said, looking at Andrea. He showed them up to the penthouse and rapped on the door.

'It's open.'

Julie Keigel, unlike the doorman, was unable to mask her consternation.

'Mr Spargo. I wasn't expecting—'

'Mr Spargo?' Andrea and Detective Lev asked the question simultaneously. Only one of them sounded amused.

'I'm afraid you may be mistaken as to my real name.' With a rising sense of dismay, Greg realized that he wouldn't be able to sit down. If he did so, he would drip rainwater mixed with concrete dust and soil on to the white leather furniture. He stood awkwardly in the living-room doorway while Andrea and the detective, who'd flashed her badge on the way in, made themselves comfortable. Julie, after a moment's hesitation, marched to the opposite end of the room and stood with her back against the sliding glass doors that led to the front balcony. She folded her arms across her chest. Behind her, the storm continued to build in the gathering gloom. There was a distant flash of lightning.

To Greg, Julie Keigel looked like an angry Greek goddess, summoning the elements to strike him down.

'What do you want?' she asked, her voice harsh.

'To accuse you of being an accessory to murder.' Gritty water was trickling down the back of his neck.

'So,' Julie said, glaring at Andrea, who had the decency to look mildly embarrassed, 'when your so-called assistant called to say there was some insurance paperwork that needed filling in, *this* is what she meant? To drag me all the way from Ohio to face a bullshit murder accusation? I did not kill that man.'

'No. Not directly. But you were here.'

'That's a lie.' Julie wasn't looking at Greg; she was directing her remarks to Rachel Lev. The detective gazed back, her expression neutral.

'It's not a lie, Julie. Although I'm afraid you've told quite a few of them.'

'Like what?' Julie's cheeks carried a hint of color. A gust of wind-driven rain rattled the glass.

'Let's start with Tuesday afternoon, the last day of Alan Mester's life. You said you came to visit him and got into a row with an ex-boyfriend, Bill Marbury, at the entrance to this building.'

'I did.'

'A lie. Bill Marbury doesn't exist. Or if he does, that's not who you met with that day. You met a member of the Russian mafia, who blackmailed you into giving him your keycard. Though "your" is a loose term. It was originally the ex-wife's. Did you know that?'

Julie rolled her eyes.

'Who cares? I didn't give my keycard to a member of the Russian mafia. That's such a load of—'

'A member of the Russian mafia is currently a guest of the Pittsburgh police, so don't bother trying to deny it.'

He ignored Rachel Lev's sharp look. As Rachel Lev understood things, the mafia member who blackmailed Julie Keigel and the mafia member in custody were two different people.

Lies within lies in the service of truth.

Or if not truth, exactly, then justice.

'Well, what if I did?' Julie said, changing tack. 'What business is it of yours? I didn't know he was Russian. He sounded like a normal person to me. And if this mafia guy is in custody, then you *know* I didn't come up here. I couldn't. *The man had my keycard.*'

'True. I'll get back to that. When did you learn that Mr Mester had died?'

'You know when. I told you already. On the Thursday. It was on the news. I came out here and cleared away my stuff.'

'And how did you manage that, given that someone else had your keycard?'

'I . . . I got shown up.'

'And the doorman will vouch for you, will he?'

'Maybe he doesn't remember me. But that's what happened.' She glanced quickly at Rachel but couldn't quite meet her eye.

'I'm quite sure the doorman doesn't remember you because it didn't happen. And I know it didn't happen because that same doorman gave me copies of the security footage. When it comes to the Thursday, you are nowhere on those tapes, Julie. *Nowhere.*'

Julie Keigel flinched just as surely as if he'd struck her on the face.

'And yet we can all agree that you did clear out your stuff, minus a Louboutin pump, of course. So when, I wonder, did you manage that?'

'Yo. Slow your roll, dude. Forget the when. What about the how?' Andrea was leaning forward on the edge of the white leather sofa, her gaze traveling from Greg to Julie and back again like it was some sort of tennis match. 'You've already told us the Russian guy strongarmed the keycard off of her, so, like the gal says, how'd she get up here? Riddle me that, man.'

Greg found himself smiling. The water leaking from his clothing on to the immaculate floor seemed suddenly unimportant.

'The when and the how are intimately connected, Andrea.

'The when is two o'clock on the Wednesday morning. Isn't it, Julie? That's when, for whatever reason, you came back to Seaford Court and found Alan Mester out in the parking lot.'

'No! I—'

'We know, because he's already confessed, that a member of the Russian mafia used your keycard to come up here at just after one a.m. And the man's story is supported by the security records, which show that the card – your card – was used to enter the penthouse at exactly that time. He beat poor Alan senseless, rummaged through the apartment for valuables and other things, and then tossed him over the balcony forty-odd minutes later: at one forty-seven, to be precise. From one forty-seven until his eventual death a couple of hours later, Alan Mester was laid out on the parking lot, helpless, probably paralyzed and fading away by the minute.

'Which presents a bit of a puzzle because, even though Alan is sprawled out in the parking lot, someone uses his keycard at the rear entrance and then accesses the elevator. This is at two fourteen a.m., twenty-seven minutes after Alan "fell" from the balcony. That someone, Ms Keigel, is you. No one can access this apartment without a keycard. And no one can access the apartment without being caught on video – except on the night of Mr Mester's death when the video, for whatever reason, wasn't working. And yet, somehow, without a keycard of your own and without being caught on video, you manage to access this apartment and remove your belongings.' Greg knew that his expression had become tight and unforgiving. 'How did it feel to rummage through a dying man's pockets looking for his keycard? Did you feel even a little bad, or are you just cold-blooded to the core?'

'Of course I felt bad!' Julie blurted out.

The room was suddenly quiet.

Her wide, gray-blue eyes roamed the ceiling, as if searching for words. 'I'm not a bad person. I'm not. And I didn't kill him. I *liked* him. After that guy made me give him my keycard, I went home like I said, but I couldn't stop worrying about it. I called Alan a few times, but he didn't answer, and I couldn't let it go. Eventually, I got in my car and came all the way back here. I parked in the parking lot and I . . . I found him.' Her head bent down then, and she wept, inconsolable and unable to speak. With a surprising gentleness, Rachel Lev walked across and coaxed her into an armchair, where she rocked back and forth, hugging her knees. Only after the sobs subsided to sniffles was she able to speak again, her voice little more than a whisper. 'He was such a mess. There was this horrible gurgling sound, and I knew he was dying. And I knew, I *knew* there'd be publicity, and it would blow back on me if all my stuff was found in there. I'd be the little whore no one would hire.' She took a deep, angry breath. 'I didn't really expect to find the keycard in his pocket, you know? But it was there, and it was, like, like a sign from God, so I took it. I went up there, tossed my stuff in a bunch of trash bags, loaded up my car, went home and spent the whole day in bed, crying.'

'How did you know the cameras weren't working?' Rachel asked, her voice as soft as Julie's.

'I . . . I didn't. I didn't even think about them. I just needed to get my stuff and get out.' She looked around the room, eyes clear now, if a little red. 'Don't you understand? I didn't *plan* any of this. I just didn't want to be involved. Like I said, I'm not a bad person.'

'You're not a good Samaritan, either,' Greg said, his voice in harsh contrast to Julie's.

'A good Samaritan?'

'From the Bible. A man went down to Jericho and fell among thieves, who beat him up and left him for dead at the roadside. A number of so-called "good" people walked by without lifting a finger to help. Only a Samaritan, a person of lower social standing, was good enough to help the guy out, to take him home and tend to his wounds.'

'I know what the good Samaritan *is*. I just don't get it.'

'If you did, then you'd understand how badly you failed. Alan Mester was alive when you found him. You could have helped. You could have called an ambulance, but you didn't.'

'It was too late.'

'You can't possibly know that. You found Alan Mester alive, and you left him there to die. It was two a.m. when you found him. He didn't die until twenty to four.'

'If I'd called, they'd have known it was me. They can trace calls.'

'And your career was more important than this man's life?'

'Like I said: it was too late. Besides, finding someone injured and doing nothing isn't a crime.' Her voice grew in confidence as she continued speaking. The voice of a law student answering a question in class. 'There's no duty of care. And I can't be an accessory after the fact: I had no idea there'd been a murder, and I didn't help cover it up. I had no intent. I may not be a good Samaritan but I'm not a criminal. Legally speaking, I'm innocent.'

The faintest of smiles ghosted across Julie Keigel's face.

Rachel Lev got to her feet. Produced a pair of handcuffs from her pocket.

'The DA can deal with all the accessory-to-murder BS. But as far as I'm concerned, you stole Alan Mester's keycard, burglarized his apartment and interfered with a crime scene. That's good enough for me. You're the law student – at least until the news gets out – you know how this goes.

'Julie Keigel, I am arresting you for robbery, home invasion and interference with a—'

'No! You can't do this. It isn't fair!'

'You do not have to say anything but . . .'

The rest passed Greg by in a blur. Uniforms arrived at some point and escorted Julie Keigel out. Rachel Lev made to follow on behind. She paused by the door to retrieve her umbrella.

'There's something not right about you, Mr Abimbola. I've said it before, and I'll say it again. I can't put my finger on it, but—'

'"But your help in solving not one but two murders, not to mention uncovering a burglary and an interfered-with crime scene, has been absolutely invaluable. And I am *so* grateful." Yes?'

Rachel Lev glared at him.

'Oh lighten up, Lieutenant. Or should I say, *Homicide* Lieutenant? No Nuisance Bar Task Force for you. Not now. Not after this.' He threw her a cajoling smile. 'Just admit it: I'm not a bad guy, and I helped you out of a jam. For no other reason than you asked.'

The detective mulled that over for a moment.

'You didn't have to help,' she agreed, slowly. 'And you did get our perp to confess.'

'On video tape,' Andrea interjected, bouncing up and down in her seat. 'Dude here did all the work and all you can do is throw shade. That's cold, lady. *Cooold.*'

Rachel's thoughtful gaze raked Andrea Velasquez from top to bottom. Andrea stared back defiantly.

'I guess you're right,' she said at last. She turned to face Greg, one hand on the door handle. 'You did good, sir. Real good. And I couldn't have done it without you. So maybe if you keep doing good, you and I can find a way to get along.' She favored him with an unsmiling glance. 'Honestly, I don't know which is worse: Russian organized crime or Russian language teachers.'

And with that, she was gone, the door swinging slowly shut behind her.

'What a b—'

'Can you get me home?' Greg asked. 'I really need to get out of these clothes.' He looked down at the pool of dirty water spreading out from his feet.

'Sure thing, man. Once you explain something.'

'OK.'

'You got the time of Mester's death, the time he went over the balcony, all that stuff, from the dude's watch, yeah?'

'Indeed.'

'But Mester's watch shows he went over the balcony at ten forty-seven p.m. Not three hours later like you said. That watch makes a lie out of pretty much everything you told the biatch.'

'Not if you know anything about where Mester had been. I couldn't understand how the watch and the keycard timings could be so badly off until I went to Stayard and spoke to Julie Keigel. When I went to see her, she told me that immediately prior to visiting her the weekend before his death, he'd been on a business trip to LA. He'd set his watch to California time, which—'

'Is three hours earlier.'

'Exactly. And he'd either forgotten to reset it to Eastern time, didn't know how to reset it to Eastern time or expected the watch to do it for him and it didn't. Either way, when you account for the time difference, the watch and the keycard match up perfectly.'

'Cool. Bet she wouldn't have confessed, though, if she'd known you were basing your timeline on a sketchy piece of beta tech.'

Greg couldn't help smiling.

'Maybe, maybe not.'

'Which goes to prove that fancy-ass law school of hers is no great shakes.'

'Why would you say that?'

'Because first day of school at Law one-oh-one has to be: when someone accuses you of being an accessory to murder in front of a friggin' police officer, ask for a freaking lawyer before you say *anything*!' Andrea's face broke into a mischievous grin. 'Do you think she cut class?'

TUESDAY, THE TWENTY-FIRST
3:47 P.M.

Greg made sure to sit underneath the camera platform, safe from the prying lenses of the news crew and Caitlin's AV setup. Did he need to? Probably not: the people he'd been hiding from knew where he was. But old habits die hard. The thought of sitting in full view of the cameras again made his skin crawl.

He'd reluctantly accepted Lynn and Demetrius's offer to take him out to dinner by way of a thank you. If he'd known the invitation meant sitting through a basketball playoff game beforehand, he might have refused outright.

The very thought of doing so prompted a wry smile and a shake of the head. Expectations had been made clear. Not a single teacher would be skipping the game.

On the other side of the gym, Principal Eisner, sitting with most of the faculty, threw him a friendly wave.

Or was it more than that?

He put the thought to one side, to deal with later. Though whether there'd be a later depended on Polukhin. Polukhin, so far as was possible in this line of business, was a man of his word. Greg had neither run nor ratted him out to Western intelligence, so his mother, thank God, was in the clear. That was the deal. Part of it, anyway.

The other part had required the very public, very bloody execution of Oleg Dobrygin. Given that Dobrygin was alive and mostly well in the custody of Pittsburgh PD, Polukhin would definitely mark that down as a fail. Which meant that Greg's time on this earth had a very definite end date. Unless—

Demetrius, with Lynn Spargo in tow, climbed up the bleachers to reach him. Basketballs thumped on the court as the teams warmed up. Demetrius sat down on the cold aluminum, rubbing his hands.

'Ready for this, brother?'

'As I'll ever be.'

'Just you wait. We'll make a fan of you yet.'

'I doubt that, Demetrius,' Lynn said, smiling. 'But thank you for making the effort, Greg. And for everything else.' The smile flickered a little. 'Al will get justice now, at least. And that little bitch of his will get what she deserves. She as good as killed him.'

Greg nodded. 'As good as killed him' was a matter for the lawyers, but there didn't seem much mileage in pointing that out. Even less in reminding her that justice for Alan Mester involved trashing his reputation as a pillar of the community. The man had laundered money for Russian oligarchs. If he hadn't, he'd still be alive, going toe to toe with Clyde Leclerc over the future of the Edgeworth School and spending time with women who were far too young for him.

'Man, I was so sure this was about PEACE and their critical race theory bullshit,' Demetrius said. 'White supremacists and murder? Easy. But Russians? In Pittsburgh, of all places? Who'd'a' thunk it?'

'It's a smaller world than we thought,' Greg said mildly. 'Everything is a lot closer these days.'

He stared out at the basketball court, thinking about Moscow.

'How are you feeling about the Edgeworth School?' he asked. 'Still going?'

'Still going,' Demetrius said, face determined. 'Like I said before, that ship has already sailed. But the boys are staying here. I don't want them going near that place. Not till I've figured out what the hell kind of school it really is.' He pointed across the court at the massed rows of faculty. 'Principal Eisner said we could work it out. Some kind of scholarship. Not full, but something I should be able to afford.' He gave a bemused shake of the head. Eisner, unaware of their scrutiny, laughed at something Ms Tsai was whispering in his ear. 'He's not a bad guy when all's said and done.'

'No,' Greg said slowly. 'He isn't.'

The referee blew on his whistle. The players got ready to start. Caleb, tall and imposing in his team uniform, grinned up at the camera platform and waved.

Demetrius watched him, a small frown playing on his face.

'Say, Greg,' he asked. 'Caitlin Bell is one of your students, isn't she?'

'And a very good one.'

'Do you think . . . do you know if there's anything going on between her and Caleb?' Demetrius stared at him intently. 'They seem kinda close.'

Greg set his gaze on the electric glow of the scoreboard: fixed, for now, at 00-00.

'I teach foreign languages, Demetrius. Russian and sometimes French. What could I possibly know about a thing like that?'

11:59 P.M.

Traffic on the Sixty-Second Street bridge was light to the point of non-existence. It was cold, though, and Greg was bundled up to the nines. He stood on the sidewalk, leaning against the bridge's high, no-nonsense railing and staring into the blackness below. Bluffs rose steep on either side of the river, dotted with light.

The rideshare driver who'd dropped him here was just polite enough to rein in his concern. He'd driven off, leaving behind a morose, middle-aged man leaning over the side of a bridge.

But as Julie Keigel would doubtless have reminded him, no one owed Greg Abimbola a duty of care.

It was a long way down. Enough, if you were scared of heights, to set off butterflies in the stomach.

Morosov was lucky he was already dead when Dobrygin dumped him over the rail. Falling alive, he would have had too much time to think, and the water would have been hard as concrete when he slammed into it.

Like Mester falling from his balcony. He thought of the high, fluttering beats recorded by the heartrate monitor as Mester plunged to the ground, the immediate change after he hit it. The long, agonizing death.

Greg took a long swig from a flask of vodka. A lonely toast to a colleague and adversary.

'You were spared that, at least,' he murmured.

Out of the corner of his eye, he noticed a light winking out on one of the bluffs.

Midnight. People would be going to bed now, preparing one way or another for whatever faced them tomorrow.

But in Moscow, tomorrow had already begun. And certain people were creatures of habit.

Greg pulled a burner phone from his pocket. Dialed the number.

'Allo?'

'Good morning, Colonel General Polukhin,' Greg said in Russian. 'I trust the weather is good today.'

'This is Moscow,' Polukhin griped. 'The weather is shit, as it usually is at this time of year. Springtime in Moscow is more myth than reality.

'So, Grigoriy. You have news for me?'

'Oleg Dobrygin killed Morosov. Total fuck-up. He'd been tailing Morosov and the Americans. The Americans were repairing a flat tire. Morosov escaped. Dobrygin tried to help but was mistaken for an American himself. There was an exchange of gunfire. Morosov missed, Dobrygin did not.'

The silence at the other end stretched to the point where Greg wondered if he'd lost the connection.

'Fuckwit. You have dealt with him, I trust?'

'Pittsburgh PD have him.'

'I beg your pardon?'

'They arrested him before I could bury him in the grave I had him dig for himself. He apparently killed someone called Alan Mester, a local banker here.'

Another long pause.

'This was not our agreement, Grigoriy. I am very disappointed.'

'I fear, Vladimir Vladimirovich, that you are about to become more disappointed.'

'How so?'

'I have Alan Mester's hard drive.'

'What is that to me?'

'Everything, I suspect. You ordered Alan Mester's death because you discovered he was cooperating with the US authorities in a money-laundering investigation.'

'So?'

'So, Mester documented everything he was doing. Not only on the hard drive but also on a USB he'd hidden with a girlfriend.'

'Useless to the Department of Justice now that Mester cannot give evidence. And apart from a few Americans, everyone involved is Russian. The Americans can't touch them.'

'True. These are oligarchs for the most part. And loyal, which makes them untouchable.'

'So why are you bothering me with this?'

'Because you, Colonel General, are not an oligarch. You are not untouchable. Particularly when said oligarchs discover how much you've been stealing from them.'

'A handling fee, for GRU protection, nothing more.'

'Of course. So you won't mind if I divulge this information to them.'

Another long pause.

'What do you want?'

'To be left alone. For my mother to be left alone. Nothing more. If anything happens to me, or to her, the information gets out – in Russia, not here – and consequences will follow. I don't imagine you will enjoy falling to your death any more than Alan Mester did.'

Greg was surprised to hear laughter coming out of his earpiece.

'I will miss you, Grigoriy. Whenever you are put on the board, the results are invariably . . . interesting. Your mother will be fine; you have my word. Enjoy your new life.' The laughter grew louder. 'Major Grigoriy Adamovich Petrov of the GRU. Ending his days as a small-time teacher in a small-time town in Pennsylvania. Who would have imagined such a thing?'

Polukhin was still laughing when the line went dead.

Greg stared at the burner phone for a moment, scarcely crediting the sudden lightness in his shoulders. He took a celebratory swig from his flask and then tossed the phone over the rail.

He neither saw nor heard the splash.

ACKNOWLEDGEMENTS

Despite the fact that my name appears on the cover, books are a team effort. Especial thanks to my wonderful colleague, Irina Ignatieva, for keeping me honest on the Russian and saving the audiobooks from disaster; to my friends Shelly Geppert, the very best of America, and Lyndsey Ratcliffe, who makes Scotland seem sunnier than it is; to my agent, the esteemed Brady McReynolds, his assistant, James Farner and all at JABberwocky Literary; to my editor, Rachel Slatter, assistant editor, Tina Pietron, copy editor, Katherine Laidler and the fine folks at Severn House; and last, but not least, to my family: Barbara, Alex, Amina, Alima, Tom, Nadia, Max, Elliot, Henry, Bex, Harriet, Angus, Corey and Margot, whose support, be it enthusiastic, disbelieving or otherwise, is very much appreciated.